LINDSEY COLLEN was born in 1948 in the Transkei in South Africa, where she led a tumultuous life as her father was transferred to wherever there was unrest in the land of apartheid, and to where no pro-government Native Affairs Commissioner would go. Her mother encouraged her interest in the political situation wherever they lived. After a boarding school education, Lindsey Collen went to the University of the Witwatersarand, where she studied law and literature, and where she became a student leader. As well as living in South Africa, she has lived in New York, on the Seychelles island of Mahe, in London, where she studied at the London School of Economics, and in Mauritius where she lives now with her husband, Ram Seegobin, a doctor and trade union activist. Lindsey is known in Mauritius as a writer, feminist and enthusiastic campaigner for adult literacy and other causes.

Lindsey Collen has been writing since the age of six and teaches reading and writing. She edited *Critique* literary magazine in South Africa, and is a regular contributor to *Revi Lalit*. Her first novel was published in 1990 and is called *There is a Tide*. *The Rape of Sita* is her second novel and was published in Mauritius in 1993. It caused such controversy that it was banned by the government and temporarily withdrawn by the publishers. In 1994 it won the best book in the African category of the 1994 Commonwealth Writers Prize.

LINDSEY COLLEN

THE RAPE OF SITA

Heinemann

Heinemann Educational Publishers
A Division of Heinemann Publishers (Oxford) Ltd
Halley Court, Jordan Hill, Oxford OX2 8EJ

Heinemann: A Division of Reed Publishing (USA) Ltd
361 Hanover Street, Portsmouth, NH 03801–3912, USA

Heinemann Educational books (Nigeria) Ltd
PMB 5205, Ibadan
Heinemann Educational Boleswa
PO Box 10103, Village Post Office, Gaborone, Botswana

FLORENCE   PRAGUE   PARIS   MADRID
ATHENS   MELBOURNE   JOHANNESBURG
AUCKLAND   SINGAPORE   TOKYO
CHICAGO   SAO PAULO

First published by Ledikasyon pu Travayer in 1993
Published in this edition by Heinemann Educational Books in 1995

British Library Cataloguing in Publication Data
A catalogue record for this book is available from the British Library.

Cover design by Touchpaper
Cover illustration by Mark Surridge
Author photograph by Dominic Williamson

ISBN 0 435 909 584

Phototypeset by CentraCet Limited, Cambridge
Printed and bound in Great Britain
by Cox & Wyman Ltd, Reading, Berkshire

95 96 97 10 9 8 7 6 5 4 3 2 1

I am Time
Ever being born
Being thus incessantly born
Torn from the world's womb
Being ever born
Born out of the eternal
The universal
Yoni.
Om.
I am Time
Who knows no good nor bad
Nor right from wrong
I move forward
Ever forward,
Onward, upward, downward,
Never backward.
Om.
I am time
I allow high, wide, and long
To be;
Without me
Where would they be?

And for that matter
Without me
Where would you be?

You oh human,
You plural,
I put form in you
And
You put form in me.
You are the meaning.

Watch out what you do
Watch out what you don't do.

You oh human.
For you plural
For you
There is past, there is present, there is future.
For you
There is better or worse.
For you, woman,
For you, man,
Cocooned in time,

Are poised in eternal dilemma.
What action for you
Would be moral
Would be true
Would be good
Would be right?
What action for you
Would be wrong,
Lies, bad,
Immoral?
Know, oh know,
See, yes see,
Feel, now feel,
Hear and speak,
Be,
Always be aware
Of each dilemma
And thus act,
Or refrain from acting,
In knowing
There exists
Just there
A dilemma.
Will this act
Make history progress
Or allow us
To slip back

Into the mud of the past?
Which act?
Which omission?
Om.
I am time,
I am Kali,
Creator and Destroyer.
For I,
I being time
Move on.
I am time.
I do not stop.

Time

Preface

◆

Please do not read this preface unless you are already a fanatic novel reader. You will notice that the print is small specially to discourage everyone except the most persistent reader.

Goldswains told me not to talk directly to the reader in my novel. They said it's old-fashioned and that even when it had been fashionable a few centuries ago, it had, even then, they informed me, been in bad taste. They said novels aren't like that. 'This is not some kind of a letter to a close friend,' they said, 'Nor is it some kind of a political leaflet designed to get someone to leap up into action. There is just no need for addressing readers personally and directly. We're after novels,' they said. 'It is a modern novel we want from you.'

I, the undersigned, Iqbal of Surinam, will address you directly quite often in the course of this novel, reader. Not to spite Goldswains. I've thought a lot about whether or not I can oblige them in their request, but I don't think I can. I will address you directly. I am already, even at this early stage, absolutely certain that that is how it will happen. I'm the boss of this novel, and I just happen to know I will want to talk to you quite often, reader. They can call me old-fashioned or in bad taste, Goldswains can. I don't mind. They can even say it isn't a novel I've written. I don't mind what they call it, for that matter.

Since when did writers and publishers get on, anyway?

Another thing Goldswains said was that they don't want diversions. 'A novel must flow,' they said. I can already see that I will need diversions in my novel. Otherwise how will you know who Sita is, who I am, who Ton Tipyer is. In any case, readers and listeners, *interrupt me*. That's a fact.

Publishers will have to jump off.

If no publisher wants to print it, I have decided to do fifty print-outs of each page on my home computer, collate them, then glue the pages together with contact glue and sell the novel without a cover. It's quite nice to have the left-hand page blank anyway. We could still call it a 'novel', I should think. I have about fifty readers who will buy copies like that. They are the people who personally informed me, after reading my first novel *Mauritius Cyclone Eye*, that they were looking forward to another one. They said they liked the structure of it: a kind of plait, they said. Well *The Rape of Sita* isn't a plait. Its structure's more like a bunch of grapes. Some critics may like the bunch of grapes structure even less than they liked the plait one. That's their look-out.

The first thing I want to say, dear reader, without any pretence at my clairvoyance is that I can predict that while some critics and busybodies will spend their time saying this book is autobiographical, and therefore not the kind of stuff a novel's made of, and that I am certainly a rapist myself, others will say that this very same book, being an obvious bunch of lies, is just too far-fetched to be a convincing realistic novel.

Sita and Dharma and Rowan Tarquin, for example, are obviously made up. They *were* made up. At least that's true. But they were made up a long time ago by better writers than me. Even then, their story is a very old one, older than the people who made the characters up. Shakespeare wrote it up beautifully in 'The Rape of Lucrece', which was based on an older tale, and long before these tales, when Valmiki wrote it in sloka metres in the equally beautiful Ramayana, he was only retelling melodically what Narad had told him before.

My only qualification for writing this story, other than the fact that Sita taught me to read and write when I was only three, writing in the sand at Rianbel, is the fact that I used to stand around a lot, leaning on my bicycle, just watching and listening. That's my main qualification. I was also once umpire of a famous wrestling match in Surinam. This is my only other qualification. The reason for my writing is another matter. Dharma wrote a short story about me called 'Iqbal the Umpire', and gave it to me, as you will find out later, and I decided to write a long story down as well. As a kind of present to him. When he wrote about me, it helped me. So I write for him. When I showed Sita a rough draft, she just laughed and said 'What a load of rubbish.'

Poetry is better for this sort of story than prose. But I can't write poetry. That's why I had to put a quote from a woman called 'Time' at the beginning of this book.

Iqbal the Umpire

◆

Once upon a time talk was in all directions.

Talk is, when the story starts, in all directions. And time is running out. How to get their attention. Are they already too raucous for a story? First, I must get the floor. It's not as easy as it used to be. Some people say it's because of television.

I feel myself stand up and move into the middle of everyone. 'Put on a saree and dance, Iqbal the Umpire,' there came a snide remark from a neatly dressed man who may well have been a car salesman from Porlwi. I control myself and don't make any mean remark back at him.

I whip round and stare at him.

'*Sirandann? Sirandann?*' I sing out. Loudly, as if an attack on him, but addressed kindly as an offering to the others.

This is a magic word in Mauritius. They call it 'the call'. And it means 'Can I tell you a story, everyone, can I tell you a story?'

'*Sanpek!*' comes the response from under one tree. '*Sanpek!*' again from on a bit of granite rock.

And so I've got the floor now. All I need now is their attention. Even more difficult these days. Don't know what's in people's minds anymore. Or even on them.

I whip around again and take them all in in my sweeping look this time.

'I'm going to tell you the story of the rape of Sita,' I begin. '*Sirandann? Sirandann?*' I call the words again hoping the theme will catch more of them.

'*Sanpek!*' More of them call out the magic response. Go ahead, they mean. '*Sanpek!*'

'Once upon a time there was a woman called Sita.'

'When?'

'Now.'

'Where?'

7

'Here.'

'So why did you say "Once upon a time" then?'

They won't let me get on with the story.

'Because,' I say, 'it's an old story. I'm telling a very old story. Ancient. Only it is my duty, my bounden duty, to make it more true.'

And this is how I start my first digression, when I tell them how there are two types of people in the story business. For every one story-teller, as you and I know him, there are two trainees. One to remember the story as it was, or as it is. And the other who has to retell it anew, and never the same. I am the second kind. Dharma, my friend, is in charge of remembering stories exactly as they were, or as they are.

'Get on with the story, Iqbal, get on with it. Who was her father anyway?'

'Is.'

◆

This two-letter word hooked them. I let the silence bite, too.

◆

Her father. The places they make you start a story. The places. The times. But I've got their attention now.

'Start with the father,' they chorus, 'and you aren't allowed to stop until the ending. Start with the father.' Good. Delays my having to take her on. Because I, the teller of the tale, must almost become the heroine. Like it's a mask, or a character, take it on. And it's difficult, this metamorphosis. This reincarnation.

A Beatles tune suddenly started to run around inside my head, like a rat. *Jojo was a man who thought he was a woman*, but instead of Jojo the word Iqbal rang in my head, *Iqbal was a man who thought he was a woman*.

◆

Start with the father. 'Is.' The way the word got them riveted. How come a rape makes them think of the father?

◆

Like the Nuvel Frans police station needs the vantage point of where the road up from Surinam and the road up from Maybur meet and makes an upside down Y with the road up to Kirpip, so Mohun Jab Brakonye, the poacher, surnamed Janaka, needs the same privileged spot.

But the police got there first.

His land, therefore, had to be a bit wider, which it is, because the triangle in the middle behind the police station gets wider immediately behind the police station and then gets wider and wider, and goes on getting wider and wider, until it gets to the bottom two corners of a triangular Mauritius main island.

Mohun Jab Brakonye's land is a wide but thin bit. It doesn't have to be deep. All it has to be is wider than the police station's so that he can see right up all three roads just like the police can. He's got the apparent disadvantage over the police of having to move from one side of his bit of land to the other side so he can see all roads, but he's a very fit man, and walking's never a problem for him. To sit still would be. The policemen on the other hand love sitting down, the stiller the better, and despite their fine position for spotting robbers and, more to the point, poachers, they often miss them. The wooden counter of the police station, behind which they sit on heavy wooden chairs, being a high colonial piece of massive woodwork bars their view in any direction whatsoever. And in addition Mohun Jab Brakonye's land has the distinct advantage of being just behind the back of the police station; this, as every poacher knows, is a policeman's weakest spot. The closer behind, the better.

Mohun Jab's verandah runs all along the police station's back, and juts out just enough on each side of its shoulders, so to speak, to see up the Kirpip arm of the upside down Y.

9

Mohun Jab Brakonye is Sita's father. That is how he gets into this chapter. He is the father of Sita.

He's a bachelor.

He lives with his brother, Extra Large Janaka, who's also a bachelor and who's also a poacher. The fact that there have always been the two of them means that when things hot up, they can each stand at a different end of their thin wide bit of land and keep an eye on two out of the three roads, each one of them, and that Mohun Jab doesn't even have to walk from one end of the land to the other to see around the police station, when there isn't time to walk. While Extra Large's immense frame is what frightens the police and the *gardyen sase*, employed to keep poachers out of private land, and what inspires terror into the *gard forestye*, employed to keep poachers out of Crown Land, Mohun Jab's cleverness is what really strikes a cruel fear into the hearts of all of them.

Mohun Jab is said to be a genius.

He is also reputed to be able to talk an enemy into anything. One day the two biggest and worst bruisers of a *sase* owner came around charged with the specific mission of beating him up; he talked them out of it. *He persuaded them against it.*

'Got powers of reasoning,' his enemies say, shaking their heads, as if it was supernatural.

The poachers' mother, Mowsi Renuka, is a girlish woman. She's in her late eighties now, and still high-spirited and loud-laughing. She lives with her two sons, the poachers, and keeps the *marmit*, the big three-legged pot, on the boil over logs of wood on the ground, so that there's always boiling water for tea, vanilla tea, when they get back from the woods. She could start the fire with just half a page of *Le Dimanche* and some *juri* wood balanced on top of the half page. One blast of the *pukni* and the whole kitchen lit up. Vanilla tea in smoke-tasting water. That's what they like best. She grinds her own spices daily, and is permanently in a state of full mobilization, ready to prepare a venison curry at a moment's notice, and to serve it with homemade unleavened bread, *faratas*, which she tosses around on a flat griddle iron, with a conviction close to violence. She always has known which road they'd be coming home along, so, till now, she still keeps herself in preparation for sudden cooking action; she walks to

10

an ideal vantage point on the verandah for that one of the three roads that she knows will produce her sons. She shakes her head and says, '*Baap-re-baap*, sons poachers.' And then laughs. 'And, worse still, they won't get married.' While she had become accustomed to their dedication to poaching, this not getting married business she thinks is not right. 'They could marry any young girl in the place. They've got plenty of cane-land at Plenn Mayan. They are planters. This bachelor-hood of theirs is just a vice. A vice. Rather they had other vices. Why can't they just smoke *gandya*. Like the others. Or get drunk. Like other men. Or even gamble. No, on second thoughts, not gambling. Anyway, why do they *not* marry, why do they refuse to marry. It's not that I'm moaning about the housework. Or even if they just set up a *menaz* with some nice woman. Even that would do. Even if he brought Sita's mother. I don't mind what woman they bring. And that Mohun Jab's got too much lip. Imagine him telling me he doesn't want to *own* a woman. Who told him to own one. I only told him to marry one. Any one. And he said that means owning, and he is not going to own any other human being, he said. Enough of slavery in the history of this place, he said. Just words, if you ask me.

'Tinerate,' she would say, 'At any rate, they bring me wood to cook on.' Then she laughs again and says 'already on government pension, and still not married. Huh.' Her deep freeze's always full of frozen venison. For the off season. 'They're obsessed,' she mumbles, and then, as she always did, she laughs.

As a pet, Mohun Jab, as anyone who knew him well could probably have imagined, has a deer, a female deer, a doe, which follows his mother, to her chagrin, around inside the house. On its wild face is this guileless expression, she notices. His mother doesn't approve, of course, but then she just laughs at it, as it walks around amongst the rattanware chairs in their lounge, watching her doing the housework. The children of family visitors love the doe. She's called Baby. She is at home, and other people are visitors, and she keeps up this feeling. Just standing, or just strolling around the house like a dog might. She is house-trained, and of course not allowed in the mother's bedroom or in the tinshack kitchen she cooks in.

Mohun Jab was, and always will be, a bachelor. This I, Iqbal of Surinam, can vouch for. I know him. He is against the institution of marriage. He says it's *mofinn* which means 'bad luck'. He is even pleased that Sita and Dharma aren't married. I know him well. Like a father to me, he is. I was the only person they nearly took on as a partner, the two brothers. But then, because of my being in the movement, I couldn't afford to be doing illegal things, which was what they did every day. Mohun Jab understood this. He had not always been a poacher. Nor had he started being a poacher as a vice, like his mother used to say he did.

Mohun Jab was an important man in the first Mauritian mutiny against the colonial government. The movement started in 1937. He was the Rozbel sugar estate train driver who was famous all over the South for his role in the mutiny. When the strike order came through from the other workers on other estates, Mohun Jab had already thought out what to do. The mutiny is not just against the sugar estate bosses, and he knew this. It had to be against the state, as well, he said. Not every person who can't read and write knows what the state is. But Mohun Jab knew this better than the colonial secretary himself. He certainly knew better than the police commissioner. He could even explain it to people.

Even his enemies said it: He is very clever.

And so that's how come he knew where to have his train at the beginning of the strike so that the strike would begin properly. 'You need panache,' he said. He could choose a Frenchified word with the precision of a wine-taster. He therefore, after a loud pull on his steam-run whistle, braked his train, and brought his engine to a complete halt, with a load of sugar cane piled high on its carts in tow behind him, on its way to the mill, at the very point when he was right in the middle of the level crossing at Rozbel. All traffic was stopped not only on the rails in the south but also on the road to Maybur. He jumped down and walked off with his hands, it was said, in his pockets and his hat askew on his head.

As planned, he met his brother Extra Large at the entrance to the Rozbel sugar mill, and they stood there and gathered a public meeting around them to launch the strike. Extra Large had been schooled, naturally, by his brother as to the question of exactly when he was to go on strike. Extra Large was a crane driver, who lifted great bunches of cane out of the train's rolling stock and swung it round through the main entrance into the mill. He had, after listening to his brother's irrefutable arguments, left his crane in the middle of an operation: swinging a load of sugar cane over the main entrance way to the mill. Shows, Mohun Jab said, where the power is. Or should be. Or can be. Extra Large had then climbed down from his crane, and walked off to meet his brother.

They met, and all the other workers came to meet at the same place. The workers' meeting was a success. The strike was hundred per cent. And the retaliation against the workers, like the wrath of the gods, was immediate.

They weren't just sacked.

Mohun Jab was put on the police 'wanted' list for arrest on charges of high treason for leaving his train on the level crossing inside the Rozbel sugar estate. This is what the poster in the Post Office said: Wanted Dead or Alive, Mohun Jab of Rozbbel. This confirmed him in his knowledge of what the relationship was between the sugar cane bosses and the state.

And for the next six years while the movement got stronger and stronger, he was on the run. He went all around the countryside with Emmanuel Anquetil, building up the trade union part of the movement. They were inseparable. Mohun Jab would translate into fluent Kreol and Bhojpuri for Anquetil, because Anquetil had lived in England so long that he couldn't even speak Kreol properly anymore, and Mohun Jab would add step-by-step arguments, if ever Anquetil skipped over them. He and Anquetil left their imprint on history. Meetings by day and meetings by night. Why you need a union. Why you should join the Labour Party. How to become a militant for Labour.

And so it was that during these six years while he was carving the path that Mauritian history was going to take together with workers from all over Mauritius, that he also at the same time, learnt to play cat-and-mouse with the police. They didn't ever arrest him. If they saw him, he was right in the middle of a crowd hostile to the police, and when he was on his own, they didn't see him.

And when the war came, and Anquetil was given a banishment order to go and live on Rodrig Island, a kind of warm Siberia, and when Mohun Jab, being very clever, knew that the importance of the anti-fascist British war against Hitler's Germany came and made anti-

British activity in Mauritius politically wrong, he felt stymied. History sometimes does that, he told me. And it was then that he took to being a poacher. In any case, he was on the sugar boss's black list, so there wasn't anything else he could do for a living.

So, it wasn't out of vice that he started poaching, like his mother said it was.

And it was only by the end of the war, after five or six years of very tight poaching, against strict and heavily armed wartime forest guards with martial law behind them, that this occupation had finally become his complete passion, his love, his life, his dedicated work. And so it was that in 1946 he and Extra Large sold half their inheritance caneland from Plenn Mayan and bought the wide thin bit of land just behind the police's back at Nuvel Frans.

Of course, Sita's father, Mohun Jab, wasn't a cad. He declared both her and her little sister. They've got his surname and everything. And he loves them. This is proved beyond all doubt by the fact that he had always brought them venison, the best cuts, every time he got a deer. Which was often, because he is and always was a fine shot. He never took a shot that he might miss. And then Sita's mother, Doorga of Surinam, couldn't complain in one way, because it wasn't just *her* he wouldn't marry, he wouldn't marry anyone else either, and he didn't marry anyone else. In any case, in Doorga's family, they didn't have men. Mohun Jab had loved Doorga because she was independent and strong and had a reputation for beating people up. They never had a single argument or row. He gave money for the kids. And more important, he came and told them about his life in the past, and taught them how to think. Check if things follow, he said. Don't believe any old junk, he said. He's always been good with the kids. And he never ever hit Doorga. Who would have? He never even shouted at her, nor moaned about food she served him when he came around. He had none of the traits of a husband, and this had pleased Doorga. He even agrees with Sita living with Dharma. He liked the man the moment he met him. Yes, he actually gets on with Sita's man, and everything. This was not expected. There is no other man that he would have liked like that. Everyone was scared for when Sita would fall in love with someone. Mohun Jab won't like him, they said. But he liked Dharma. He respected him and accepted him as his daughter's friend, lover and informal husband. Dharma was brave enough for his liking, and tough enough, and intelligent, at the same time. And Dharma could crack a joke, and shoot straight, two things poachers like. But what he likes most about Dharma is, as he puts it himself, that 'Maybe you, Dharma can take up what Anquetil and me went and got out-manoeuvred in.' That was his dream. He was referring to the War having made their movement so difficult. Dharma, Mohun Jab said it aloud, was not a sucker-up like all those other young creeps that the country produces these days. Do anything for money, or for a place in government. Sell their souls. Dharma is perhaps a great leader of the poor, or a prophet of the people he says. Who knows, he says. When he says this, people sometimes smile or even laugh. *Short-minded* people, *short-minded*, he repeated, just don't realize, he added, when they see someone who has vision into the future. Vision, I didn't have enough of it myself, he likes to say, but some of you guys have got a good deal less; you only see to the end of your own noses, like cattle.

Mohun Jab spoils Sita and Dharma's little girl, Fiya. For example, he made little miniature deer out of pipe cleaners and corks for her, and she kept them on her bedside table. She keeps them next to two beautifully carved bits of granite rock that had belonged to Sita when she was a baby girl.

Mohun Jab never made or makes any scene about Sita being in the movement either, like other fathers would have. He loved it. Even when she was locked up in Line Barracks he got wind of it, went to see her, and took a *katora* of venison for her and her seven woman friends locked up with her. He felt that she too had taken on the police like he had, and in his way, still does. More openly, and thus, he concludes, in a way *better* than he ever had. He was proud of her. 'My Phoolan Devi', he called her. And when one member of the family or other, in suit and strangling tie, said something about his daughter being in jail, he just said, 'At least she believes in something, which is more than I can say for a lot of people around here.' And after a short hesitation added: 'Including myself for that matter. Good luck to her.'

♦

'When you were over there, were they already separated?' Dharma asked Sita, calling across the room. There were lots of people around when he asked it. No-one else noticed anything, I shouldn't think. It was in that soft-talking lull just before a committee meeting starts if I remember rightly. And I was perhaps the only one that noticed their conversation. Or at least paid any attention to it. She didn't hear. He said it again: 'Sita, when you were over there, were they already separated?'

'When?'

'In 1982.'

'Where?'

'Reunion.'

'Who?'

'Rowan and Noella Tarquin.'

She was cross. Yes, she was cross. She was cross for nothing. I saw it in her face. And there was something else wrong. It was the order of her questions that was wrong. For her, anyway. She wasn't a literal sort of person, never had been, and she knew the question should have been 'who?' But she asked 'when' first, and then 'where' and then only 'who' last. Putting the answer off. Or even, or even, was it almost as though she had difficulty understanding the question? It seemed to elude her grasp. She even put her head to one side. Like a meerkat that's heard a twig crackle. Or maybe she already knew very well who, when and where, and was only asking the questions to delay, after all, having to give an answer. Maybe she just didn't want the original question to have been asked at all. Wanted it to go away. That was what it seemed like, anyway.

She snapped a reply. *'How should I know? I was only there a couple of hours. Time for a meal at a restaurant.'*

16

Then she stared into the middle distance ahead of her for a long time. As though startled by what she had said, herself. Or as though she thought she had had some kind of mental fault, a short-circuit or something, that had caused her to imagine Dharma's whole question and her answer. As though the whole thing were made up in her own head, like a *déjà vu*. And then, almost as though nothing had happened, or worse still, as though she wasn't there, she sort of went absent. It was as though she switched herself off, or as though her mind took off into space, leaving her body like a sloughed skin. It made me shudder. No-one seemed to see.

But I had noticed. She had been cross. Distinctly cross. Why? And she had asked questions in the wrong order.

Odd, that. And then the way she looked into the distance as though trying to place something somewhere someone someplace.

Then she looked at me, and said: 'Iqbal, why on earth do you look so odd. *Ki to gayne, Iqbal*? What's the matter?'

I, by the way, am a friend of Sita's. I grew up in the same village as her: Surinam. Her *dada*, paternal great-grandfather, that is to say, Mohun Jab's grandfather, and my *gran nana*, great-grandfather on my mother's side, were *dahajbay*, or boat brothers. That meant that our families were closer than blood relatives. The two old men had as young lads come over from Calcutta to Mauritius on the same coolie boat. They were survivors of the sea-trip. They hadn't thrown themselves overboard. They hadn't died of typhoid fever on the way over. Nothing had killed them. They didn't die in the depot at Porlwi either.

'Nothing's the matter.' I spoke quietly, as I am accustomed to.

◆

Two months later: 'You go, Sita,' they all said. 'You go to Paris. It's important. There's the war about to break out. The States,' they said, 'has already mobilized hundreds of thousands of men. No-one knows when or even how it will end once it starts. A movement like ours can't be isolated at a time like this. It's an important congress. You can do it, lass. You'll represent us well.'

All the delegates from different regions said so. They mixed the two points, she noticed. That someone should go, and that it should be her. Everyone was pleased to say this to her. I also said: 'Yes Sita, we must be there and you are the person needed.' I noticed something menacing in the way she looked at me. I shuddered, as if someone had walked across my shadow. We all looked at her to see what she would say. Everyone else thought she would be pleased. Maybe honoured. At worst, neutral, about it.

She hesitated for a minute.

Even the hesitation caused a wave of anxiety in everyone in the committee. We all looked up at her. Something was wrong.

What was wrong?

Then, quite suddenly, as if to prove us right, she burst into tears.

'No, no, no' and then 'No, no, no.' Great big tears of dread. And horror on her face.

A few seconds later, Sita was mystified by what she had done. Bursting into tears like that. 'Good grief,' she whispered. She looked perplexed. 'Well I never,' she said. And it blew over. Like a sea-squall. There one minute, and gone the next.

When she was two, her first memory, mother gone away to Suyak to get a little sister for her, she gone to her great aunt's house and she sick with scarlet fever, mother come back again, but Sita in quarantine, peeping through a slit between the wooden door and the tin lintel, in the threshold, seeing her mother sitting up in bed on the coconut mattress: 'Grit your teeth, Sita, don't cry. You not a crying kind of girl.'

True.

Forty years later, an adult woman, 'No, no no,' she had said, and had cried, cried like a baby.

'Don't, don't ask me to go. I won't. I refuse. I can't.' She was serious. No-one present could believe their eyes. But there it was. In front of us all. Seeing was believing.

'OK,' they said, 'OK. No-one's forcing anyone. No need to get all upset.'

'She's being ridiculous,' I heard one of the men mumble.

I personally saw her face the day of that committee meeting. I have known her the whole of our forty two years. I never saw her go like that before, never. I can vouch for it. In her, I noticed these things. She would have in me, too, I should think. Two Surinam kids. Her face

18

was sudden. There was something that got set off. Like a detonator. But like the detonator of a time bomb.

◆

It was two months later, again.

I was about to see her face get another odd expression. A strong emotion. But hidden, or masked quickly afterwards. This would be the third time.

As everyone around us became despondent, and said, with reason most likely, 'But how can there be any future for mankind? What with the US army preparing to invade and destroy Iraq like this?' The vast devastation was still ahead at the time of the third thing that I noticed in her, the third oddness. The wholesale destruction was still ahead. There was the size of the army. The numbers of tanks. Of soldiers. Of Patriot missiles. There was their name. Kill in the name of the country. The bombs. Carpet bombs. Dropped like you lay a carpet. Like a rape and murder. Nothing will crawl out from under alive. *Not suffer anything to crawl upon the surface of the*. The mindlessness of the media and its control of the minds of perfectly good people you met in the streets. The deafening propaganda about a clean war. Clean destruction. Clean death. Clean war. *Cleanliness is next to*. The falsified news broadcasts. The god bless us, us, us, stuff. And the nominated ministers like Baker striding around in our homes, coming into the privacy of each person's verandah with their words. And the nominated war chiefs like Schwartzkopf talking talk about sucking Saddam into the desert. Prior to the rape. Prior to storming the desert. Storming the body of the earth. On first name terms, I noticed. Saddam, your old friend. Saddam who you helped. Saddam whom you'll.

And no-one seeming to be able to stop anything and no-one being able to act. Just as we were all realizing what was happening, and lamenting. As if war was being sent like a pestilence by an angry god, we were left doing nothing but lamenting. Lamenting is a very *old* thing to do. Old crises demand old reactions. But this was a new crisis, and we treated it like the old plagues. Fire and brimstone. Locusts in the desert air. Frogs.

So, in the beginning, we were lamenting. We felt a scourge had been sent upon the earth. It was before we had even managed to call an anti-war front. Before we could adapt to the new vistas of domination looming up ahead like in a science fiction film, not just in the case of Iraq, but from now on everywhere. Before we could get our patience back, before we could summon up our internal resources again. Before we could act as an organization. Just then, just at that very moment, the news came in. To every action, a counter-reaction.

Sita could not believe it. I saw her face the day she heard that news. She was as if in a trance. She was vindicated. But then, I am too. Are all of us socialists not vindicated by such a thing? And yet we didn't all look like that. Just she did. Again it was sudden. She went odd. For her, it was more of a vindication than for anyone else. She began to dance a strange dance. Sing a strange song. In front of everyone there and then. In a round, an imaginary circle drawn in the middle of the room. Legs and arms flying. *Spiyaking*. She always could dance. Then she calmed down, but was left looking like the statue of victory. People knew she was impulsive. Jidit laughed, throwing her head back, and crooning, straight out of Africa, handed down from mother to daughter: a laugh. Then leaned forward and clapped her hands just once. In distinct support. Maybe she understood something that no-one else understood at the time. Certainly it has taken me a whole year.

The news that had come in was that the children, the little children, the poor little children, the poor little children of the Sodron had had enough.

They have put their feet down.

They have acted.

They are putting a stop to their accepting.

They have set Sendeni alight. On fire.

Those very children born into the heart of submission, Reunion, the colony of colonies, known to submit there more than any colonized people anywhere, held up usually as an example of *intégration, assimilation, départmentalisation*, by the French rulers, those very children, the most down-trodden, unblessed of us all, have risen up by themselves like immense giants striding across the firmament. Against not ordinary masters, but against the most difficult of masters, colonial masters.

Not just standing up.

Fighting. Against six storey concrete monstrosities. Like Goliath, buildings brought down.

Whether they are winning or not is not known. It is certainly not at all likely. But what is known is enough. There is mutiny.

The child is not dead.

Do not despair, Sita, she said to herself You needn't have despaired, Ingrid Jonker. The child is not dead.

The child is a giant. Each child.

And this was when she sang and when she danced.

And together the children control the streets. Their city.

The car importers have been burnt to the ground. The French army has run away. More soldiers are being imported from Mayot.

The Reunion firemen have refused to put out fires.

The timid, poor, apologetic housewives, mothers of these children, mothers who behind shy handkerchiefs usually hide even their own language in public, so spat-upon they feel, these women are wheeling supermarket trolleys off. Heads held high. Goods are free now. In the broad daylight of the tropics. Up to the slum flats in their part of Sodron. With a smile of victory on their faces. The smell of a future victory. One day.

One woman was even overheard saying to Bishop Aubry, '*Bondye la done*', gift from god.

The children have, in all their innocence, revolted.

The colonizers are afraid. Cowering in corners. Paying thugs to be night watchmen. Installing electronic fences. Buying more guns. Being petulant on television. Sometimes the children give warnings. They spread rumours. Tonight we will burn such and such a building down. Sometimes the threat is even on the television beforehand. And they do. And the army runs away. And the firemen don't put it out. Sometimes people even think it's ordained by sorcery that such and such a building should fall. Or do they pretend to think so?

The oppressed cry out.

They rise up.

They oppose.

Speak out.

In the Sodron. Even the Sodron. In Reunion. Even in Reunion.

We were all vindicated. The US army may destroy the whole of the Iraqi army and flatten a whole civilization. And yet, as if in counterpoint, the most unprepared-for resistance comes out. At the very same moment in history. The French army, concentrating on the Gulf War, is being forced to handle a mutiny in its most docile Indian Ocean outpost. All this to say that vindication was necessary. We all felt it.

But Sita was more than just vindicated.

And I saw Sita's face that day.

Some kind of detonator went off. Not an immediate effect to it. Again, not immediate. But it, too, was like the switch setting off a time bomb in her head. If I hadn't known she was a Surinam girl like I'm a Surinam boy, I'd have thought maybe she was a *Reyone* herself. What else could explain this ultimate vindication she was celebrating.

◆

At this point in the story, usually there's one listener or another, when the story is told live, that is, and not just written down on paper for later reading by unknown (even if dear) persons like you, reader, who will ask me, the story-teller, a certain question, which other listeners will invariably nod at, meaning it needs an answer. It is always the same question: '*Who are you anyway?*'

This question does not mean *how do I know the things I'm writing about Sita*. Listeners already know that this is a matter of mere convention. They know that at the very end of the story I'll have to come up with some kind of a lame excuse as to how I know all this. The kind of thing like '*Then the king gave me a kick in the arse, and that's howcome I landed here in front of you to tell the story.*' This traditional kind of ending preempts that particular meaning of the question 'Who are you anyway?'

What the listeners invariably want to know when they interrupt early on like this in a story, is am I telling the truth. Am I an honest person? Can I be trusted? And more particularly, would I tell the truth about *myself*. For how can I tell the truth ruthlessly about, say, Sita if I am not known to be fairly brutally truthful in relation to myself? Am I trustworthy: that is the question. Would I tell the whole truth about myself? Because, hiding things is lies. And nothing but the truth? Because inventing bits is lies. You can only add on bits that make things more true.

It is customary in our archipelagoes and islands for us story-tellers to give a short and cruel introduction of ourselves, through a sub-story, at round about this point in someone else's story. I see no reason to deviate from this tradition.

My name is Iqbal, as you know.

And I'm going to tell you my very first memory

23

It's night time.

My mother stands in the dim moonlight night. A very young wiry widow. She is centre stage. She is projecting her voice, loudly. She is standing shrieking arguments at the top of her voice. One hand's on her hip and the other's in the air. She's fighting the enemy. Loudly in the middle of the night. The enemy, in the form of my *two uncles* from Kannmas who had come smelling of drink in a taxi, and *my cousin from next door* and *a policeman*, who he had gone to fetch. Four against one.

Me and my two little big sisters shivering by the tin shack house, barefoot in the rags we slept in. My mother midstage, ranting and raving. She has truth on her side. At this point, anyway. And she knows it. 'She might even win,' I think with a sudden pleasure replacing the fear I feel.

Out of the blue, I'm summoned to centre stage, myself. '*Garson*, Boy,' my mother shouts to me 'Boy. Fetch my sugar tin. Go on, fetch it.' I am honoured. I have been given a role in the play. I run inside, climb up on the only chair in the house, and take the sugar tin down from the *machann*, cradle it in my arms and run into the spotlight. It's an old milk tin, now used for keeping sugar in, because we haven't had milk for a long time. I give it to her. The moon gets brighter at this point. And she takes the sugar tin, rips its lid off, and holds the tin up in the air with one hand and points at it, or rather inside it, with the other hand which is, at the same time, clutching the lid. 'Do you see this tin? Do you? Lost your voices? Men! Family! What's the matter with you? Answer me. Can you see this? Can you? When Inoos was old, and sick and dying, and then when Inoos finally died, and was gone, did you ever take the trouble to so much as look into my sugar tin? Did you? It's the only question I want you to answer. Did you even once check my sugar tin?'

There was the cry of bats fighting over ripe litchis. This makes the four men get the shivers. Bat cries make them put their heads on one side. Make them look in the wrong.

'Family! Huh! Brothers!' she goes on now, getting a certain extra lilt to her voice from the fact that the bats are clearly on her side. 'Do you know what it is when you haven't even got a few grains of sugar to make *dilo disik* with a glass of water from the fountain for the kids?

Sugar paradise island indeed. Do you know? Flaming hypocrites. And now you talk of shame. *He* gave me sugar. That's what. *He* checked in my sugar tin and saw I didn't have sugar to give the children. That's what. And now you tell me I'm a shame. He gave me sugar for the little ones. Is that true or false, Iqbal.'

'True,' I say. I am proud of her. 'That is true.'

The policeman is the first to lose his nerve. 'It's not really a police case this!' he starts to mumble and shuffle his feet around. 'She is over 18, and she's got the right to meet anyone she wants to. She can do what she likes.' He fiddles with his heavy leather belt that's swinging around, unbuckled, in slovenly style.

My mother sees he's weakening. She's not going to let them off that easily.

'Calling policemen out in the night because I'm a shame. Making a laughing stock of a poor policeman in the middle of the night.' She is smart, my mother. 'It's you fools that are a shame, that's what. Bring shame to the family. Pah! Say I'm a whore, I keep him. I am a woman. I'm proud of it. See what you can do. None of your business. If my sugar tin isn't your business then nothing of mine is your business. *Tande la*? Do you hear? I have to leave these tiny ones, hardly more than babes in arms, that's what they are, I have to leave them, abandon them, I have to go out to work. And then you punish me, punish me, bring policemen out in the night.'

By now a fair-sized audience has developed all around the moonlit clearing between the *alfons* mango trees in which she holds her soliloquy.

'Let her be,' the policeman continues, desperately trying to make way for a retreat from the all men's alliance he has got into. 'She's right really. It's not in my scheme of duties. We policemen have a lot of problems as it is. I have to find transport home in an hour or so.'

But she interrupts him. She flies off again, keeps him standing there gaping along with her two brothers and her nephew neighbour, the pathetic still life of patriarchy against the primal mother. And I, Iqbal, the primal child, admiring the mother. My sisters stand there upright like heroines now, glaring at the enemy. Firoza is five, Begum, four, and then there's me. I am nearly three.

'You say I keep a Hindu. No, you don't say Hindu, you say I keep a

Malbar.' She is getting provocative now. In for the kill. I can feel she is about to make a mistake in her new tactic.

'I'll do what I want to, and you keep your noses out of it. You say I'm a shame to the community. Well, I'll tell you what. I'll damn well tell you what. You hypocrites. That is no longer a worry of yours. I'm fed up now. I have an announcement to make.' I sense the drama. She's going to do something irrevocable, I know it. And probably erroneous.

'Don't speak like that, sister,' one brother, rather the worse for alcohol, says. 'Look there's even a policeman come to try and make you see reason. Your children are neglected. You don't send them to prayers or anything.'

'Don't change the subject, you hypocrite. You know what I'm going to say, and you are going to hear it. Because it is the truth.' Her voice begins to take on apocalyptic tones. Even as a child I am horrified at what she might say. The power of the word. In that weird light. Under the *alfons* mango trees. With a large audience riveted.

'I,' she intones, 'I, Salma, widow of Inoos, hereby formally tell you all. I am from this minute onwards no longer in your religion. Keep it. I'm joining *Mission*, Assembly of God.'

This had the effect of a thunderbolt. On everyone. On me especially. What does it mean? What can it mean? *Mission?*

'So you just hold your mouths with the shame to the community business. And my children will go to Assembly of God prayers. Twice a week,' she adds, 'And,' for dramatic effect 'to church on Sundays.' There is a kind of silence I've never heard before. No-one even breathes. 'And so you can all just piss off.' The contrast of religion and her last words is for added effect: juxtaposition, it is, and it's noticed even by me, a child. But, something gets hold of me, some awe at my mother's courage, and, before I know where I am, I step forward into the moonlight patch she's standing in and I proceed to say my first ever theatrical words:

'Yes, piss off.'

At this point, the taxi driver starts up his engine. Anyone can tell the curtain is now coming down. My two uncles squirm back into the taxi they had come in. My cousin disappears into his house. And just the policeman is left gaping in the middle of the night.

He walks off in an undignified way. Head down. Shuffling untidily, groping for the other half of his leather belt, to buckle to the first half around his uniform. The denouement unbalances him. I hear him mutter: 'Women aren't what they used to be,' and then 'Mind you, never anger a mother with small babies. They get like that. What brokendown cart have I climbed into. I'm getting out of here.'

And so it was.

My mother went on seeing Ratchetaran, as he was called. And he did see to it that there was sugar in our tin. He was a foul sort. And we were terrified of him. We had known him since we were born, and called him uncle, because as far as we could make out, he was a sort-of husband of our father's sister, Fatimah, and they lived in Sime Giriye in a concrete house. And he had a bicycle. And registered scales. All of his own. In his name. Ratchetaran. And he sold vegetables door to door. I mainly remember slices of pumpkin and dubious tomatoes. And he gave credit, and had a little red notebook that he pulled out of his back pocket and that he wrote down how much people owed him in. His debtors were mainly women. Mainly single women.

Everyone called him 'Ratchet', making the first vowel resound, as in 'rat' and the second sound more like an i, and making the ch sound like sh. It was his character that made this name stick.

Ratchet was probably the man from whose sperm I, Iqbal, sprang. I am not just saying this because I want to get your sympathy or to be shocking or anything. It is not even that I am proving that I tell the whole truth in saying this. It is just that I turned out the spitting, splitting image of the man.

And my father, Inoos, was already old, had been sick for three or four years before he died, too sick for any strenuous exercise like begetting, and, another proof, he was not getting much pay either. And vegetables were being bought on credit. And so my mother, very young and I thought pretty, came to start laughing and flirting with Ratchet. Very open about it. And my father ailing in the tin house.

And this is what, as I got bigger, and understood more, intrigued me.

Those uncles and cousins of mine never did anything to put pressure on my mother to stop her acting up with Ratchet while Inoos, my father, was still alive, even though she clearly, and I always thought cruelly, flaunted her 'keeping' him, to use the expression of the uncles during the later offensive against my mother. Why not? Why didn't they say anything earlier? Why didn't they tell her to make a choice? It would have been a reasonable thing for any relative or neighbour to say. Such were my thoughts as I grew up. A good woman, a fine member of the community, her husband dying, unable to work, and she blatantly carrying on with the vegetable seller. And no brothers, cousins, neighbours told him to lay off, or her to quit it. Their silence was a mystery to me. And it was more than silence. It was collusion. They agreed.

Maybe, I had thought, it was for the vegetables. They all knew how little my father brought home, being absent from work all the time, until he hardly went to work at all. And they all just shut up so that they didn't end up having to fork out to pay for feeding our little mouths with vegetables, themselves.

Or maybe, I had pondered as I got bigger, it could be put down to the fact that my father's sister having already become Ratchet's mistress, in the open, before my mother also did, maybe this put my father into a difficult position. But still, that was just my father. What about all the other neighbours and family that usually intervene to prevent complicated set-ups? What happened to them. It stayed quite inexplicable. Because, with the exception of this one thing, everyone used to tell everyone else off for anything that wasn't approved of. Just like that, on the spot. This was, I think, a good thing, that they were frank. It's a kind of truthfulness. She should have been told off while my father was alive, I think. What do you think? But no, when he's dead and gone, she's a widow, free to do as she pleases, as far as I can see, then, at this point, they make a posse and intervene like some kind of a lunatic lynch gang against my mother, in the middle of the night, drunk, by taxi, with a policeman in tow.

I might never have known.

But there was someone very truthful who I know.

Sita's father, Mohun Jab.

He told me. One day when I was walking in the woods with Sita's father, Mohun Jab, checking out the situation before a poaching expedition, I asked him. Just like that. I was twelve, and I asked him. Why did no-one say anything to my mother when my father was still

alive about her and Ratchet. Was society just becoming degraded I
asked, like they say in church, and no-one even bothered anymore to
tell anyone else off when they acted in a way that was inconsiderate,
to say the least, and potentially dangerous, given that my fatber, Inoos,
was very angry about it. I still remember him raving on his sickbed.
'What could they say,' Mohun Jab said. 'What could they say. The
silence had started long before you were born. And people are
superstitious. And they thought your father was paying for his past.'

'I can't understand a word of what you're saying, Ton Mohun Jab,
not a word.'

And then he told me something. A funny thing. Funny peculiar.
That my father, who was a great deal older than my mother, had when
he was young, done just what Ratchet had done in relation to my
mother, to another woman. As a young man, he had actually moved
in with this woman, while the woman's husband was dying of
tuberculosis in the next room, and had stayed on as husband, after the
husband's death. And many years later she had died, and after more
years had passed, Inoos, my father, had remarried the young woman,
Salma, that was my mother. And so, out of some kind of collective
spite, no-one said anything to my mother or to Ratchet about their
carrying on. 'Inoos got, in their view, what was coming to him,'
concluded Mohun Jab.

◆

So, you see, I tell you the truth about myself. As I understand it. So
why shouldn't I tell the truth about Sita?

That is who I am anyway. And I am used to it. Can I go on now?
And, as I come to the end of this diversion, the strange song starts up
once again, ringing in my head: *Jojo was a man who thought he was a
woman*, only instead of singing it right, I sing it: *Iqbal was a man who
thought he was a woman.*

I took my mother's side. More sinned against than sinning, I thought
of her.

Can I go on now?

◆

She dived. Sita dived down under water. One hard pull with the arms. Strong arms, strong will, and swivel down like a propulsed arrow. Then swimming strong breast-stroke with her legs, keeping her arms ahead of her like a blind person in an unknown place. Her ears rang with the depth. The water was dark and murky. Yellow brown. She didn't know where to look. Where to begin to look. But she searched. She searched everywhere. She didn't know where, didn't know where. Where? Visibility was appalling. Where? She couldn't see a thing. But it was somewhere down there. She touched around in the water, twisting in the slow motion imposed by water to the left and then eel-like to the right. She felt in front of her as she dived, felt with moving hands. Braille. Wasting no time. Where is it? Where has it gone? Where on earth is it? What is it? Yes, worse still, *what is it*? What is it? She must find it. It is down here somewhere. No sound. Nothing to be seen.

And yet she knew it was there. Lost, but there.

She had lost something somewhere.

Somewhere down here. A great big hole. A nothingness so strong that it was a presence.

She had to come up again. Can't stay down there too long. A dizziness came over her as she came up. Didn't want to get the bends. So that she'll only be able to move smoothly at 33 feet underwater. And a cripple the rest of the time.

She found nothing. But she knew it was there. She would prepare to dive again.

It wasn't a river she was diving into. Not the canal outside Cambridge when James or someone had knocked another punter's glasses off. And, with Dharma watching amused, she had taken off her long skirt and in the same swift movement, dived in, autumn and all, had seen the murkiness, had felt the wildness, the wild mess at the bottom, and had felt around in the dark until she got the glasses and came up. But she knew there was something in there, just as she had known the glasses were in there. She even knew the place, just as she'd known the place where the glasses were. And she would find it, just as she had found the glasses. Or would she? What was it?

Nor was she diving into the Patat River just outside Surinam. But it was as muddy as it was after floods in the hills behind Surinam, when water came pouring down, washing all the topsoil off the cane fields on the way down into the river. That was before she had known Dharma. Long before. When she was a little girl. And maybe she would have to dive into the underworld itself, as she had done once then so long ago. Maybe she would have to dive through an underworld, underground bit of river, like she tried to do under the smaller falls just beyond the Rochester Falls on the Patat River. Just where the river itself, like a snake into a fissure, dived under its own pool at the foot of the waterfall, and disappeared into the underground. Under the ground. Completely. Where the river became an underground river. And maybe she would have to brave it, underwater underground, until like where the river came up to the surface again thirty yards downstream, she would re-surface again. And then it would be like the glades when she came up to the surface again, the glades in all their greenness. She hadn't got through then. I hadn't either. Too narrow a trip. Would she now?

It wasn't Lake Erie up-state New York either that she was diving into. Not the vast dull water-mass that had been clogged with weed so thick it was like diving into a solid rather than a liquid medium. The weeds had gone mad, unbalanced by the chemicals continually spat out by the heavy factories for a century, when she had dived in just to see if a person could dive into such a thing, her being a life-saver, to know what to do if someone fell in one day when she was there. It wasn't Lake Erie she was diving into now, with 'Save Lake Erie' friends from the conference, one of whom became her second mother, looking on, in case she had to do life-saving, but it did feel a bit like diving for a somebody. Or rather diving for a body. For a corpse. Of someone unknown. Something dead.

◆

'Buried in the recesses of your memory,' Dharma had said, 'Buried.'
'Did you say *buried*?'
'Of course I said *buried*.'
He was right.
That's what it was.
Buried.
There was a hole.

◆

There were hours missing. But it was worse than that. Because the very word 'burying' rang and rang in her mind like a persistent alarm bell. She couldn't turn it off. And then it went on and on coming back like a haunting spirit: 'buried'. Why dive for something buried underground? Or was it underwater after all? It was in the thickness of blackness of murkiness of something.

The lost day. At least twelve hours missing from her memory.

Clean missing. 30th April, 1982. The eve of May Day, of Labour Day. The eve of the first of May. One night missing.

No, not completely clean. Because otherwise why should she have been angry. Why should she have replied angrily when four months ago before he went away to Paris, Dharma asked her a question about Rowan and Noella Tarquin. Why anger? And she replied '*How should I know? Was only there a couple of hours. Time for a meal at a restaurant*.'

Four months later, quite calmly Dharma turned on her, and, she took it as such, though he didn't mean it as such, he accused her. 'It is you. You are jealous, but it is inside you.' He said that. 'Isn't there something missing?' he asked. 'Don't you avoid something? Evade something. Something has got away, escaped, perhaps. Haven't you lost something. Missing in you. Don't you see it isn't in me, it's in you,' he said. What was it? Something was lost. Had she passed over something important? Had she failed to take a decision, perhaps not seen it? Was she hiding something in herself? Had she missed a dilemma? About something? About someone? He told of the missing hours. Missing. Quite neutrally, he said it. He did not accuse. Of anything else except projecting something. He didn't need to accuse her. The missing hours themselves were the accusation.

She stood accused.

He didn't use the word *lies. He wouldn't think of it that way. She did. There is a moral error somewhere. A wrong action or omission.* 'I feel,' she thought, 'that there is some kind of a lie. I lie. I am guilty of a lie. Plead Guilty? or am I Found Guilty?'

Sita realized, a knowledge descended on her, a conviction was born and grew up in a few seconds: she had been in Reunion not for 'a couple of hours'. Nor just 'for a meal'. What she had said was not true.

It was not a few hours.

She was, of course, there, *overnight*. For a whole night. She doubted it for a while. But then there were air flight schedules to prove it. She looked them up, and there they were.

'I lied.'

But what happened, then.

No memory was left.

Nothing.

A blank.

Only the knowledge, the new feeling of this great big black hole. The nothingness.

So that night, she went to work on it. With a will of iron. And she dived again and again all night. Diving into her memory. Relentless, she was. Diving into the unconscious. With cold determination. Diving into that opaque, dark, murky underworld.

It was a fateful night. Owls hooted. Cats spat. Bats in the litchi trees shrieked. Dogs put their heads up to the firmament and, like wolves, howled.

It was on the eve of the declaration of war against Iraq, the 16th January, 1991. Just before the bombs would go diving down. And she was plunging into the past. It was also the day Ton Tipyer was given a new suit top, and after looking at it from all angles, had decided to keep it, had taken off his old one, rolled it up into a ball, and stuffed it right there and then, deep down into the nearest garbage can. And she was diving into the past.

She dived and searched. Came up again.

She dived again. She had only three clues, or what seemed to be clues. First there were obviously The Missing Hours. Then there was the word 'Burying' which went on and on banging away in her head forcing itself into the status of a 'clue'. How could a word take on life like this word had: '*buried*'. It was like a haunting ghost. The very word.

And then there was a third clue. As if to confirm that there was something to look for, there was a memory from 1987. This memory was not faded at all. In 1987, five years later, that is five years later than the lost night, Dharma and Sita had gone to Reunion, and she had had an episode of illness of some kind. An episode of feeling completely bizarre. Almost of madness. This bizarreness she had hidden. She had masked it. She had tried to cover for it. It had lasted about three hours in its extreme form. And now, right now, it was still there, a clear memory. Sitting there in her mind. The memory of it was there. The memory. As clear a memory as the sea is, just outside the reef at the *kulis* outside Black River at midday in summer after calm seas for a week. Crystal clear. And never having been so much as looked at, let alone interpreted, worked out, analyzed, it was as alive in her memory as if it had been yesterday. She looked at this memory. This clue. She had had a bout of transitory madness. Insanity. Psychosis. No less. Which had evaporated hours later. The only time in her life. I know this for a fact, because I have known her throughout her life. It was only once. But now, after all these years, the memory of this state of lunacy, was her third clue. Why did she go bizarre in Reunion in 1987? Why? Five years after the missing night? In that same island, Reunion?

Sita dived down all night

With the determination of someone who can hypnotize herself to sleep. Sita could do that. Who can have teeth drilled without injections. Sita did that too. With the same will she can apply to other things. She dived. When she was only two, Doorga, her mother, tucking her saree into her waist, roughly as she did when she set about a new task, would say: 'Sita, where have I put my scissors?' and her mother would watch her, and she would, even then, dive into her memory, even then as a toddler, and after a minute or two, start to walk around in a trance-like state, and then find the scissors, 'the bleeding things', as her mother put it. Once Sita's mother called me over to watch Sita remembering where she had seen something. 'Sita, where have I put my hairbrush? It isn't in the bathroom.' It drove her mother mad just to watch her. What a weird little head she's got. Her mother called her Sita, short for 'Sister', because her mother didn't want a child really, so preferred to have her as a sister. She specially did not want a daughter like this one: all this concentration the little girl had. Her mother didn't like to think she was responsible for producing this. She was scared of her. Proud, but scared. Even then when she was a little girl. She stood completely still, staring into the air in front of her, and then walked around distractedly, got irritable when I tried to say something to her, and then all of a sudden a confidence came into her footsteps and she went to the bedroom and fetched the hairbrush. Her mother knew she, herself, had put it in an unusual place the day before.

And now, Sita took another breath, dived down again. There was no let-up in her.

She was looking for lost hours. Where had she put them? She hunted like Diana. Without ceasing.

Must it be, she thought in horror, for a memory of some form of duplicity? Of lies? Was there shame in it? Was their guilt?

She found nothing.

Nothing.

She dived down again.

She studied her three clues in trance-induced detail.

◆

And then she met something.

She drove into it with her whole self. Something large and dense and hard and terrifying and real and unknown.

She bumped into an illusive heavy, dense, *presence*. Like the big hole in the universe. The presence of an absence. The hole.

It was Anger. It was Rage. It was Fury.

That is what the hole was.

It changed its texture as she studied it. Its substance changed, or her perception of the matter it was made of changed. Like after eating psychedelic mushrooms.

Mainly it was a dense hole. With a heavy gravity around it. So that as you approached it, new things could fall in, and get lost in it.

But as her courage grew and she got closer, it would change. First she felt she had bumped into a great *ball* of anger. Wound up tight like fine single-ply wool, having been worked out of a loose skein, and wound into an immense, fraughtly tight ball of fury. As if you couldn't knit from it. The wool wouldn't get unwound. It was stuck.

And then it turned back into a hole again. She got vertigo at the edge of it. It wasn't just a hole below you, like a mineshaft. It was a hole on every side of you, vastly wide and vastly deep and as if you got a premonition of falling down it, so that it was above you as well as below and on the sides.

Now it takes on the form of a knot, a gnarled knot of sinew. Slippery sinew tied into endless knots, like nylon fishing line. How will I ever undo that, Sita thought. There isn't even a loose end to start with. Knots of rage.

And now it turns into a great wall of anger. Up against it. Iron and steel anger. You couldn't dent it. Or move it. It was heavy and inert and unresponsive anger. It was absolute.

And then it was a hole again. Always becoming a hole again. Dizzy edges. A hole of lost thoughts, that more thoughts would fall into. Or would she herself fall into it. She stepped back.

And then, as she calmed herself, controlled the vertigo, and studied the hole. It turned from a hole into a *hall*, a great hall of anger, with walls on all sides. Infinitely large and long and concrete. The main feeling of this manifestation of what was lost was that it was of concrete. But it hung, like curtains, only they were concrete. Concrete anger. Rage of reinforced concrete. How could she open concrete curtains and look behind them?

Whose anger was it? She wondered, looking at it. She looked at it. She went up to it and touched it.

And then she knew. She recognized it. Like it was her own hand, only seen under water with goggles, all big and frightening. She knew at once. It was *her own* anger. A violent, tripe-devouring anger. A memory so vivid as to hit her across the face. Struck. The memory of a wild anger so terrible and a murderous rage so ferocious, as to make her tremble. Even eight years and nine months afterwards. She felt it.

It moved from outside her to inside her, and back outside again. But what was the anger for? Against what? Against who? *What dread hand and what dread foot?* But she couldn't remember. She couldn't remember what about. Nor who with. Nothing. Nothing. If she added together all the anger she had ever felt in her whole life and multiplied it by anything she could imagine, any immense number, it would not reach the vast scale of the anger she now faced. She faced it.

It came into her again.

An animal cry of rage built up in her throat. And her hands had an itch to commit an act of violence.

And then something else became clearer. Got set free by the rising rage. It started to take form in the formless hell she was in. Closely knotted into that anger, was imprisonment. The hands that were hers and that wanted to perpetrate an act of murder, were trapped. She saw herself trapped, or was it locked up, or tied down physically, or handcuffed, or ball-and-chained, or paralyzed, or perhaps with a rock on her chest under water. Or being buried alive. A weight on her. Gyves.

◆

What she had found: Rage. The rage of the history of wounded womankind. And with it: Slavery. The slavery of humans historically doomed to be unable to move.

◆

Then came the word.

She spoke it.

She never thought it. She just found it, lying there like the rage and like the chains.

'The Word' just like an object. It came to the surface. Not the content of the words, no.

They were words she had intended to say. Once long ago. Words already composed and then, for some reason, instead of having been said, they had been abandoned. Deferred. *What happens to a sentence deferred?* Put into limbo? The whole composition was there now. She came across it. Reified before her.

The words had been an introduction, prepared and never spoken.

And now, when she came up from the last, deepest, and most exhausting dive, just when the first light of morning came up, eight years and nine months after whatever it was that had happened, without knowing what it was an introduction to, she said the words:

'Dharma, something terrible happened in Reunion.'

'What?'

'Something terrible happened in Reunion.'

'What happened?'

'I can't remember.'

'Can't remember what?'

'It's the word "buried", the word "buried". When you said I had buried something. It's true. The word "buried" haunts me. I've buried it. I've buried something. Or someone. And then now, now as I say the words to you, I find something else. It's from a T.S. Eliot poem, *The Waste Land*, I think it is, funny I haven't thought about that poem for twenty years, something about a corpse buried in someone's garden. There's something about that poem, Dharma. I think I killed someone. Murder, I think. I think it's murder. Maybe I killed Rowan Tarquin,' she said to Dharma. 'Maybe I buried him in the bottom of his garden.'

'What are you talking about, Sita,' he said, 'for god's sake?'

How could she answer.

A small, unkempt, garden, she now remembered. The first picture came through, a tiny bit of veld, outside a flat in the Sodron just outside Sendeni in Reunion. 'I murdered him.'

'Sita, you've been having a nightmare,' Dharma sat up in bed, and turned his head back to look at her.

Then the second image came. It was a visual image, this time. There were three knives. Daggers. African curios, perhaps, in three sheaths on the same holder. The two outside ones pointing slightly inwards at the pointed bottom ends. The middle one bigger. Did she use them? The spot? Just between two ribs, perhaps, find a soft spot, and then punch hard with the other hand. Or was she afraid of them being used on her? She put her hand to her side in self defense. Or maybe not curios, maybe one of those sets of kitchen knives. But definitely displayed in that way, laid out like a fan.

So it was, that after all the diving, she had come up with just that: raw, unclassified, violent anger all mixed into a feeling of trappedness, complete imprisonment. Like in a nightmare when you can't escape. She couldn't escape. Perhaps a murder. And a picture of a bit of back garden. And three short daggers. And a T.S. Eliot poem, of all objects, more vivid than anything else. She got out of bed and went to look it up: 'That corpse you planted last year in your garden, / 'Has it begun to sprout? . . .' It was in Part I of *The Waste Land*. Part I was called 'The Burial of the Dead'.

'Something terrible happened in Reunion, Dharma, on the night of 30th April, 1982, the eve of my favourite day of the year and I can't remember what it was. I think I murdered someone.'

'Sita, come back to bed into my arms, you've had a bad dream. It'll pass. Let it be.' They lay still like that.

◆

There was a knock at the door.

It was Ton Tipyer. Dharma went to the door. Let him in. He sat down. And then said to Dharma: 'I'm quite old now. Will you bury me when I die, Dharma, you and Sita?'

'When you're dead, you won't have any problems left, Ton Tipyer.' But the word *bury* disarmed him.

Then they both laughed. 'That's true,' he said.

He felt the atmosphere strange.

'I've got a flute now,' he said.

'A flute? Who do think you are? Krishna?'

'I play the flute now.'

'Be down at the stream watching the women washing and bathing soon. Where did you learn?'

'By myself. A bamboo flute. Is Sita all right?'

'She is having strange dreams, it seems.'

'Call her for me.'

When Sita came in, he asked her if she would bury him when he died. 'Will you bury me, Sita?'

'Bury? Did you use the word *bury*? Why did you say bury?'

'Yes, you have been having bad dreams, Sita. Forget it. I know you and Dharma look after me in any case. Forget it. Pretend I never said the word bury.'

'You said it again.'

Then, consciously pulling herself together, she said: 'Let's have a nice cup of tea.'

◆

There is no limit to the interruptions allowed to my story. This is normal. It is a story. You have your rights. So now you want to know who this Ton Tipyer is. By what right, you ask, does he pop up like that in the story? He also has his rights, I say. More rights than most. He is the chorus, folks. And so you want to know how someone becomes a chorus. How he earns this status. It isn't easy. It took him a lifetime.

He was a stone mason. He was *the* stone mason at Linyon Dikre sugar estate. Uncle Tipyer, the Rock. *Ton Tipyer Ros.* That was his name long ago. Stone masons in any case have a habit of being allowed anywhere. Absolutely anywhere. They can walk through any place with a trowel in their hand. Through a church, right through a cabinet meeting, through a trade union assembly, through a women's meeting. Stone masons have the rights of the creator. They make bridges and churches, school steps and sculptures. They make mills out of stone and it is them that make gravel. They make chippings. By hand. Even god doesn't do that.

By the age of eighteen he had become the master of rock. He could do anything to granite. He could do anything *with* granite. He could even talk to a granite rock. I have to tell you all frankly, by way of confession, so that you know the truth: Ton Tipyer was my god. When I was a child, I worshipped him. This makes it hard for me to tell about him. Forgive me. He meant to me that mankind could form his destiny; he meant man could cleave rock; he meant tools; he meant man is not ape; he overreached Hanuman, the ape-god; he meant transformation of nature; he meant creation; he meant birth of new life out of rock. He was a man like a woman: he could do with his own hands what women can do with their bodies: produce, reproduce, create, make, invent. He was magic. And as I tell this, the song words

41

come back to me, the words about myself that haunt me. I wish I were not bound to tell the truth, the whole truth, but the words are here, and I am doomed to tell you: *Iqbal was a man who thought he was a woman. No not thought. Not thought I was.* Not exactly that. But what then? Wished I was?

The field manager walked around the fields with Ton Tipyer, looking for a rock for an important job. The fields were full of huge granite rocks. The medium-sized ones had been piled up into pyramids by previous generations of slaves and indentured labourers. But the big ones were left for future generations who would toss them all around with monster machines. But, in the meantime, the cane just grew around them. They all just stood there. They were like the original inhabitants. Or Stonehenge.

Old rocks stood still, waiting for the pair of men to check them over.

Ton Tipyer didn't want any old rock. The field manager walked slightly ahead, with his head turned towards Ton Tipyer in a mock-respectful tone, thus making it obvious to any field labourer who might not know that he was a field manager and Ton Tipyer was only his stone mason who was who. Otherwise, so grand was Ton Tipyer's carriage and so imposing his demeanour, that you might have thought the opposite true, respective skin colour of the two or not.

They visited one rock and he looked at it from one side, and then from another, and then he said: 'This is a sick rock, Sir.'

That was it. The diagnosis was pronounced.

And they went on to another examination. He would take his hammer along, and in cases of difficult decisions, he would sometimes leap up onto a rock, and sit on his haunches against the horizon, looking down at the field manager, and then putting his ear to the rock, would tap one face lightly with his hammer. Sometimes a sad expression would come over his face as he announced the news with resignation to the field manager as though he were a close relative to the rock: 'It's ill, very ill, on the inside. It's an internal matter. Nothing can be done. It's a pity. But there it is. A fact.' When he found a rock, a real rock, a real granite rock, with no disease or disability, his face would light up, as if he had had a vision. 'Oh, what a rock. Rock of ages. This is it.'

And the field manager, would arrange for the rock to be taken to the front garden of Ton Tipyer the Rock's house in Surinam. And there he would carve what had been ordered. The only tools he used were a hammer, an ordinary hammer, and one very short chisel, which he held in his clutched left hand. He would sit in front of the rock for hours on end, for three or four days before he got to work on the rock. The field manager said behind his back that he was lazy. But he couldn't say anything direct or to his face because what if Ton Tipyer stopped doing his stone work, and went off and started lighting slow-burning woodpiles to make wood-charcoal at Samarel instead. What would he do then? Ton Tipyer said he had to *see* what he was making inside the rock before he could chip it out, he said. And so for three or four days he had to look for it. Specially he said, when he wasn't just looking for what might be in the rock, by nature, but when he had to look for what the boss ordered to be got out of that particular rock. A difficult task. But he inevitably saw it. Sometimes it was a huge mortar to use for crushing maize. Sometimes a huge circular mill, a *janta*, and sometimes it was a geometrical form for decoration of the sugar estate entrance.

Once he made something he saw inside a small, perfect rock. He made it for Sita when she was three. You see even from then, Sita was his little girl. That's why he's in the story. That answer your question? He cared for her. He was always there, near her. This was to stay true throughout the time I've known them. He made a jewel for Sita. It was a *karambol*. A perfect replica of a *karambol* fruit; star shaped in cross section; and along its length, it had that twist that characterizes a *karambol*. And when she loved it, and wanted not to let go of it at night when she went to bed, and when she had fights with her mother, Doorga, about it, he made a deal with her. 'You put it down at night, because I'll make a friend for it. It won't have to sleep on its own anymore.' 'A friend for my *karambol*?' 'Well, do you agree?' She did. So he made one. He made an avocado pear, a half of an avocado pear, with its stone in the middle, out of a separate piece of granite. She still has them. You can go and ask her to show you. Her little girl, Fiya, keeps them next to her bed.

Ton Tipyer's bread and butter task, when he didn't have a particular sculpture to make, was to break rocks up. So he, with his huge granite

43

hammer, would be escorted into the field by the *kolom* who was wearing shorts, and presented to the rock that he wanted demolished. I once went with him, and had the chance of seeing him working. He was given a rock six foot by seven foot by five foot. The rock was sitting all crooked in the middle of a cane field, the rock itself like an ancient god. The *kolom* walked off and left Ton Tipyer and me. And he, Ton Tipyer sat and looked at the rock. He didn't even talk to me. I was young, and was afraid. I thought the rock might really be a god or a *kalimay* or something worse than either. He sat and looked at it from one side, and then from another, and then from a third. I got the impression he was preparing to fight it. And then he jumped up on to it. And then down again. Then he lit up a cigarette. I looked around behind me to see if we were safe. Then, all at once, he took up his granite hammer and looked at it in his right hand. 'He's going to hit it,' I thought. But no he paced round and round the rock and then up onto an angled side of the top. 'I've found its *latab*, its main side,' he said. Then he stood up tall against the sunlight, and breathed deeply again and again. And in one vast movement, he swung the granite hammer in both hands up into the air, it hesitated at the apex, and then, like a crack of lightning, it split the air downwards and struck the rock. A strange sound came out of the rock. Like a sigh of pain. Like a deep fracture. But you couldn't see anything. Ton Tipyer started breathing deeply again, standing tall as a giant against the sunlight. I put my hand up to protect my eyes. And then he swung his granite hammer up again, again it hovered at its highest point, again it tore through the air and hit into the rock. This time, the rock cleaved in two. I was in ecstasy. 'It's broken in half, it's broken in half.' He came and sat down next to me, and didn't say anything. He just sat, looking half pleased, half sad.

His two assistant masons were alongside by now; they weren't allowed to hang around close while he was concentrating on the first hit. They had to hide behind the nearest rock pile until the big rock cleaved in two like this, and then they could come forward, greet Ton Tipyer, shake his hand, and set to work, separating the two halves with crow bars; and preparing each of them, for the next halving. Then all four of us sat and listened to the stories of one of the assistants. Mainly stories against himself, as a bad mason, stories that made us all laugh and feel pleased to be alive. We were sitting around, and the cane labourers in the field right next to us, hidden between the rows, were head down, hard at work, finishing their piece rate weeding. One shouted across, swore at us, calling us lazy goddamned artisans. To which the storytelling assistant said: 'Come and split the next one, mate.' In his tea break, the big-talking labourer came over and said, tongue in cheek, 'OK, where's the granite hammer, folks?' He was a huge young labourer, twice the size of Ton Tipyer. He climbed on to one of the two halves of rock, swung the huge hammer up mightily and down again. It only jarred his hands. He laughed and said 'Each to his work,' or something like that. To which Ton Tipyer said: 'Work slowly at it, mate, the cane won't go away. Tell the others to work slowly at it.' He couldn't stand being rushed, or even seeing them rushing. 'You've only got one life,' he called across at them all.

When I got big, I, Iqbal, myself had a few swipes at a granite rock with his hammer. At most a chip flies off, and hits me on the cheek; but usually it's just a spark.

And then, with his money that he got as a master stone mason at Linyon Dikre, Ton Tipyer bought his horse. Well, it was called his *horse*. Because he treated it like a horse. Like a cowboy in films treats his horse. It was a second-hand, very old, black and silver, Harley-Davidson *motorbike*. No-one else in Surinam had a motorbike. And that was the only Harley-Davidson I ever saw in the country. And it was a thoroughbred. He kept it beautifully groomed.

'He looks just like his horse,' I would say, and everyone would laugh. Because he and his motorbike did look alike. Ton Tipyer's hair was black and silver, just like the Harley-Davidson, and he dressed in well-preserved old suit materials that had the same aura as a Harley-Davidson saddle. And on his leather jacket he had thongs on the sleeves, near the elbow, that blew about as he went past on his motorbike. And the motorbike, on its handle-bar grips, had leather thongs as well. They also blew about as he went past.

And this was how, at a certain point, his name started to change. At first imperceptibly and then conclusively. He was not called Ton Tipyer, the Rock anymore. He was called Ton Tipyer, the Horse.

He never lent his horse to anyone, and he never carried a pillion passenger.

And when he drank too much, it was said that it didn't matter because his horse knew the way home. Which it did. If his horse was sick, Ton Tipyer wouldn't go to work. And his horse was often sick. And if Ton Tipyer didn't go to work, he would drink more, and his horse would bring him home drunker and later. And this was how his wife got fed up with Ton Tipyer, although he was the nicest man in Surinam. He took to drink.

She would stand inside the verandah room, the *godon*, and watch him sometimes, because it was incredible, when he and his horse came home. And people said she exaggerated, and laughed. And she also laughed. He would have been out, and would have been so drunk that he could hardly get onto his motorbike. But he finally would. And his drinking friends would sigh with relief, because his horse would take him home. Which it did. And he would drive all the way home from anywhere, back into his street, and right into the bit of garden in front of the house and bring the motorbike to a stop, and then frozen still, once there was no more forward motion to keep them up, he and the motorbike would fall over really slowly. To the ground. Like two lovers. And they would both go to sleep. Ton Tipyer snoring loudly, and the motorbike engine ticking over in neutral.

His wife would go and turn the motorbike off, and chuck a blanket over them both, and leave them outside. People said his wife was jealous of the horse. But maybe she was just cross about the drinking and not giving money for food for the kids. But in any case, this was how his getting kicked out started. And how it finished, for that matter.

But I must get back to stone-breaking. We have only got to breaking it into two, and then possibly four big rocks.

But he would make gravel out of it.

Gravel.

The sugar estate was making a new road. And the foundations of the road had been laid, with rock prepared by Ton Tipyer and the other masons, and the gravel chippings, or *makadam* were now needed.

And Ton Tipyer would make them. He turned huge granite rocks into gravel. Into chippings. By hand.

He sat on a gunny bag, hammer in hand, feet out in front of him.

And then pulled one stone the size of a tennis ball down in front of him from the pile of stones all the size of tennis balls on his left side. He pulled the stone down with his left foot. He held it between his two feet, and hit it with his hammer. It split in half. He aimed at one of the halves, then the other. Halving each one. When the pieces were small enough, he pushed them over to his right side with the outside of his right foot. And gradually the small mountain of large stones on his left side became a small mountain of small gravel chippings on his right side.

I loved this man.

◆

Sita, our heroine, was standing on the ledge along with the others. They were, it felt like it, all gods and goddesses. Of modern times. Not immortal. No. Not all-powerful. Not at all. Not in any other sense except that they were aware of their place in the universe. They had a vantage point. So many humans have lost this, that it now seems a quality of the gods.

A tenderness melted the atmosphere between them all, that tenderness that you get on a good work site, on an old work site. The proof of love. Love amongst work mates on a dangerous site. Work. Mates. On a site that had been around a long long time, enough time to grow organically.

There were transport problems again for Paris vegetable workers.

'Why do you do it, Sita? Why do you agree to do this work? Why accept in the first place? Why go on?'

'The helicopter's late again,' she replied. 'Don't worry about me. Mind your own business, mate.' She laughed. You could hear her laugh explode and then ripple over the whole of the centre of Paris. 'Can hear you from the Mediterranean,' he said. 'And the *korbey* they give us is bigger now, with more cauliflower fitting into it. Why, I repeat, minding my own business, do you do it? Why are you a vegetable seller?' The *korbey* was a sort of round tray made out of woven rattanware, an enormous replica of the tray people use for winnowing rice, a tray woven out of bamboo slats. They were given it by the vegetable bosses for carrying their cauliflowers in.

'And in spring vegetables are heavier, with all the April showers. Someone has to be a vegetable seller. I've got to get back for May Day that's why. You also do it. Work is work. Who else will do it? Why should *anyone* do it? Anyway I've got to be back for Labour Day. To Dharma and for Labour Day, don't you know?'

48

'You're mad to do it, Sita. You accept too much. Me too. We all are. We all do. But look at the view. Even up here, at this height, we are like fallen gods and goddesses. Why are we so abject as to accept this? Must we humans be like this? Maybe we do it for the view? The little Eiffel Tower and Arc de Triomphe. And look at the little traffic jam below. Dinkey toys. Tourist's curios. Magnets somewhere pulling iron filings in concentric patterns. What is May Day to you, Sita, anyway?'

Transport was late. Again. They were sixteen storeys up waiting for it. The ledge was very narrow. They were in a long line, all having to lean back slightly so that the weight of their cauliflower baskets didn't pull them off the ledge.

The helicopter was late again. When it came, one by one they would hook their baskets into the big hooks hanging down from the helicopter, and then hold on as if for life onto the other side of their baskets, or *korbey*. They would be transported to the Marche Central de Paris. This kind of transport had, like many other abuses, been reported to the Labour Inspectorate, but they had said casual workers are not always covered by the law. It was as if they were free-lance vegetable sellers, they were told, and as if they voluntarily exposed themselves to such risks, the Inspectorate men said. They were, they were informed, more like a small businessman, technically speaking. The country's free, they said. The government's not going to come and say people aren't allowed to stand on narrow ledges, or carry vegetables in *korbey* under helicopters. It's a free place. If people want to do it, they do it. And so it was that it went on like this every day.

'I'll fly to Dharma,' Sita announced, 'I'll fly to May Day.' At this thought she laughed a second time. Ripples over Paris a second time. 'It's not any old May Day there this year. History moves fast sometimes and someplaces and slow othertimes and otherplaces. It's been moving fast there lately, since 1978 and 1979 and 1980, and it's about to slow down. I've got to be there for the last fast bit.'

Then with the concentration that was the so-called gift of the gods to Sita, she floated off the ledge, waving goodbye, leaving her cauliflower basket balanced where she had been standing.

She flew off. With grace. Like a turning dolphin, off Kolonnday.

Only sheer concentration did it.

She had to move her arms, she knew, in order to fly.

She had to steer.

The feeling was divine.

She would fly to Dharma, she would fly to May Day.

'You can't stand around waiting for transport your whole life,' she called back to the others. 'There are limits. I must act. *Namaste*.' And as she flew off, they heard her saying to herself, 'May Day in Mauritius here I come.'

She went on flying.

And so it was that she set off, concentrating with all her might, up over the Alps, down past the foot of Italy, over the Mediterranean pool, across the corner of Egypt and Ethiopia and off Africa, and over the Indian Ocean. She saw the Carlsberg Ridge which rose like a mountain range under the sea off to her left, as she followed the edge of the Somalia Basin. She flew over the Seychelles Islands. Way over to her left, she saw in the far distance the Mauritian islands of the Chagos Archipelago. Amongst them the horse-shaped Diego Garcia and then Salamon and Peros Banos and she flew over more of the Mauritian islands, over Agalega, Tromelin, and the Cargados Carajos Islands; Rodrig, the second biggest Mauritian island, in the meantime was over to her left. Past the vast fishing banks, the ships had let their boats down, like mother whales with their young, to go out fishing around them, and she flew on towards that part of Mauritius commonly called Mauritius. The main island.

Like an emerald, Mauritius was ahead.

She concentrated on her flying more, and then started the descent. She flew over the bright green northern planes, where sugar cane and rocks and sugar cane and rocks lay basking in the sunlight along the northern part of the west coast, over Porlwi, snuggled roads, cemeteries, police headquarters and mango trees, into the foot of Montayn Sinnyo, over the Gran Rivyer Mouth at very low tide, rocks all jutting out, up over Laferm reservoir, past the Black River Gorges, round the Lemorn rock, and before coming down lower, she looked across over the whole of the south of the island, wildly and crookedly thrown together just like when the volcano vomited it up out of the bowels of the earth, and she glided along the south coast, past Rivyer Degale, when the sound of the rocks rubbing against one another in the backwash, came up and met her, and into Surinam under the *badamye* tree into her tin house, and just in time for the sun to set and the moon to rise, into her bed. Next to Dharma. Under the safe covers of her sheets drawn right over her head.

◆

Where, she thought, would the dream have gone if she hadn't dreamt it then? If, say, a dog had barked and woken her up?

◆

She would have to look at her three clues again.

The missing night, she knew was the night of 30th April, 1982. The eve of Labour Day. She also knew she was, at the time, in Reunion, the French colony. She was in transit between Seychelles and Mauritius.

What was she doing there? In Reunion. At that time Ton Tipyer, having been kicked out of his house by his wife, was living in large pipes that were being stored in the lowland near the Kodan warehouses, and he had met Sita near there and told her not to go through Reunion. It's a bad place, he had said. Kept slaves there after we were free, he said. And now keeping it a colony. Since he didn't say much usually, Sita had listened. And then she had laughed. Put her head back and laughed. 'I'm not going through Reunion,' she said. 'I'm going direct to Seychelles.' Ton Tipyer had also laughed then, at her laugh.

On Sunday 25th April, 1982 a week before the fated date, she had taken a plane to the Seychelles to go on a one-week conference on Women's Liberation. There there was a motley crew of academics and social workers. She was the only person there, it seemed, involved in opposing the political aspect of the repression against women. It would be lonely. She wasn't very keen to go.

In fact it almost broke her heart to go.

Significantly, she was originally scheduled to be back on 2nd May. This was the difficulty. She wanted to be back by 1st May. I don't blame her one bit. On 1st May, there would be the birth from out of a *tendency* within the big Socialist Party of our *organization*. Maybe it would turn out to be an important historic birth. Like the phoenix out of the ashes. The spirit of the 1979 strike and the 1980 mass protests, burnt to ashes by the new alliance between the Socialists and the Social Democrats, would live on. Will live on.

We were even preparing our manifesto for that day, Labour Day,

May Day, when we would distribute copies. I was in charge of roneo-ing them. We would be present at what we already knew would be the huge public meeting of the Socialist-Social Democrat alliance.

Our organization was also having public meetings for the first time under our own banner, a few times a week to encourage people to leave the Socialists, to support our organization, and nevertheless to vote for the Socialist-Social Democrat alliance against the right wing parties in the coming elections of 11th June.

What was most important for Sita was that she would, on her present schedule, miss the birth of our organization on 1st May. From the beginning, she told everyone she would do everything to make arrangements from the Seychelles end to get back for the 1st May meeting. She had to be present. Had to be there. When the organization would be born. 'As if you were the midwife,' I said to her teasingly.

Only Ton Tipyer, as he picked my stompie up out of the gutter I'd just thrown it in behind me after stubbing it on the edge of the rock wall by the canal, and as he straightened it out, mumbled that he was not going to that meeting. Waste of time, he said. Then he said he didn't have transport money anyway. When I offered him some on loan, he said his clothes might get wet if it rained. 'Gaspiyaz', was his exact word. 'Useless.' But I knew he might change his mind. He liked to get the atmosphere of meetings, in person. He would probably end up going.

We now celebrate the organization's birth as having been 11th April, 1982. Funny that. That in another way that day has been volatilized. We only chose this date, 11th April, afterwards. We decided that it was ambiguous, which it was, to have the organization's birthday on the same day as Labour Day; this, we quite rightly afterwards thought, would be spreading confusion between the working class and our organization. I had, in the beginning, personally not agreed to change the date. I was probably wrong. Sita wanted to change it. But she never gave her reasons. Odd that. She usually could. I was wrong, because 11th April had also been an important date in any case. It was a Sunday, and on that Sunday, 11th April, at the Socialist Party's delegates assembly, we had announced our collective resignation from the Socialist Party, on the grounds that we didn't agree with the leaders' politics of what they pompously but accurately called New

Social Consensus with the bosses, nor with the alliance that we had bitterly fought to prevent, with the right-wing populist party of Huriasing, the Social Democrat Party. We would go ahead and form an organization, but, in the immediate, we had only one alternative: to tell everyone to vote for the Socialist Party and its partner. We had to support the alliance because it was significantly more favourable to working people than any other party or alliance. We even had a list of ten specific political points on their platform on the basis of which we called on people to vote for the alliance. The transition from a tendency in the Socialist Party to becoming a separate organization was very much part of all our personal histories at the time. It was certainly part of mine. I, myself, had a sort-of midwife, or midhusband, role. *Iqbal was a man who thought he was a woman.* The song intruded again. I pushed it aside. I was midwife, because I had been on the Socialist Party Central Committee, the spokesman you could say, for our tendency; I had been personally responsible for the steering of the Tendency towards a clear political and ideological split from the Socialist Party on the 'new social consensus' issue. Sita was midwife in a different way. She toured the country holding talks, she spoke at public meetings, she drafted leaflets. Sometimes Fiya in tow, sometimes on her own. Just like she had been like a sister to her mother before, now Fiya was like a sister to her. 'Oh, I didn't know you had a daughter, Sita,' people would say.

Sita went to the Seychelles Conference to represent the women's association that she was, and still is, an active member of. The All Women's Front had received a phone call from a certain Mrs. Philippa Mionne of the Ministry of Women's Affairs in Seychelles who transmitted the rather belated invitation to the All Women's Front to delegate a member to attend. From the Seychelles end, they would pay the airfare. In brackets, one could say that in general whenever the All Women's Front ever gets past the usual official boycotts against them for being too workerist, then the invitations are invariably late. The All Women's Front very much wanted one of its members to go, but they were all very busy and it was not easy to spare anyone. In particular, they were preparing an important event: on Sunday 9th May, they would be holding an all-day Colloquium at the Louis Leschelle Hall in Porlwi. There would be Ragini Kistnasamy, Rajni

Lallah, Pouba Iyasawmy, Anne-Marie Sophie and myself Iqbal, the only man on the panel, speaking. The late Ah Fong Chung would preside. And there would be an exhibition, and group discussions. But everyone, including Sita, would be doing preparations.

The All Women's Front delegated her to go to the Conference. The choice fell on her for a number of rather minor reasons. But it fell on her.

Whoever it fell on, the All Women's Front wanted its member back as soon as possible to give a hand with organizing the Colloquium.

So it was that she went to the Seychelles on Sunday 25th April for a one-week conference, even if it was reluctantly that she went. Even if it broke her heart.

Here is the first dilemma, dear reader. Should she have gone to the Seychelles at all? Can a person know what will happen as a result of this decision to go to a conference? Is there any error yet on her part? She didn't really want to go. She really didn't want to go. Let us be clear about this. But could this feeling of refusal be taken as a warning? Can we believe in prophesies, like some ancient tribe does? Sita, like so many of us, may have been a goddess of sorts, that is to say, amongst those humans who want all humans to be in control of their destinies, but how was she to know that this feeling of not wanting to go was an omen? Can this threat of 'even if it broke her heart' be taken to be a sign of something? A premonition. A warning to be heeded? And can we, modern people who don't believe in prophesies and auguries, fault her for going? And can we say that what Ton Tipyer said about not going via Reunion was a soothsayer's warning, one that Sita ought to have taken more seriously? He was, after all a wise man. He is the chorus. He associated the trip to Seychelles with a stopover in Reunion. He said 'Beware the end of April. He said April is the cruellest month.'

The Conference, though worth attending and though historically very important in a way, was also rather trying. Half of it was academics being very competitive with one another about their women's studies and theories and research, all very clever and also very boring, and the other half was rather mindless pragmatism, going on and on about what had been done for the sake of it having been done. It was one of those piously anti-political and thus intensely cowardly conferences. And there were, among the women there, broken women from colonies, women who never breathed a word about the fact that they were still relentlessly colonized. They seemed to be used to it. If you didn't know better, you could almost say they seemed to like it. Be honoured by it. Like a slave, she thought.

She was obsessed from the beginning by something else. How to get back in time for May Day.

As soon as she found out the earliest possible time she could leave, that is to say, that the resolutions would already be prepared by Thursday 29th April, and that after that, the conference had only rather ceremonial parts, she went to a travel agent's in Victoria during a lunch break to try to change her ticket to get back for the 1st May. Sita, the determined, was at work. And she found a way to get back for the public meeting. The only way she could possibly manage this, was to fly to Reunion in the middle of the day on the 30th April, to transit in Reunion until the morning of the 1st May, then to fly over to Mauritius in the morning. She could arrive in Mauritius in time for the second part of the big public meeting at Rozil. She didn't think of Ton Tipyer's warning.

She changed her ticket. She would unfortunately, although only for twenty or so hours, have to be in the colony. She would even have to pass through the hands of the French colonial authorities, always something to be avoided, but she wanted to be back for the 1st May, so it didn't matter.

Here, dear reader, is the second dilemma. Should Sita have changed her booking? Should she have left a conference a day early just so that she could be back in time for the 1st May public meeting? Is this a case of stubbornness? Is this a case of cussedness? Culpable persistence?

And then, even more pertinent, should she have done this knowing that she would spend 20 hours in Reunion? She knew only too well the dangers and the traps in this. Is there some error that has crept into her actions? Can we blame her for anything yet? Why did she not think about what Ton Tipyer had said? His warning had been specific.

Sita telephoned Dharma at his brother Lutchman's house in Surinam; they had arranged that she would do this. 'I'll be there with you, Dharma, and with all of you, for the birth of the organization. Give my love to Fiya.' So it was that Sita told Dharma she would be back on Saturday, 1st May and would meet him at the public meeting. On the roundabout itself. Before putting the phone down, he gave her the address of Rowan Tarquin and his wife, Noella, so that if possible, she could contact them again while in Reunion. Useful to get into contact with them again he said. It turned out she already had their address routinely transferred into her 1982 diary, just over the page. They lived in Reunion, just ordinary colonizers, and in 1979 Dharma and Sita had stayed with them and their three children for a week. She had, in fact, at the time been invited to give a one-week teacher training course for preschool teachers in Reunion. It was a course she was used to giving, and it had gone well. It was held at the flat of a woman who lived in Lepor, a friend of the Tarquins.

It would be good to be in touch with the Tarquins again, and to find out how the kindergarten work was going. Rowan Tarquin was a probation officer and a dabbler in politics. Now that the organization was being born, it would be necessary to start developing more systematic links in the Indian Ocean. At the conference no-one from Reunion, or anywhere else for that matter, was very interested in politics; there were careers, and there was do-gooding social work, but no political contacts. Rowan and Noella were the only people she really knew in Reunion. You have to start somewhere to develop contacts, she thought.

Sita and Dharma had got a card from the two of them the year before to announce the birth of a fourth child; it was one of those 'far par' cards that French people send out. On the back Noella had scrawled a fond message in her spidery script, 'Mon grand frère est très intelligent, mes soeurs sont toutes douces, mon père est parfois brute, et ma mère gargarise des bêtises sur une carte', signed by the new baby. (My big brother is intelligent, my sisters are sweet, my father is sometimes cruel, and my mother is writing rubbish on a card.) Sita remembered the card clearly, because she and Dharma had been impressed by the strange poignancy of Noella's joke. *Sometimes cruel.*

These thoughts flashed through Sita's mind as she looked at the telephone in front of her. Then she right then and there picked up the telephone again, and this time dialled Rowan and Noella's number.

Should she have done this, dear reader? Should she have phoned them? Is there any possible mistake here?

She got Rowan on the phone and said she would be in Reunion overnight, and would it be possible for her to stay over at their place? Certainly, he said. He would meet her at Zilo Airport on Friday during the day.

Another dilemma, dear reader. Should she have invited herself to stay? This must be considered seriously. Now, eight years and nine months later, she knows only of a meal in Reunion and she doesn't even know if Rowan and Noella were separated or not then. 'How should I know?' she had replied angrily to Dharma. Why was she angry? 'How should I know? I was only in there for a couple of hours, time for a meal at a restaurant.'

False.

She was in Reunion overnight.

Only she can't remember it. She can't remember anything. She can't remember nothing, nothing, nothing. Except a meal at a restaurant. And that also, a strange elusive memory, unlike other memories in her head.

She remembers getting back to Mauritius, being met at the Plezans Airport by Dharma's brother Lutchman, who took her to the 1st May meeting. To be there. She remembers being angry with an unreasonable, fleeting anger, that Dharma was not there at the airport to meet her, himself. How could he have been though?

A week later she got a card from the only friend she had made during the week of the conference in the Seychelles, the nightwatch lady at the small hotel she had stayed at. The card only had seven words on it. It said: '*You must find again your lost day.*'

The words, while innocently referring to her having left the conference a day early, seemed so eerie to Sita ('Spooky', she had said to herself, not knowing why she said it) that no sooner had she got the card than she forgot about it as well, just like she had forgotten about everything that happened in Reunion. The card slipped into the hole. I suppose it was just too near the edge. Like the black hole in the universe. It sucked in everything nearby. Specially light.

A hole.

Missing.

Nothingness.

◆

How, you now ask (What questions!) did Sita become an activist, a militant? For goodness sakes, a story's a story. You folks really make me work for my money. Another diversion, but when will I get finished? I'm telling you about the *rape of Sita*, and you want to know how and why she was a political activist. That's not what the story's about. She just was one. Can't you take anything as given? And in any case, what story can I tell about that.

OK. OK. I give up.

Obviously, there were many reasons. And the main ones are easy enough to see. Why d'you even bother to ask? She, as you jolly well know, had the luck of having a father who had been Anquetil's right hand man. Wouldn't she have learnt on his lap about political struggles? You can expect her to have a penchant. It's not necessary for me to come up with a story. She even had the distinct advantage of having had Doorga as a mother. You know Doorga, of course. Well Doorga had personally, as you know, suffered the specific effects of the Public Order Act. Oh, you don't know what I'm talking about? Well, skip it. Sita would have been obliged to have understood a lot from this. Her grandmother, oh, you don't even know about her grandmother? Well, well, well. (Sorry I mentioned her, you'll be along with more interruptions later, if I don't watch out.) What could you expect from a grandmother like hers except political education handed down? And Sita's a direct descendent of Ana de Bengal. Of course any direct descendent could be expected to have every chance of being a political visionary. You don't know who Ana de Bengal is either? Well, that's your bad luck. All I'm trying to tell you is there is no need for a story on this point. Her family obviously and clearly formed her perceptions young. That's why she's a militant now. That's all there is to it. No sub-plot needed. May I continue. There's the story of the rape of Sita to get through.

What, you ask, about her sister. Her sister, you say, is interested in nothing but making chutney, bottling jam, pickling *bilinbi*, waxing her floors, beating her clothing on a rock down by the river, and cooing at her two angelic children. Not that Sita isn't also like this. Her sister sings and dances and beats the *dolok* and *ravann*. We know, you say, that Sita does too. But her sister'd rather, you allege, put henna in her hair than go to a public meeting. She'd rather, you accuse her, go on a pilgrimage than a demonstration. She's got gods all over the house and yard. Of all denominations. Just in case, she says. And she loves bright sarees and skimpy *choli* blouses. And puts a stick-on *tika* on her forehead to go to weddings. And she sticks it to the mirror in the bathroom when she takes it off. She paints her toenails with glitterful nail polish. And she doesn't know anything about trade unions, politics, world affairs, or anything. She's not even in the women's movement.

And her sister's got the same father, the same mother, the same granny and the same ancestors, you say, as Sita.

Correct.

So you accuse me of talking rubbish.

OK, you win, I'll tell you a story. I give up. You want a story. It's like a thirst you have. A story, a story, a story. And I have to pour it out. The story as to why Sita got interested in politics.

Newton saw an apple fall off a tree. It fell downwards. And so he saw gravity. Everyone else had just seen apples falling off trees and seen nothing more than apples falling off trees. His sister also just saw apples falling off trees, I add for spite.

Let us start with definitions. Definitions. Because gravity itself isn't clear yet. Being interested in politics, what does it mean? It means only one thing, a human being who hasn't yet given up on the general issues facing humanity, our nature and our culture.

Sita hasn't given up.

One day when Sita was four years old, Doorga took her around to Suyak to the bit of rocky beach just on the other side of the river mouth. Sita already knew how to swim, from splashing about in the Patat River. 'It's high tide, Sita, and it's noon. I will teach you something about life.' The sea was navy blue. 'What you mean life, ma?' There was a signpost cemented into the rocks, right near where the waves crashed in, a signpost which read 'Dangerous to bath here. You may be drowned!' She had read it aloud to her mother, and translated it into Kreol, not noticing the spelling mistake. Doorga was very pleased that Sita could read. Impressed in the way only illiterate people can be. 'That's it, my girl,' she had said, 'You will make history move forwards. But you must learn about life as well.' Sita frowned up at her. 'What *forwards* are you talking about?' Then she undressed Sita completely, and took off her own sari, took off her petticoat and *choli*, and they both stepped out of their *savat*, sponge sandals. Together they went and stood next to the signpost, on a big black rock overlooking the heavy south sea as it hit in and swirled off the rocks. Two naked humans. Mother and child. There were people in the distance, here and there, but they didn't notice anything odd. Doorga had two bits of light wood in her hands. 'Watch, Sita,' she said, and threw one in about as far as a person could jump, and they watched it sink, shoot up, hesitate and then get whirled around by the current in a dash, and get drawn down the gully, like into a vacuum tunnel, rush along the gully, and wash up out of it, abruptly on to the sand patch between the rocks. 'Don't jump until I tell you to.' This was the first Sita knew of what she would be asked to do. Doorga jumped off the rock down into the water four feet down, a wild, swirling current, that she turned around and swam against, holding the wood in front of her, and called 'Jump here!' to Sita, pointing down current from herself. Sita was calm. She jumped out to where Doorga had pointed down current. Sita was calm when she came up from under the water after jumping. 'Hold on to the bit of wood, Sita,' Doorga said, and so it was that she put her hands out on to the bit of wood. She looked Doorga right in the eyes. Straight. Doorga looked at her. Confidence was born. Then Doorga and Sita in delight began to kick and to swim in the same direction as the current, and with two speeds, that of the sea and that of their legs and Sita's right arm, like lightning, they whooshed around the rocks in a wild arc, laughing heads back both of them, and they were propelled along the thin gully, and were coughed up by the rough wave that broke suddenly on the beach. They lay on the sand, looking into one another's eyes. 'That kind of forwards,' Doorga said. And for years and years, this experience was the central well from which Sita drew lessons. You have to decide whether or not to listen to instructions from authority. What does 'do not' mean? Under what conditions does *do not* hold. It's a good thing that they put up the signpost in a way. Because what if someone tried to swim against that current. But then again, if you can swim, and if you know the current, and if you check on it like Doorga always did with a bit of wood, the danger was less. And if you know the current, and if you can swim well, when you add together those two things, then you can get up real speed. Danger is not necessarily a bad thing, is it, girl? Nature's force can be used. Understand it. Know it. Test it. Harness it. You must also be able to train yourself, for example, to swim. Practice hard, girl. And what is the meaning of being able to read? And who do you trust when they say 'jump'? Who exactly. You must have judgment, girl. And why act? Why not just sit on the beach. And what do clothes mean? No-one thought it odd that Doorga took her sari off and swam. Or were they too scared of her?

And now you ask about her sister. Did her sister not get the same lesson when she was four years old? Well, yes, probably. But maybe she didn't think about it as much. In any case, Doorga always had more intensity in her way of dealing with Sita.

One day, the very day Sita was born, Ton Tipyer told me this, because it somehow stuck in his mind. And so the second story begins. One day. On the day of her birth. She was born at midday. The day she was born, Doorga was on her own, and pulled her out all by herself. A huge woman, she was, and strong. Crouching on a mat on the floor, she pulled her out and put her on a bit of clean cloth next to her. She tied the cord between the little girl and her own body in two places with a bit of clean cloth and cut between the two knots. Then she pulled out the afterbirth. And went and washed herself, put a half a clean sheet between her legs, got dressed and picked up the newborn Sita and went out into the midday sun. And what Ton Tipyer swore she did was she carried the little girl, that wasn't yet named Sita, up in the air above her own head, a little ahead of her, proudly, on her open right hand, clutching her head with her index finger, and her body with her thumb and little finger, and walked out into the street. She held her just like a puppy, he said. He saw her carrying her. Just like a puppy. And Sita cooed, eyes still tightly closed against the midday sun, relaxed and happy right from birth. Then she was taken inside again, folded into a clean sheet and held against Doorga's hard breast. She felt her mother's pride in her. She felt the sun and the Surinam air on her newborn skin. Confidence was born in her on the day of her own birth.

You, see, you need confidence in yourself to be interested in politics. And where does it come from? This confidence? Sita got it free, at birth, carried around in public, her mother saying, 'Look what I made.' So when people say, and who do you think you are to be interested in politics, woman, she just laughs. And if people talk against her politics, if they're in good faith, she answers, and if not, she just laughs again. That's the kind of confidence you need. And she has handed it down to Fiya, I see. Fiya just runs around on her own when she wants to. But, whether this confidence will take a political form in Fiya, well, that remains to be seen.

One day, another day, another story, also true. One day, Sita sat on a sand dune at Lapwent and said to Ton Tipyer who had taken her down when he went fishing, 'The sand dune wasn't here at the new year.'

Ton Tipyer told her why. Sand dunes are always on the move. Just like human society. Only you don't always see it. Only after cyclones, everyone says, Oh look, a new sand dune. Or, Oh look, where's our sand dune gone. But you, Sita, you have noticed that the sand dune is new. It took a year. The south east trades, relentlessly blowing, the south east wind picked up sand on the seaward side, and ran it up the dune, and dropped it on the other side. It's just like a wave. It's always moving. You must know, Sita, that everything you do, can be with the south east trades, in which case, you have a helping hand, or against them, in which case you are wasting your time. But, Ton Tipyer said, please, Sita, do do things. Find out about the trade winds in society, and work together with them. Don't be like those sugar estate cows grazing over there, cows that don't even know there's a south east trade, let alone how that might help them.

It's like a dam, Sita, he said. Well not like a dam, more like a watershed. Think also of a dam, Sita. At the end of the dry winter season, there is sometimes no water at all, and the ground is parched and cracked. Every drop that gathers in the dam after the rains start falling, every drop stays inside the dam. There is no waterfall. And yet every drop that gathers there helps towards one day, one day, quite suddenly, making the first drop rise on to the wall, form an extended lump of water the whole length of the wall, hover with surface tension, and then cascade down in a waterfall. This is what a watershed is. In human society it's the same, he said, said Ton Tipyer.

From raw dough, with fire, comes a *farata*.

From mixing glycerin and Condi's crystals comes fire. Or from the bottom of a glass bottle and a dry bit of straw comes fire.

From fire, he said, comes heat and from fire and heat come ashes.

◆

Then he went on. There was slavery. Now there is not. There was indenture. Now there is not. There was colonization. Now there is independence. There was no right to vote. Now there is.

And now, there is no way to control our futures. There will be.

And now, there is no equality between humans, some of whom sell their labour, others of whom buy labour. This also will not be.

Study what moves in the good direction. Feel it. Know it. And then lean on it, Sita. Help it along.

◆

Said Ton Tipyer.

♦

It had been prophesied that Rowan would *not* rape Sita. But this wouldn't necessarily stop him. Prophesies only worked long ago.

He had been a destructive child, when he was little. Restless and aggressive. Why, no-one knew. No doubt there were reasons. And after he had raped two young girls, when he was only fourteen, although he had not been found out, nor prosecuted, nor accused, nor anything, he had been warned. He had been given a formal warning. Do not rape anyone again. You will not rape her. If he did, the prophesy said, his head would split in two. Therefore he would not. Therefore he could not. Therefore he did not rape Sita. So much for mythology.

This prophesy did not come from the Sibyls, nor from a soothsayer. Nor did it come true.

Prophesies no longer govern stories. And prophesies are found in such unexpected places these days. Rowan found his on a bubble gum paper. He himself interpreted it all by himself, without help from any intermediaries. He opened it and read it direct off the 'Did you know' bit of a bubble gum paper. This was in Reunion when he was still only fourteen, not long after he had perpetrated the first two rapes. The bubble gum paper said: 'Did you know that if you, repeatedly and of your own free will, do something you do not agree with, you can become a schizophrenic?' This was obviously addressed to him, he thought. 'Did you know, if you,' it said. *Me* know if I. When he asked his mother what a schizophrenic was, she said, being a vague sort of a woman, that it was someone with a split personality. Later the same day, he asked his mother what his personality was, she said, after thinking this way and that, and not really being able to explain what it was, its basically your *head*. Head split.

'You.' Me. Me, head split. It gave him the distinct notion that if he,

65

Rowan, and the feeling was very precise, if he, Rowan ever raped anyone again, his head would split in two.

He had never after this wanted for any length of time to rape anyone. The thought of raping anyone always and invariably made his head hurt. As if it would split in two. So he would stop thinking of it. It was self-induced aversion therapy.

Of course there was his wife, Noella. He raped her. But as far as he was concerned, that wasn't rape, and didn't make his head split in two, which proved it wasn't. Because, he said, you can't rape your own wife. She's yours. 'In any case, she goes out and comes home late; doesn't respect me enough. What does she take me for anyway, sitting at home waiting for her?' And then what he did with the girls on probation under his care. What about that. But whenever he got near thinking of full scale rape, a migraine split his vision in two, bored little holes into one side of his visual field, and tore one side of his head from the other. So what he did to them fell short of rape, in his own mind. He had a lot of justification of one kind or another. 'She deserved it, anyway. She got what was coming to her. She doesn't respect men enough. Now she will respect me.' And that type of thing.

Then came Sita.

It wasn't that he wanted to rape Sita. No, that was the last thing he wanted to do. The last thing he intended to do.

He admired her. He hated her for this. He looked up to her. For this too he despised her. He hero-worshipped her. But, he didn't like doing this. He didn't want to have to admire, look up to, hero-worship her. He wanted her, and any other woman for that matter, to be unimportant and inferior. He wished Sita would therefore go away. He wanted her to disappear, to disintegrate. Vanish.

Could he own her too? Like he owned Noella? Take her, make her his own. Or take her, make her disappear. Or, should he, would he invite her. Ask her. Propose her something. She may well agree, he thought.

But what if she didn't? What if she said 'No, Rowan, not today thank you' or something like that?

The very thought made him feel humiliated. He was already humiliated. Could he bear this refusal? From a woman. Could he bear any refusal from any woman.

He would not rape her. He didn't want to hurt her. He would ask her just to hold his hand. But what if she said 'Thank you for your kind offer, but . . . no', what if she said she would prefer not to. Then what. He would, he knew it, he would have to rape her. Why risk the refusal, he thought. She would have to be annihilated. If I ask and she refuses, then it'll be rape. But if I don't ever ask.

Another thing, he thought, how come she accepts sex from Dharma, then. What's so special about him. 'Why should she accept him and not me,' he raged inside himself. 'There's nothing inferior about me.'

I will rape her, he thought.

His head already started to ache from the minute she telephoned him. He became agitated with the pain. No amount of pills abated the pain the least bit.

The person he wanted to rape was Sita, so if he raped her, his head would split in two.

Pain sheered into his skull.

'No,' he thought, 'I won't do it. I swear it. I'll just ignore her. Hope she goes away.' She and all the feelings of hope and despair, love and hate, tenderness and annihilation, and all her threats of rejection. His head still ached.

And he became distant, cold and reserved.

Silent. Grim. Introspective. Uncommunicative. He sulked. He was sullen. He sniffed defiantly, like a five-year-old, and stood up trying to look imposing. He touched his limp balls furtively.

He walked over to his mirror and looked at himself in it. He jerked his head back behind his glasses, like a child being hit in its cradle, unable to escape behind anything except his own eye-lids. He blinked defensively. Then he turned his profile to the mirror. This inflated him. A he-man. I am a he-man. Who is this woman anyway to disturb my peace of mind. I'll kill her.

His head burst into pain.

He went and pissed into the wash basin.

◆

No one listening to my story asked me who Dharma was. They all knew him already. The older son of Dasratha, the son who was hero of all tales. They knew what his name meant, and that he had *dharma*.

But, although they knew who he was and all about him, and although they didn't therefore ask *who* he was, they nevertheless, and in no uncertain terms, asked for a story *about him*. 'We want a story about the hero. A story that tells about how he met Sita and about how he is part of the planet,' they said.

Demanding, you are.

Hero. And not only that. How he is part of the planet.

I moaned.

You know it's difficult to tell stories about heroes these days. Heroes are a kind of human who are either out of date or in advance of their times, or both. They are in a way, not part of the planet, as we now know it. But of course, Dharma was.

These days, I continued my lecture at my unwilling audience, in order to inspire awe and be a hero, you have to be out for a quick buck. And you have to get one. And that's not awe-inspiring or heroic. It inspires instead of awe and admiration and wonder, disgust and loathing. And it makes humans feel like worms. This is the main contradiction, listeners, these days. If you set out to be a hero, you won't be one, because the word's changed meaning. Anyway, I'm not going to tell a story about someone out for a quick buck and getting it.

I wasn't so much cross with them for asking for a story with a hero, as cross that being a hero was so difficult these days.

If you're a professional, say a surgeon, in this day and age, I went on, in order to inspire awe in people, you don't have to help them get better after an accident. You don't have to save their lives by

68

interventions. What you have to do is to run a private clinic. You have to be in with the drug companies. Give them the back-up they need to sell their products. On a big scale. Do trials. Supposed research about useless products. Prescribe them. Then, in your clinic, you take money from patients as a direct and sole condition for caring about their health; sell health care on the free market, it's called. Or, more profitable for the surgeons, rip out an organ or two a day in exchange for a fee. Specialize in it, they say. This, too is not exactly heroic. It's not the stuff stories of human glory are made from. Makes humans feel like fat frogs, croaking in the mud. I'm not going to have any hero with this kind of propensity to grab at money over other people's sick bodies.

They seemed to agree, and looked glum.

And today, it is sometimes held in awe to be rich, to act rich, to have things, and to move in certain circles. This isn't very heroic either. Say if you got rich the quickest way, through running drugs, or arms or women, it still means you're OK. Because you're rich. More like a villain. Certainly not hero-worthy. Makes humans like vultures. And I am not going to write about scavengers who feed on the human misery of others. They were pleased about this, they said.

Or to be held in awe today, you have to be a contractor or a factory owner, enslaving more and more men and women, and taking a dollar or two on the labour done by each head of human per day and keep it. Sell the labour of your neighbour. And keep a cut. A cut of your neighbour's arm-power. A shameful role. Makes humans seem cannibalistic. I'm not going to sit here and tell about slave dealers and their slave trade in human flesh.

Most of them said they work for people like that and didn't think they were heroes. They had a lot of epithets for them.

Or lazier still, you don't even have to do anything. You just take interest, money interest by lending money to those who need it when you've borrowed from another person at a lower rate: hire purchase dealers, banks, money lenders, merchant bankers, pawn brokers, insurance companies, and so on. This is not heroic at all. Although the sons and daughters of these people stride across the planet as though they own the place.

Money-lending, too, is hardly heroic. The World Bank. The IMF.

Their men and women peddling money at interest rates the world over. It is a creepy crawly profession. Sometimes they even have immoral conditions on money-lending: "Starve the workers, make public pension funds become private, stop subsidizing basic food."

We, said one listener, are the idiots. No, said another, we are the benevolent ones. Don't own the skin off our own arses, he said, and we give away to rich people. We are benevolent. We work for a pittance, and give them the rest. A compromise was reached on us being benevolent idiots.

And then there are others who take a quick percentage as money changes hands, in that famous split-second, when it isn't anybody in particular's money, you grab: agents, representatives, stock brokers, notaries and so on.

They said all right, all right, but tell how he was part of the planet anyway.

These, I continued even though they were letting me off the hook about a hero, are the modern day success stories, and they aren't the stuff that heroism is made of. Everyone thinks they're lower than shark shit.

Dharma was a hero.

And the story *is* therefore about a hero.

But it isn't my story. It's the story told to me by Jojo Treebohun. Jojo, his name, that's funny, and the words came back *Jojo was a man who thought he was a woman* and then *Iqbal was a man who thought he was a woman*. Jojo Treebohun was the greatest storyteller in all of Mauritius. He was a seaman, an ordinary officer of some kind, and was home for months on end between jobs. And then, wake after wake he sat around outside the house where the body was laid out telling stories until the sun started to come up, while other people wasted their time gambling and playing Bingo and drinking.

He always had an audience.

He told me a story about Dharma. It isn't my story, it's his. A true story, although he made it up. The reason I'm telling it is that it in fact tells how Dharma was part of the planet.

And this is the yarn he span. 'It was a dark and stormy night, and the skipper said to his mate, spin us a yarn, Jojo, spin us a yarn. And this is the yarn he span. It was a dark and stormy night and the skipper said to his mate, spin us a yarn, Jojo, spin us a yarn. And this is the yarn he span. It was a dark and stormy.' And so on. Audiences loved this kind of beginning.

◆

'It was a dark and stormy night, and I, Jojo, was walking down the main street in Cambridge. You know, the University town in England. It was grey. The street, I mean. And I was dressed in grey. And the whole world was grey. And inside my head it was grey. There was rain in gusts. There was lightning and rumbling thunder. My umbrella had just turned inside out. It was also grey. I felt as though I were walking on the surface of the moon. A grey moon.

'Let me remind you, skipper, that before I went to sea, and long before I became mate on this trawler, and before I grew this beard and got wise about the world, and before I knew there was no land that I was happy in, and before I took to this life of eternal roaming, I was a student at Christ's College in Cambridge, an unhappy student, and I was also, I believe, a thing called an *eligible young bachelor*.

'I was also what is commonly called a dweat. Or do you spell it dweet. This was a cross between a twirp and a drip.

'But mostly I was down. I was depressed. I was miserable. I heard sad notes of cello music in my head. Specially that night on the main street.

'I felt completely out of my element. Like a fish out of. Like a sailor ashore. But mostly, with a puffed up chest, I felt a Mauritian, and nothing English agreed with me. I yearned for Mauritius, and knew how happy I would be if only I were home amongst all the people and all the things I knew. Instead of in this hostile, strange world. I thought of *zasar legim*, and *vinday*. I thought of *konfi bilinbi* and processed Kraft cheese. Like a child, of food I thought. And I was homesick.

'The rain wet me, the wind turned my umbrella inside-out, I couldn't stand the food, I had no friends and I was homesick. I, Jojo, the Mauritian could have stood there and wept, right there with my umbrella inside-out.

'I was on my way to a meal to meet this Mauritian who was the manager of the Bank of Mauritius, the Central Bank. He was on holiday in Cambridge. He was, I believe, the first Mauritian ever to hold the job, and he, it was rumoured, was going to offer me his daughter in marriage. One of his daughters. And one of her brothers would then marry my sister who was getting a bit on in life. She, Premila, his daughter, is now my wife.

'At the very moment, when I was struggling there in the middle of the main street with my inside-out umbrella, I saw in the middle distance coming out of the grey, a striking figure emerge like a giant. I recognized him at once. In red shirt, black scarf, and tight blue jeans, no jacket, no gloves, no umbrella, heading forwards, as if it wasn't even cold. Striding along in perfect harmony with the world, towards me. It was Dharma. A warmth and happiness came into my heart. A Mauritian. And Dharma, he is at home here, he can help me.

'As I started to raise my hand to say hello to him, warmth at the thought of using the Kreol language again, I can't say whether he saw me or not, he suddenly, as if struck by an important thought, crossed the road, walked blithely over to the other side and there he met three people, obviously his friends, all joking and laughing, and calling out "Dharma, the Great, why are you late" and things like that, and "Dharma, how's your lingam". They hugged him when they met him. As though he were part of them. They were going to go off to a pub, I thought. He was happy. He is a real Englishman, Dharma. And he's only been here as long as I've been here. And he's only a scholarship student, from the poor Dasratha family. His mother selling cakes at the Lagar Dinor and his father working his own cane land. But just look at him.

'I had been standing right in front of him, fiddling with my inside-out umbrella, and he didn't even see me. Or if he saw me, he crossed the road on purpose, and was engulfed into the English landscape and lost to me.

'I cried. I admit it, skipper, I cried. It was a dark and stormy night, as you know.

'And I wiped my eyes, and went on my heavy-footed way to the dinner at the visiting Bank Manager's invitation. There, he didn't speak to me only about the daughter he wanted to offer to me, but also about his younger daughter, that he intended to offer to Dharma. But, he said, Dharma was not free to come to dinner that night. So, I thought to myself, he crossed the road on purpose. That's what it was, the sudden, important thought.

'And what was left carved in my mind, throughout my three miserable years at Cambridge, was that Dharma had a place in the universe where he was happy. Here in Cambridge. And I was a fish out of. I was miserable.

'I tried to forget about him, but a kind of persistent envy of him grew inside me. He was a scholarship student. But it wasn't that, what got me was how happy he was there. He was handsome. But lots of people are that. He was part of the place. He played sport. I could have, if I'd wanted to, but that was not what made me jealous. He was part of the social fabric of the place. He was in the chess team. His neighbour on the stairs liked him. He went out drinking and he was at home. He had friends who were in the Dramatic League and who put on modern plays. There were always girls talking to him. Serious-minded girls and laughing girls. He made jokes that they laughed at, and when he laughed, his eyes closed with pleasure.

'I saw the three years of my studies through.

'He stayed on some eight years in all doing advanced studies in science and literature, Dharma did. Who else did science *and* literature?

'And when finally I did get back to Mauritius, yearning to get over the homesickness I'd suffered in England, and when I tried to settle down, I couldn't. I hated the place. I loathed Mauritius. I took up my job as Librarian in the Parliamentary Library in Porlwi, and when I looked around the place, it was full of hostile people and I felt lonely. I wasn't Mauritian at all. Everyone was strange and unknown to me. I felt like a fish out of. I felt miserable. Again, miserable. I looked out of my bedroom window in Katborn and saw a bamboo hedge, and a depression, a tropical depression, settled on to me and my whole being.

'It was a dark and stormy night. Yes, it was. But a hot and sultry stormy night. The storm making it hotter and heavier. I had to do some unpaid overtime, a night shift, at the Library because there was a Commonwealth Conference the next week. I had to walk through the Company Gardens. As I got nearer the Gardens, a gust of hot northerly wind, a *vannlor* turned my umbrella inside-out. I was so low

I left it like that. I decided to leave it like that and to just go on through the Company Gardens. Imagine that: I was too depressed to even bother to turn the thing right side out.

'The desolation at night of the Company Gardens, a desolation that had set in since the 1960s race riots, would make me feel at home. The Company Gardens at night are as desolate a landscape outside of me as I am on the inside, I thought.

'But no. Tonight it was different. Something strange was going on. I was taken aback. On this dark and stormy night. The Company Gardens were alive. Pulsed with human movement. Calm, deliberate movement. I noticed that in the dark there were people, perhaps tea plantation workers, women and men, bus conductors, there were dockers, and cane labourers and women labourers, hundreds of them, moving around organizing something. And they were assembling, as if for a quiet demonstration. In the dark and stormy night.

'A cold loneliness gripped my heart.

'I felt left out.

'Suddenly I felt English. Like a colonial servant, imposed on this strange place, rejected by its people. Strangers, they all were.

'What is this Mauritius I live in? Who are these people? What are they doing? I feel like a fish out of.

'Should I go and look, see what they're all doing? In support of what? With whom? By what system of communication did they all come here? What are these lanterns they've made?

'And so it was that I walked over, my umbrella turned inside-out, towards the group of people. They won't notice me in the dark, I thought, and they didn't. Even though I looked like a scarecrow.

'Everyone was crowded around a square of tarpaulin set up like a tent, and underneath it, were people on grass mats, beginning, it became clear to me, beginning, I realized, a hunger strike. I don't know what made me realize that that's what was going on.

'I felt like a foreigner. I understood nothing about this country. What do they want? Why do they stop eating? Who are all these well wishers? Where will this lead?

'And I peered under the tarpaulin, into the dim light thrown up by a petrol lamp and some home-made lanterns. And my eyes caught his for a second. "Dharma," I whispered. I saw him on the ground. A labourer's hand holding his shoulder. His own arm on the man's knee. They stared into one another's eyes as they spoke. And then they put their heads back and laughed, a deep laugh of the universe. A deep love of the universe. They all love one another, I thought.

'There he was again: Dharma. His whole body touching the earth. Part of the planet. Of nature. One of the people. Among them all. I felt the loneliest I have ever felt. "You really have got *dharma*."

'Again, a second time in my life, I cried. I walked on to the Parliamentary Library crying like a baby. Lonely as a cloud.

'That very night I took my decision to go to sea.'

◆

That's the story Jojo told, about how he went to sea, and about how Dharma was part of the planet. Wherever he was, he was in it.

◆

'Even at sea, he's more at home than I am,' Jojo ended his story against himself.

◆

Can I go on now, I asked, with my story. No, they said. They said it was all very well what Jojo said. But how did they meet?

Who? Oh, all right. How did Dharma and Sita meet? And was it love at first sight? I reply that I'm not here to be like some women's magazine, telling how couples first met and first fell in love, I'm not. But then you all reply that it isn't the question that's wrong, it's the hollowness of most people's answers that's wrong. People, you persist in it, are quite right to ask the question. Therefore, you say, tell. In any case, you say, you want to know because you can see they love one another now. Well, when did it all start. No one else loves their mate like those two, you say, so tell us.

The listener, say I Iqbal the storyteller, is always right.

True.

How they met, then.

They first met twice.

Twice? you all chorus at me.

Yes, twice.

This may sound like a contradiction, but it isn't. Their first meeting was like when you come across a person in a dream, when in your dream you seem to know a character very well, and he or she is present in flesh and blood, a whole complete human being, only when you wake up, you're sure the person doesn't exist. And you wonder how your own mind can make up a face, features, expressions, a body form, a voice, a frame of mind, and a way of being and a way of acting. Is it possible to invent a whole person without even concentrating on it?

You should know, you all yell at me, you're inventing them all the time. But don't change the subject, they go on, how did they meet?

◆

It was like this.

'I'm late,' Sita whispered to herself, stopping next to the glass box of bread rolls on the pavement, and picking up her watch which was around her neck on a chain, looking at it just under her nose, in the dismal light of the Luxor tea room, whose bread it was, jutting out in its aquarium on to the pavement. A loud soprano from an Indian film squealed out into the deserted Porlwi Sunday evening. A tired cashier and an even more tired child waiter stared at one another under the fluorescent tube. The child had a filthy serviette on his head, and pretended to be an Indian film star actress, singing love songs to his boss, the cashier. He and the cashier then both turned to her and nodded hello, recognizing her. The cashier made a gesture to show what conditions he worked in in the tea room. She signalled understanding by a nod of the head. Then, quickly, she put her head down and set off again, crossed the road to the Moontaza side, and went on turning into Lasose. She shuddered as she looked down the deserted street, seeing the pall that the Sunday and the time of night had imposed on it. The usually crowded street you could hardly get space to walk down on weekdays at shopping time was now all heavy metal anti-riot shutters, each anti-riot shutter with ten or twenty padlocks of all ilk battening it down. Always expecting a civil disturbance. Ever since 1968. Special insurance premium for riots, but you have to have rolling metal shutters. And lots of padlocks.

As the Indian film music soprano got further away, she became aware of another sound, a kind of scuffling, which made her stop. She put her head to one side and listened.

From across the road. It was four well-dressed young men who, running across from the car they had just parked, were attacking an old man who was lying on the ground, groaning. She ran towards them. She had thought for a moment it was Ton Tipyer.

'Take your hands off him,' she cried. It was a man who looked just like Ton Tipyer in fact, dressed in very old rag-like clothes.

'You shut up, mind your own business,' the big one of the four smartly dressed men turned on her. One of the others hesitated, and started stuttering an explanation: 'He was trying to open our car door. We shouted at him and he ran away. Got to teach them a lesson. Teach him a lesson, that's what. We just ran after him. He tripped, all by himself.'

'What exactly are you saying he did wrong?' she said, standing between the old man and the four youths. A second or two of stunned silence. 'You can't just beat up a defenseless old man for nothing you know. That happens to be my business, I'll have you know.' She turned on the big, bullying one.

'For nothing? He touched our car, that's what. For nothing. He's a thief. A no-good. They are bringing the country to ruin. Can't even be at the office after hours without worrying about your car these days. And what are you, a woman doing out at night.' He leered.

'If you've got anything against this old man you've thrown down into a doorway on the ground, go and give a statement to the police. Your car, your car, your car. Is that all you can think of,' she said. 'Get out of here. Your car.'

'We'll give you something to think about, young lady,' the big one said, leering. A threat. She was defiant.

'Shut your mouth,' she said.

At this point, a young man walked up to them. It was Dharma. He had caught sight of the posse of order-keepers charging out of their car down Lasose, and had gone and stood at the corner and watched the confrontation.

THE RAPE OF SITA

He took the old tramp by the hand, pulled him on to his feet, and said 'Oh, it's you, is it? Would you like a cup of tea, a *roz tjed*,' in fact, he said. 'Any problem?' he asked the four men, sarcastically.

'No, no, no. No,' they replied, pushing their smart clothes into place and backing away.

Sita laughed at them. Right in their faces. A laugh from Africa, that shook her shoulders. The four men shuffled off, trying to get back their veneer of authority.

'Petty bourgeois city slickers,' she said of them, in mock heroic swearing tones, turning first to the old man and then to the newly arrived young man.

'A cup of tea?' Dharma asked her. 'You did very well.'

'Be nice. But l'm late. A meeting in Plenn Vert.'

They stood and looked at one another for a full minute. In complete silence.

And she was gone.

Would you call this love at first sight?

It definitely was.

And yet, Dharma's memory of Sita and Sita's of Dharma were like the characters only a dream can invent.

They thought of no one else but one another from that moment onwards.

◆

second time they first meet unbelievable

he or she sita for there is no he nor she but only both sita all alone lying on sand-dune between sea and land in hidden hollow under sole *badam* tree hiding sun no cloud she sita lying naked half asleep shade from leaves caressing his or her body letting heat and cool dance on his or her tummy and hand of one side touches nipple of the other which stand up and hand of other side turns lips of yoni inside out for sun to see for sea air to breathe thereinto and to cause rivers to flow thereoutof and to wet the sand and like time ever to be born from the universal woman round and round the clitoris round and round and eyes closed she or he loves oneself fully and comes

he or she dharma for there is no he nor she but only both dharma all alone lying on sea itself floating feeling unseen with the woman sea caressing buttocks and back of neck and thighs and small wavelets over the top arouse his or her nipples and lingam which swells and stands out of the water proud and is the oval egg of creation and hand of one side on nipple and hand of other side on lingam eyes closed she or he loves himself fully and comes

◆

and as sita all alone comes down to bathe and as dharma all alone comes out to dry they meet and make love

◆

for they are separate and fulfilled and their love is therefore whole and they live together from that day onwards ever after

◆

such a meeting was their second

◆

Somehow when Dharma accused her of burying something in the recesses of her memory, it sounded larger than life.

'Funny,' she thought. 'Most odd.'

The word, as I have said before, was all alive with meaning for her. Even when Ton Tipyer had come in and harmlessly asked her to organize his burial when he died, she had got all confused. The word was still there: 'Buried'.

It was true.

True. In some deep way, it was true.

She knew it.

She had buried something.

A memory?

Something. A thing? Or somebody. A body?

And the word 'buried', the very word itself, took on the form of some kind of a living monster. A creature. She'd never known a word do that. It echoed around her head, haunting her and taunting her. It seemed to inhabit her mind. Walking to and fro restlessly without ceasing. Like a ghost, she thought this for a second time. I can't be haunted, she thought, laughing.

'Burial.'

Two sets of meanings jostled for her attention. The metaphorical. Burial to cover something up, to hide something, to forget something, to put something out of sight and out of mind. To cover something up. For example, a revealing mural she'd just painted, and being horrified by her creation, had covered up with a sheet of wallpaper. To rub a word out. To hide a cigarette stompie in the sand. To cover a stain on the sheets. Guilt. Shame. Pain. Bury them all. Thou shalt love. But there is hate. Hate. Bury the hatred. Put soil, thick earth on top of it, whatever it had been. Soil. Soiled. She looked it up in the dictionary now. *Bury*: 'To dispose of or to hide (as if) by covering with or depositing in the earth', 'To cover from view; conceal; to put in obscurity; to put completely out of mind'. That's it. She's put it completely out of mind. Out of mind. Gone out of mind? Going out of her mind, if you ask me.

And then the literal sense. Burial after a death. Or perhaps even after a murder. Digging a hole. Surreptitiously. Dragging the body to it. Burying a corpse. Burying somebody's body. Or someone burying her body. Six foot under. Or was it a shallow grave? In a tiny bit of veld outside a flat in Reunion. In a shallow grave. After being stabbed with a dagger supposed to be ornamental from a series of three. Her, dead, buried, and gone. Lost to the world. But, she is still alive. Or was it her killing someone and burying his body. Positioning a dagger carefully between someone's ribs on the left side, just behind his arm, holding the dagger in place with her left hand, and then puncturing it hard and sharp with the clenched fist of her right hand. One hard punch. And proceeding to the burial. Digging and digging in the night. Cover it up. Surreptitiously. Thou shalt not kill. But there is kill. Kill. And bury the body in the garden.

She remembered taking a book from Rowan Tarquin's bookshelf. Taking it and going and sitting in a chair. Not on a chair, but in a chair. She remembered the exact place in the bookshelf where she had spotted the book. *The Waste Land and Other Poems* by T.S. Eliot. She hadn't so much as glanced at *The Waste Land* for more than twenty years. Didn't even like it. But she distinctly sees herself taking it. She took it out of the bookshelf by tilting back the top of the back cover with the middle finger of her right hand. She remembers. She remembers this very clearly. And she went and sat in a Madagascan chair. Made, if she remembered rightly, out of one piece of wood. Two interlinked mobile parts, carved out of one light-coloured log, so as to lodge into one another as a wooden deck chair. A comfortable chair, but not easy to get out of. And she lay back against the back of the chair, and began any old where to read *The Waste Land* at the spot she happened to open the book to. And in there somewhere there was 'the burial of the dead' and there was a corpse in the bottom of the garden. *Had it begun to sprout?*

'It's to do with bodies.'

81

Suddenly she said this to Dharma.

And only then did it come to her, and then she said it to Dharma again. 'To do with bodies.' Again the word before the knowledge. But knowledge must be before the word she thought. What is knowledge? After having dived all night, a phrase.

'It's to do,' she repeated, 'with bodies, with sex.'

'What is?' he asked. 'What are you talking about, Sita?'

She said it the day the United States dropped its first bombs on Iraq. Tore the cities open.

'I wasn't expecting it,' she said.

'Expecting what?' he said.

'I don't know what. But, it was a shock. It was sudden.' Was she asleep? Something to do with the safety of sheets covering her in her own bed. Where does that fit in? Pulling cool, safe sheets over her head. Or was it the shroud? Afterwards. The swaddling clothes of death? Who killed Sita, long ago? Was she in that chair reading *The Waste Land*? Did she doze off? It was very sudden. She didn't know what it was. But it was all very sudden.

And then no more pictures. No more sound. No more vision. A hole again.

She doesn't remember what happened. She can't remember.

She just had these words, the words she had composed to say to Dharma at the Rozil Roundpoint: 'Something terrible happened in Reunion, Dharma.' She hadn't said them at the time, or maybe she hadn't been able to say them. Some sort of an interruption. They were still there waiting to be said. So she said them.

'Something terrible happened in Reunion.'

'What?'

'Something terrible happened in Reunion.'

When she tries to remember now, she bumps into nothing except this, this hard ball of anger. Is it in the universe, out there, or knotted into her solar plexus itself? This call of anger, this stifled shriek of anger. It's a kind of memory but it's not like an ordinary memory. It's horrifying and recent and undigested. It's monstrous. She finds her own anger. Staring at her. Raw. Can one behold such a thing? An anger so hateful as to mean killing. To murder. Did she kill him in his sleep? This seems likely. Yes. No wonder she doesn't remember it.

Murderer. She stands accused. Did she bury his body in the bottom of his garden? A shallow grave. Worse than lies, this. Murder.

Someone had mentioned him. Implied he was still alive. It was this very conversation that had provoked Dharma's question: 'Were Rowan and Noella still together when you were in Reunion in 1982?' And the fateful answer. How should she know. Only a couple of hours. Restaurant.

Did she kill him? Could she have? Maybe she tried to kill him, but he got away. Or did she just decide to kill him. Want to. Very badly. But didn't actually attempt it. Maybe that's what it was.

At times the anger, when she saw it, even though it was 'out there', outside of her, in front of her, opposed to her, would then come in, rush in and inhabit her and rise inside her like a wave of nausea.

Or had she been afraid he would kill her? And bury her in a shallow grave at the bottom of the garden? Dispose of her.

Or did he actually kill her? In some way, kill her.

Was she a person who had died eight years and nine months ago. Been buried and all?

◆

'Where have you come from, Sibyl and Alexsina?' Sita asked, 'What's happened?'

'Stupid policemen. Stupid damned policemen.'

'I know, I know, but you look very cross right now. They're always stupid. And what's happened to your dress, Sibyl? You were both here at the midday demonstration, no? What on earth?'

They put back their heads and laughed, and Sita laughed with them. Sita laughed even louder than them. Not because she knew what at, but because their laughter was so infectious, it was victorious. She knew it was a victory of some kind. 'You've won a fight then?' Sita laughed for the victory again. *We hear you laughing at night, Sita,' says Kaveeta. 'What,' says Sita, 'from your house?' 'Even from my granny's house, we hear you laughing, Sita,' said Kaveeta.*

That was the kind of laugh they laughed. They were in the Company Gardens and their laughs reverberated up and down the Canal on one side and on the other, bounced off the British High Commission offices, over to the Mauritius Institute Museum and to the import-export dealers and back again. It was as though the laughter came out of the banyan trees, which were ridiculing the colonial statues, posturing among the trees like fools.

From slave days some women have kept the laughter as a weapon against oppression. When I hear it, a deep envy rises up inside me, and then the song *Iqbal was a man who thought he was a woman*. And then it passes, as usual.

Ton Tipyer had gone into town to fetch his ex-servicemen's pension that day, and saw them as he went past. He took up a bench in Company Gardens, and straightened out a cigarette he had picked up in front of the bench, and looked around for someone to get a light from.

'Sita, a light?' And then he sat down again. He had seen the demonstration on his way to fetch his pension and was pleased. At the ex-servicemen's trust fund they told him there was a delay and to come back the day after tomorrow. This was how he would come to be arrested along with the women.

And then after Sita had laughed, Alexsina and Sibyl, all three women had laughed some more and shaken their heads and said 'Stupid policemen' a few more times. Then they explained to Sita what had happened. Ton Tipyer overheard it all. And he told me.

They had come to visit the hunger strikers. Sita had and they had. That was this morning. Then there was the demonstration. After that they went to drink a Fanta at Luxor, then they had been on their way to visit the hunger strikers again, before going home to cook for the night.

There was a hunger strike on. It was 1981. Nine women had taken up cardboard sheets in the Company Gardens, sat down on them under the elements, and stopped eating. They only drank water. Nine days had passed. All around them were Vichy water bottles, in neat piles. Most empty. Some given by well-wishers, and not yet drunk. The women wanted to go back to Diego Garcia and the Salomon Islands and Peros Banos. That was where they came from. And they wanted to go back. They had been in Porlwi for fourteen years. 'Sometimes we only had green mangoes to give to the children. Green mangoes and salt.' 'I left my bed and two chairs there. We didn't even have locks on the doors, it was so safe, so we just left everything. The Company didn't tell us anything. Just when it was time to go back after buying a frying pan and a pot and a few yards of cloth in the shops in Porlwi, they said that the islands were closed down now. Closed down. You can't go back, they told us. The islands are closed down.' 'I liked the sea turtle eggs.' 'Women worked same as men there. Same pay. And the company paid old people to look after the children.' It was matriarchy there, Sita knew. Not glorified matriarchy, but the matriarchy of slavery. *He, she* and *it* were all one word: *li*. The man, the woman and the beast of burden. The male animal, the female animal and the inanimate object. Slavery reduced one to equality. Sita knew this. Therefore, as she said, we can be *elevated* to equality as well.

'So what happened? What about the stupid police stupid men.'

And then they told her what had happened. And Ton Tipyer

eavesdropped. They had been coming to see their friends again earlier in the afternoon. After the Fanta at Luxor. And a detour to pay Sibyl's electricity bill on the far side of the Gardens. And then as they came into the far end of the Company Gardens, it was a bit deserted there, for the heat, four policemen came by in a police jeep, stopped, ordered them into the jeep and drove off. Alexsina and Sibyl thought they were being arrested, perhaps because of the midday demonstration. But the police started to act in a threatening way towards them, like animals, they said, and drove towards Montayn Sinnyo. They then drove up Montayn Sinnyo. It was a deserted road up the mountain. They took them up the mountain to rape them.'Women should not wear the pants,' they said. They would teach us a lesson, they said. '*Pa vinn deklar mari isi.*' One of the policemen had started to undo his fly.

'What did you do?' Sita asked.

This was what Alexsina and Sibyl did. They stood up in the back of that jeep, half way up Montayn Sinnyo, and started to tear their own clothes off. Both of them. At the same time. They just tore their clothes off, and shouted: You all bloody-well try. Men. You think you're so goddamned special. See what you can do, you little shrimp-heads. Men. Bah! Brainless creatures. Think you can scare us with the threat of rape. You show us, then, smart alecs. Show us. Give a demonstration. Show us what's so special about. Come on. Get going. What's the delay. Goodfornothings.

What happened? I was worried. Fear of rape and fear of male retaliation at resisting rape caught my throat. Horror. *Iqbal was a man who thought.*

The policemen, they said, got scared, started to giggle, and to say to one another 'Let's get back into Porlwi.' '*Anu ale, zot. Anu ale. Inn ler pu nu return kazern.*' They just lost their nerve. 'Men are scared of us, you know Sita. Just Mauritian women don't know it. We Chagos women know. That's all. Then the little twirps came and dropped us here now. Stupid policemen damned stupid.' That's why their clothes were all crooked. And that's why they were so cross. *Iqbal was a man who'd rather be a woman.* The song was back in my head.

◆

The next day, after a second women's demonstration, a very nice
senior policeman was standing next to a group of women near the
hunger striking women. He was conversing gently with them. But, as
senior policemen are wont, he was beating his baton which was in his
right hand onto his left palm, as he spoke. Just a habit. Like a teacher
with a pen, or a ruler. No threat meant. Zilyet, a Chagos woman of
about thirty-five, playfully caught hold of his baton, and said, and
what if she were to snatch his baton away. He laughed and said, 'Ah,
but it is attached to my wrist by my leather strap, my dear.' To which
she replied, 'Batons more strongly attached to men than that have been
known to be wrenched away from men.' The policeman went shy.
Almost blushed. Such is the humour of matriarchy. No harm meant.

Iqbal was a man who thought he was. I tried to chase the song
away, but it wouldn't go away for long.

◆

The following day, during the third women's demonstration on the
third successive day, the women all massed in front of government
house, where the cabinet of ministers was meeting. 'Give us Diego
back.' 'Military base, out!' 'We want compensation!' They didn't
shout the slogans, but sang them. To different tunes, and at different
pitches. Some very soprano, some very alto. There were three hundred
of them that day. Chagos women and members of the All Women's
Front. I watched from behind the statue opposite Government House.

They blocked the Royal Road. So the police, on orders from their
superiors, linked arms, making a policeman's daisy chain, and because
it was women they would be easing off the road, they covered
themselves from future untoward allegations of any kind, by clasping
their own hands together behind their backs after they had woven
them into their neighbour policeman's arms. While covering themselves from one problem, they exposed themselves to another. But
these were the orders. They did as ordered. Then they moved forward.
The aim: to ease the women, squeeze them gently off the Royal Road,
into the Plas Darm garden behind them.

The women did not move.

They dug their heels in.

But the policemen continued to move. The women gave in a little. Stepped back slightly.

And then, like one woman, all the Chagos women knew what to do. They just sent out a right hand each and grabbed the balls of the policeman directly in front of them in the iron-grip of their right hands and squeezed hard.

Each policeman doubled over in pain, groaning and moaning in the agony of males. When their heads were down, one or two women, for good measure got them one with their parasols on the back of the head.

Teach the silly pricks, they said.

Iqbal was a man, who knew he was a woman.

◆

When eight of them, including Sita, were arrested that same day after a staged battle between the Riot police and the women, in which the Riot police had been defeated by the women in the famous battle later known under the name, *The Battle of Lasose*, they were taken to Line Barracks for detention.

Ton Tipyer who had had to go back to the ex-servicemen's trust fund to get his pension, was there. He was just walking past when the battle broke out. It had been violent. Police with batons and rattanware shields against women with parasols and shoe heels. But the women hunger strikers joined in from the Company Gardens side and hurled Vichy Mineral Water one litre bottles at the Riot Police. One man working as a dish-washer for Rogers upstairs, a loyal employee of the company, six storeys up, saw the fight and joined in with plates with Rogers and Co. written on them, hurled down at the police. And as was usual in all demonstrations, the paving stones were ripped up from the edges of the canals and hurled. One hit the window of Les Copains, who boldly, had not lowered his anti-riot shutters like all the other shops in Lasose.

Ton Tipyer had a hip flask, his only possession, in his right pocket of his suit top. When he found himself in the middle of the fight, he threw it at a policeman, and was immediately and summarily arrested. The women never knew he was arrested. He got charged with 'Wounds and blows', while they were charged under the Public Order Act. They only found out after his release from prison that he had been their ally. 'Why didn't you tell me,' Sita cried. 'Why?'

'It's over now,' said Ton Tipyer.

A hundred people were in the Line Barracks Police station. Eight women arrested, and Ton Tipyer who no-one knew was arrested, was also there. I was there too. Waiting to see Roselee and Sita, to leave them cigarettes. Ton Tipyer would have appreciated a stompie in there, if I had only known he was there.

♦

And what about her mother? Tell about Doorga, you all cry out. She's the one you want to know about. She makes you scared, I'm sure.

Sita came from a family of women only. Dharma is the first man, at a very late stage in family history, to join the family on a residential basis. He and Sita live together. This is an honour for him, because only women made up Sita's family. Although he and Sita never actually got married, on principle, they do live together on a long-term basis. Dharma settled into the household. But then again, Dharma would not have settled in with any other woman than Sita. He would have lived alone.

This kind of talk, makes the song words come back into my head, *Iqbal was a man who thought he was a woman.* No, I don't *think* I am, it's not quite that. *'Wished he was a woman.'* I wish I were a woman. I do. By being a man, I feel left out of things. Especially when I think of Sita's family.

And just like neither husbands nor lovers ever settled in in Sita's mother's family, so boy-children were never born to them either. This is obviously a coincidence. There were just women and girls. And they kept cows, never a bull, and when the cows calved, they were reputed, more often than not to be she-calves. This was probably a rumour rather than the truth. They always had a bitch with swinging tits and two-or-three pups gazing up lovingly at her. Their hens produced chicks by immaculate conception. Hen-chicks. There were just women and girls. Not only today. As far back as you could go. And some knew the story way back. So this bit will be a matrilinear story, it will. To be completely truthful, and to make all the women and girls seem even more womanlike and girlish, Sita's sister, who kept up the tradition of not having a man in the house, gave birth, after her first daughter, to a second child, who turned out to be a boy-child, a son.

90

A *seribin*, or literally translated, a cherubim. He was called quite simply and by absolutely everyone from his first days as a gurgling babe in arms: *Zom*, or Man. He was one of those children that glows with happiness. He made them all seem more female by his illustrious presence.

Who was Sita's mother, you ask? Tell about Doorga, you beg. You've heard all sorts of things about her, no doubt. You're scared of her? Even after her death?

Doorga was the cane labourer from the North, from Flak, who had come to live in Surinam all on her own when she was only fifteen. She was the young girl labourer, whose mother was murdered in front of her very eyes. Not just murdered. Assassinated. In the North, near Flak.

But before we come to Sita's *nani*, to her maternal granny, let's tell about Doorga, herself. Because Doorga herself was a famous woman in her own right.

She was a trade union delegate for women labourers at Sen Felix. No boss ever raised his voice to her, or called her 'twa'. No boss ever had his way with her in any way. Neither as a worker nor as a woman. And the other workers in her gang, and in the whole section, respected her. Because she could tell you what your fortnightly pay should be, sous for sous, in one or two seconds. Faster than an electronic calculator can tell you today. You tell her how many days you were present, thus basic wage for the day, which was twenty-two rupees forty seven cents, how many days you managed all your task work for task rate wages, which were higher, how many days you had sick leave or local leave, specifying if any of the foregoing were a Saturday, and she would give you the answer. To the nearest sous.

She could keep a whole register of union members without writing down a word. She could collect dues, and remember it all and go to Porlwi and hand the money over to the treasurer. People said she had a mathematical mind. She could also tell you what day of the week the 23rd August was in 1786, or any day of the week that any other date had been or would be. It only took her about two seconds from when you had finished asking her it.

So you can see where Sita got her powers of concentration from.

But Doorga's fame spread for other reasons as well. At a national level, she was famous for having being sent to prison under the Public Order Act. She was the only woman to have been imprisoned under this law, which had been voted in the previous year so as to prepare for lifting the State of Emergency by making a fairly permanent state of emergency under the Public Order Act. She was accused, along with three men labourers, of the storming of the Sime Giriye Police Station in 1974, when Sita was away at a conference in Cambridge in England to help organize support for the Mozambique liberation movement. She, Sita's mother, had, in fact, with some fifty other labourers, stormed the police station. Because during the strike, the police had arrested one of their work mates. It was normal that they should go and get him out of the police station, Sita's mother later told her. Sita agreed. And they were found guilty. This was also normal, her mother told her. One month her mother did. Mounting an assault on a police station, the charge sheet read. 'There's nothing wrong with going to prison,' Sita's mother had told her long before. 'A place made for people, not for dogs. Women go in there women, and come out women. Men go in men, and come out again, men. Your dignity can't be taken away from you by someone else. You can only give it away yourself.' So she said. 'The moral,' she added, 'is an easy one. We've got to get the Public Order Act repealed. If we hadn't gone to jail maybe no one would have believed that we needed to get it repealed. We can't even read, but we know more about the Public Order Act than most people who can read the law fluently. We don't know history, but sometimes I think we understand it more than all those intellectuals with degrees.'

Doorga hadn't wanted Sita to be uneducated like her.

She therefore went to see Ton Tipyer. She knew that Ton Tipyer knew the whole of the Mahabharata. 'I was told it by Hanumanjee,' he said, 'Hanumanjee, who was the watchman of the Pillay sand quarry.' Hanumanjee was said to have brought Ton Tipyer up in a *maray* he slept in at the sand quarry, a *maray* which consisted of two tin sheets leant against one another. Ton Tipyer was the best brought up child in the South. Every night for fifteen years from when Ton Tipyer was about twelve months old, Hanumanjee, *Gardyen Disab Pillay*, the Pillay Sand Guard, spent two and a half hours, from dusk onwards, telling Ton Tipyer the Mahabharata. 'You are an educated man, Tipyer,' said Doorga, 'My daughter needs education, Tipyer. You know stories. Please come and tell her them.' Ton Tipyer came and told the stories. Not because he was scared of Doorga. He was one of the people who wasn't scared of Doorga, because he knew her, and when you knew her well, you knew only tenderness and kindness.

And so it was that Ton Tipyer went to their house every night because he *wanted* to tell the stories of the Mahabharata, and had always been looking for someone to tell them to before he forgot them. He wanted to remember them, and to retell them the same as they were, *because they were necessary*, as he put it. Personally, I think Doorga herself wanted to know the stories as well.

Anyway this was how Sita became educated. Every night she and Doorga would listen to Ton Tipyer for two and a half hours, from sunset onwards, and he would retell, in his way, what Hanumanjee had told him by the *juri* fire in front of his *maray* down by the sand quarry. They would watch the embers glowing in Doorga's supper-cooking fire. He had started telling the stories before Sita's little sister was even born. And I had the luck, the honour you could say, to be there as well, from before Sita's little sister was born. Because my mother, being poor and having empty sugar tins, was only too pleased that most nights Doorga bathed me and fed me along with Sita, and sent me over at bedtime on a full tummy, and with my head spinning with Ton Tipyer's stories. 'You, Iqbal, have to concentrate on telling the stories anew one day,' he told me. 'You must remember the stories as they should be.' Which is what I'm doing now. The same story he told me, I'm telling it anew.

Doorga was the perfect mother. She gave the two girls love, lots of affection, and the gift of emotional independence. They could look after themselves. They got education in arithmetic and mathematics from Doorga direct, in history from her father and in literature and philosophy from Ton Tipyer, and then Doorga sent them to school a year earlier than other kids, and that's how Sita learnt to read and write at four. It would be her who would teach me to write down my ideas in the sand. She held a school class for me and her little sister. I could read *Le Cernéen* at four, like she could. This was the sugar estates' owners' paper. And she taught me to write things down, so that now I can sit and write down this story. I can perform reading and writing. So can Sita.

Her mother taught her lots of things. How to make chutney from wild fruit, and how to preserve mangoes as sweet jam or as sour pickles, and how to dry brinjals. Her mother, after working in the sugar estate fields, before doing her cooking, would also take Sita into the Rianbel lagoon, and they would spear octopus. Her mother taught her to dry octopus.

She also taught her to *know no fear*. 'Fear,' she said, 'is there for you to conquer.' And Doorga taught Sita something else: to take part in history. 'Never be like a head of cattle, Sita, my little sister.' To her, daughters stayed sisters. And it was from this that Sita got into the habit years later of treating Fiya like a younger sister instead of a daughter. 'Understand things,' Doorga had said 'as much as you can, and what does not augur well for the future, whatever it is, you must oppose it. Never give in. If you stand alone, what does it matter? It is nothing to be alone. But you must stand up, at least. In good time, the others, if you are right, will stand up too. But never just bang your head against brick walls, either, Sita. You have to think what to do if you want to oppose something. That's why I want you educated. Not schooled. No certificates, no diplomas, no rubbish like that for my daughter. I want education. Wisdom. Knowledge of things past and expectation of things to come.'

Doorga was Mother Courage, herself.

But she was more famous. You're waiting for this bit, aren't you, my listeners.

Doorga's fame spread throughout all the villages of the South for something else. For this she was a household name. She was known as the only woman *taper* in the south, a she-bruiser. Violence, she told Sita, is a last resort, but you must always know how to threaten it, or if need be, use it. Because, she said, women often have to use the last resort. *Has history made her, our Sita, go backwards from Doorga? And where, one wonders, will Fiya go?*

Doorga wore her work boots even after work hours, and had a way of tucking her *horni* into her skirt that made it look efficient, even war-like. When she walked past, men, in general, looked away from her, or said good-day in a neutral tone and went on with their business.

Too many men had been warned, and too many men had been made
to suffer, for looking at her, or even at other women in her presence,
in the wrong way. Because Doorga, after living on her own from such
a young age in Surinam, and having fended for herself, was not only
very strong physically, but she was a warrior. When she was young,
any man who made a comment about women in her presence, she
would give one warning to. Only one. And then, any further misdeed,
and she would *beat him up*. There was only one other woman who
made men scared like this, and she lived in Kirpip. She was called
Nancy Khaki. Even Gaetan Duval's bruisers were scared of her.

Doorga would sometimes, just to keep her reputation high, go into
a bar, a proper *lakanbiz*, and ask two men at the bar to buy a rum for
her. This is another side altogether of her character. 'Women's pay is
less,' she said. 'Buy me one.' This was her sense of justice. 'My pay is
less for the same work. Buy me one.' She would put one arm on the
counter and wait.

Any intelligent man would either buy her one or, if he couldn't,
explain very precisely to her why he couldn't. But from time to time,
someone would refuse. And she would ask what the reason for the
refusal was, and, if the man replied in what she considered to be an
insolent way, she would ask him to *tom deor*, step outside, and when
he did, she would beat him up.

Doorga was a legend in her own life. And what's a legend, if not
someone who tries to get into the flow of history, out of the mud of
the past, into a realm of rationality that humankind deserves?

Sita was brought up with a sense of history, and a sense of progress,
and a very sound sense of the role of the individual in society. Neither
an omnipotent fancy of herself, nor an impotent image of herself.
Thanks to her mother, and, in a way, to her grandmother before her.

Yes, I will tell you about her, too. Hang on.

Because before Doorga, was Doorga's mother, grandmother of Sita,
who in turn had been a famous woman, even more famous, now also
a legend; a woman who had lived in a house on her own with her
fifteen-year-old daughter Doorga, in the north, near Flak. Doorga's
mother was a woman called Anjalay. The sugar bosses at Union
Estates had taken up guns in September, 1943 against the striking
labourers, and were on a rampage, looking for a man called Swaraj,

who they wanted to kill, a lynch team against Swaraj, who they thought was hiding in Anjalay's shack. Who they knew was hiding in Anjalay's shack. She, Anjalay, was pregnant with his second child, which would no doubt have turned out to be a girl-child, but who was doomed never to be born, because the bosses, when she barred the threshold to her low-doored house with her own blown up body, and when she would not let them in, because she was a stubborn upright principled woman, then they fired three shots into her, and she fell crumpled to the ground in a heap, with a red mark getting bigger and bigger on her, and then stopping. She was dead. Doorga was a witness to the murder. Witness. The word rang out with warning. Witness to the assassination.

The neighbours panicked for Doorga.

For Anjalay it was already too late for panic.

They gave Doorga a handful of money from under mattresses, pushed it into her hand, for her to tie into her blouse, and told her to run away. 'Run away, run away, run for your life. Beware. Beware because you have seen too much. Beware for thou hath beheld too much. They, that lot, they won't let a witness live,' they said. And they would not have. 'Take this money, catch the bus to Kirpip, and then catch another one to Surinam. Rent a room from any woman you find living on her own, and get a job in the cane fields there. Your mother's family came from there. *Her mother is dead, but her mother's mother was called Olga, Olga Olande. Take your time, ask about her. But now, hurry up, there's no time left. Get on this bus and keep your head down.*' Which is what she did.

'Do you know my oldest relative, most long ago, Iqbal?' Sita said to me once. I said perhaps she was Eve. 'No before her,' she said. 'It was Time,' she added. 'Time?' 'Yes, time is the mother of all life.' I said: 'I suppose it is in a way.'

And then she told me who her oldest relative in Mauritius was. 'Not my mother,' she said. 'Not her mother. But many mother's mother's before.

'My great great grandmother was from Samarel. She was called Olga Olande. She was one hundred and one years old. The one they sent my mother to look for, because she was a witness. She found her and stayed at her house for two weeks, and she talked to her for two weeks almost without stopping, except to drink sugar-water and then announced that she had now reached the time to die. And she died that same night.

'In her very name is the history of Mauritius. Olga Olande, Olga the Hollander.

'She told Doorga and Doorga told me: In Samarel, a village high in the mountains in the South West, there was the only fairly big group of people left on main island, Mauritius, when the Dutch colonizers left. The Company had given instructions to round up people and slaves, which the officers did in a haphazard way, leaving odd individuals here and there, on purpose and by accident, left to fend for themselves after the last boat left.

'But the big settlement of runaway slaves in Samarel was one place where they would not even bother to go. Leave them to themselves. Not take any risks up there.

'The Dutch left because of rats. Too many rats. Yes, rats made them leave. But before they left, a fairly big group of around a hundred slaves had run away, sometimes in groups, sometimes one by one. *Maron*, they were called, *runaways*, and gone to live in Samarel, in the mountains. And started to have children. They had beautifully planted terraced fields. And there was always enough rain not to need to water them. And they had pigs and goats.

'And amongst the people at the runaway slave town of Samarel there had been long ago a young girl, who had run away in exactly the same kind of circumstances as you have,' her great grandmother told Doorga.

'There was a young girl,' Sita told me, 'who ran away just like my mother ran away as a child. *Only more-worser*, being a slave. Long long long ago. On 18th July, 1695, when she was only fifteen, she ran away. Because she was a witness. She was witness to her mother's defiant action just like Doorga, my mother was.

'She was witness to her mother, Ana's act. Ana had burned down the whole of the Dutch East India Company's quartermaster's stores and the whole of the headquarters of the Company at Maybur. The young girl, daughter of Ana de Bengal, saw her mother, together with two man slaves called Antoni de Malabar and Aron de Amboina, plot together, plan together, work out together, and then go ahead and do together their act of defiance. They took part in history. They decided to destroy the visible representation of their oppression and they set about destroying the symbol of the state: the stores and headquarters. Being thought guilty of treason, without any trial of course, they were executed. The men slaves by beating and hanging, Ana by drowning and then hanging in public.

'Ana's daughter, Olga Kleinetjie Ana, was told by the other slaves, when they knew she had seen it: "Here's some *satwa*, seven types of grain all ground together and stored for dire emergencies in a cloth bag, run. Run, girl, run. Run for your life, girl, run for your life. Take the Samarel mountain as your aim. Go and look for someone called Jan. He will be an old man by now. Maybe a hundred and one years old. Run, girl, run. Witnesses must flee. Thou hath beheld too much."

'Olga had run and run. And she had hidden in the mountains by day and by night. And drunk from the traveller's palm, which stores crystal clear water high up in its vaselike leaves, for emergencies, and had eaten her *satwa*. She ran and she ran. And when she got near Samarel, she watched from a distance, and saw a woman she liked the look of leaning over washing clothes by the river. She was singing a strange song. She was big and strong, and would put her head back and laugh loudly. To herself. And shake her head. "I'll go up to her and tell about my being here."

'Which she did.

'And so it was that Olga settled in Samarel. She had children, girl children her great granny told Doorga, and her children had girl-children her great granny told her, and all through French colonization, they stayed hidden. Because a runaway slave had only one punishment: death after torture. And when slaves were freed, by the 1835 decree, slowly over the next five years people came down the hills and dispersed, looking for contract work, as if they were coolies. And my great great granny, also called Olga after the original Olga, at the age of eight or nine years old, had come down to Surinam to settle and work as a cane labourer. And then she had a daughter called Olga, too, who then had her own daughter in turn, who grew up and met a labourer called Gassen who was her friend, and together they had a daughter called Anjalay, who also became a labourer. And when she was a young girl about eighteen years old, Anjalay fell in love with a man from the North, called Swaraj, and Olga, her granny, who had brought her up after her mother's death, let her go up to the North where the man called Swaraj lived. And though Anjalay loved him, she would never live with him, but on her own. And Anjalay gave birth to a little girl called Doorga, and fifteen years later was pregnant, very pregnant with a second of Swaraj's offspring, when she was assassinated. But because Anjalay had often talked of her grandmother, Olga, to neighbours in Flak, and told stories about how they lived in Surinam, and all that her grandmother had taught her to do, that was howcome people in Flak could whisper to the fifteen year old Doorga: "Run, run to Surinam, girl. And take up house with a woman living on her own. And look for an old lady called Olga Olande, sweet Doorga."'

So Sita told me.

♦

Sita walked from where the pirogue was moored temporarily, up the grassy, bushy hill towards the Pwentosab road. The pathway was meandering. She was wandering along, humming to herself. Dusk was coming down fast. Living on the sea for a week had made her even more self-confident, in an animal sort of way than she usually was. Doorga's daughter was a strong woman. She and Dharma had eaten well, slept well, worked hard at the sails all the way up the west coast to Granbe and back. They had even taken a bottle of whisky along. And drank a bit by moonlight. Made love in the rocking pirogue. And told one another stories and myths. In the day Dharma had caught a big dorado, and she had steered the pirogue during the catch. And the demonstration in Grandbe, which was the reason for the outing, had also been a success. She and Dharma on the sea, as planned, their sails as banners, and the others on land. I was standing there on the rocks. You can see my photo in the newspaper cuttings. I had both arms right up, and I look all pleased. The wind got into my clothes. Balloons and sails and kites alike bore slogans of protest. *No to apartheid. No to Mauritius colluding.* The demonstration had been planned so as not to blame entirely the silly-headed sportsmen in the yachts. This had also been managed. It was a demonstration with a sense of humour. It had for the first time carved a place in the minds of the people. 'What,' they had asked 'is this apartheid thing really about?' When they first got to Grandbe, a four-year-old with a husky voice had appeared. An urchin in Granbe. 'Where's the pirogue from? 'Suyak.' He had been sent by a group of fishermen watching from under the *lakoklis* trees. The pirogue was too small for the seas up in the north, which thrashed around Kwindmir. And too big for the Granbe lagoon. And anyway it didn't usually moor here and had to get here by way of the high seas, and it wasn't to their minds big enough to have got here by way of the

100

high seas. The child had been delegated to ask a supplementary question: 'And who's the woman?' The fishermen, renowned for asking no questions, were aroused by the demonstration. In person they came near: 'Why did you put up those words? What did the words say? Why did you hold up those words?' This meant the demonstration was a success. Why does one demonstrate? A question that has to be answered. A way of saying something to someone when there is no other way. An age-old method of telling the king something. In case he wasn't aware. An age-old way of saying 'No', of saying I do not accept whatever you mete out, you who have the power and the money. We had said it in Granbe. Humbly, but truly.

The sea had been kind to them. Not gentle, but not treacherous either.

And now on the way home, they had come into the estuary at Gran Rivyer and she was going to look for a telephone. Dharma was on the pirogue.

She walked on bouncy feet.

She was going to phone to say they couldn't get a mooring nearby enough because of the very low tide, and because it would go down further, and that they wouldn't be coming to meet the others, for the all-night stopover they had planned, before continuing on the high seas home the next day. I had been amongst those waiting for them. I was standing on the Gran Rivyer bridge, trying to wave at them. I saw her set off up the hill. That was all I saw. Until I saw them set off again under sail.

But Ton Tipyer saw her then. Ton Tipyer, being, as you know, the chorus, was there, drinking a bottle of wine under a *lakoklis* tree. He wondered what she was doing there. He watched her, intending to get up and walk over and talk to her.

She came up onto the Pwentosab road, which wound down in towards Porlwi. She stopped humming. On the road she saw a half drunk man. And another completely drunk man. Of course, it was Saturday night. How could she have forgotten. She shuddered. The purity of the sea. And now this. A kind of horror passed over her. A carload of men, shoulders jammed together stopped next to her. 'Where's the Golden Restaurant?' one said. Fear, the feeling she didn't know, had started to creep up inside her, and she didn't want to tell them where the brothel was. She said. 'I don't know where it is.'

And then, realizing that she was avoiding a moral dilemma and pulling herself together, she added 'No, that's not it. I do know. Only I'm not telling you where it is.' A brothel that had ordinary mothers working nights. She wasn't going to tell them where it was. The fear had receded a bit. Ton Tipyer was moved. It's all the stories he told her that made her precise like that. 'Why do I drink,' he thought. And just as Ton Tipyer was about to call out to her, she set off fast.

She decided to walk to her right, towards Pwentosab. Probably be a shop open. No, the first one was already closed. She walked faster. Then the fastener holding her skirt up snapped and as she felt it give, she panicked slightly and grabbed hold of her clothes with her left hand. As the fastener broke, it was as though the whole of her being changed medium. She had to run away. She started to run. Holding on to her skirt. Another carload of men on their way to the Golden looking like savages, went past. Who are they hunting? Not me, I'm sure. Yes, me. She suddenly knew she was running away from someone. She broke into a sprint. More and more a feeling of being prey, an almost animal fear, rose in her, and she looked behind her, then in front again, then ran faster. 'Where am I running to?' Into more danger? Then she turned around and started to walk fast in the opposite direction, back in towards Porlwi. She was still holding her skirt up, still looking over her shoulder. 'I am fear personified.' Then she started to run again. Right past Ton Tipyer. The next shop beyond the closed one was open. Three drunks inside. Dinginess. 'Wait for your eyes to get used to the dark. No telephone.' Out again. 'It's getting dark,' she thought. 'I have been here before.' The way the road curves down into the town. The feeling of outskirts of a town. The road from the Sodron into Sendeni in Reunion. Running away. The gendarmerie on the left on your way down. 'I am running away from someone in Reunion.'

Ton Tipyer tried to run after her to find out what was the matter, but he was too drunk. 'Must give up drink,' he thought. What problem's she in? The words tried to form in his head.

Panting, fear draining, she got back onto the pirogue. Relief settled in.

'Well, never mind,' Dharma said. 'No need to let them know. They'll guess. The tide's going down fast. Must get out into the bay right now. Should we really anchor here in this bay? It looks derelict, doesn't it? All these shipwrecks. Like a graveyard. Should we push on again. There's full moon, and the sea is good. Those huge swells will carry us home like a dolphin carrying Orian. They're huge and pushing in the direction of Flikanflak. We can get back to Suyak in the morning.'

'Inland it's just as bad as the bay. If not worse. Derelict and seedy.' She was trembling, as she said this, by way of report on her walk in towards Pwentosab. She added: 'Rather die by the high seas.'

'What did you say?'

'Nothing.'

'What on earth are you talking about?'

◆

The last memory she had of something pleasant, or even ordinary happening that day, was that she was talking to a woman. Just talking. She was talking to a woman who said she worked as a domestic servant, who she met at the bus stop, and just got talking to. The woman had said 'Mauritian? Rather free like you.' In Kreol. She asked about wage rates in Mauritius, which were much lower than in Reunion, but then, as she put it, there wasn't work in Reunion at all so what was the use of comparing wages. So she said again: 'Rather free like you.' She and Sita became very close in the ten minutes they spoke to one another. As only women can.

For some reason, this has stayed very clear in Sita's mind.

But, that day, in 1987, in Reunion, as she went in by bus from Senzil to Sendeni, she began to feel the bizarreness. There is no other word for it. Bizarre. I used the word earlier, and I have to use it again. It's what she felt. She and Dharma were to be in Reunion for 48 hours. Dharma was giving a series of political talks to young people in the Independence movement. While Dharma was at the Seminar, she would go in to Sendeni by bus to meet two people. She had to go in early, although her planned meeting with the two men who had something to do with pre-primary education, was only at half past one, because during the day there weren't buses. In any case, she had thought it would be interesting to spend a half-day in Sendeni. After all she had nothing against the place. To her knowledge. So at half past eight or so, she was on her way to Sendeni.

It was during this journey that she began to go mad. The journey was like a journey into madness. *Into the heart of.*

To begin with, people started to look unreal to her.

She saw a man with no eyebrows. His forehead bulged outwards. She saw another with club feet. Both feet clubbed. And then another man with one club foot. She saw a haggard pregnant woman bowed down by the weight which unwillingly she bore. She saw a vacant-looking child. Standing, dribbling. Unemployed youths stared into the middle distance. *Alone and palely*. Young girls were tarted up. As if for a stage show. Make-up covering for poverty and for expressionlessness. Poor farmers trudged to town, knock-kneed.

In everyone she saw the same feeling. The same outline. As if drawn by a good artist with one stroke of the brush: *submission*. In a word.

Deferred anger was everywhere on the faces of the people. Deferred until when? Submission and prowling anger were caged up inside them.

Even in the early morning, you wake up to it, she thought. Another day of being colonized. The word went round and round in her mind: colonized.

She felt herself during that journey become completely colonized. Journey into the heart of oppression. She felt her own eyebrows melt and then evaporate. She put her hand to her forehead. She felt her feet club. A heavy, resented pregnancy, distended her unwilling womb. Her eyes shred blankly, and she checked that she wasn't dribbling. Perhaps, she panicked, she had forgotten to put on her make-up. Perhaps her paint wasn't thick enough to resist what she felt she would have to resist.

At one she was with them. At one with the passengers of that *bis individyel*, private bus, running in its chaotic system, humiliated we all are, she thought, even in transport. Even when you are inbetween one place and another, even then, they got at you. Buses without time-tables, jamming people in, running only at profitable hours.

Past the dog-training centre. Training watch dogs for the rich. Keep the thieves at bay. Instill fear. Into the dogs or into the people? Trained to bite? To kill? Who knows. Keep people at bay.

Past the military installations. Walls. Thick walls. Barbed wire fencing. High fencing. The very secrecy visible everywhere.

Past rich cars. Shiny, insolent. Fast. To kill with.

The bus went indecently fast. Half of the road was closed to traffic. Too many rocks had fallen down. Crumbled off the cliffs overnight. Huge boulders were still blocking the motorway. After the holocaust. Daily holocaust here. Cars in both directions were on the outer lanes, supposedly reserved for traffic going out of Sendeni only. The outer lanes were in land reclaimed from the sea. Between the devil and the deep blue. Driving along, she thought, out of our element. Driven out of our element. And the mountains ominously threatening to attack the road again at any time. Boulders, like the plague, to be sent upon the unsuspecting peoples of the island, she shuddered.

Meanwhile, as the bus hurtled in towards Sendeni, she was, in fact, heading for the scene of something she knew, but didn't know. *The scene of the.* Of something she had gone through, but had lost, and which she had no idea was in her memory. Of something she had done, but couldn't remember it. Was it something terrible? She didn't know at all.

And yet this fact united her with all the other people in the bus. As though they too had terrible memories that they didn't know they had. Of submission, of humiliation, of defeat. And they, like her, remembered an anger so vast as to be impossible to keep in mind, in brain, in head. Murders.

She was inexorably heading for the scene of the crime she had forgotten. Alarm signals tore her brain apart. Her mind couldn't cope anymore.

So she went mad.

But mad or not, her memory of that day, in 1987, which is after all a long time ago is one of the clearest she has. She can picture everything exactly as it happened. As if it were yesterday. Not figuratively, literally. Like an unedited reel.

The bus conductor collected their money.

And then he did something else. He came up to the front of the middle aisle and put a video cassette in the video player. The video player was just above and behind the bus-driver's seat, pointing backwards at the passengers, like a gun trained on a dangerous enemy, just where it could focus on all passengers. Just where all passengers could focus on it. Could see it at least. Couldn't really not see it.

No-one actually watched it.

Just pictures and noises. 'Are we offended? Or do we no longer mind anything? What about our eyes and ears? Are they our own? It is not clear to me. But there we sit in front of the video machine. Seeing it all. But not really watching.'

Submission. That's what it is.

Anger lost inside somewhere.

And then the film turned out to be pornographic. Then also, no-one reacted.

Used to it.

'So we just saw it there in front of us.'

Humiliated even in public transport.

Insulted.

Again the word came, colonized.

When she afterwards mentioned the porno film in the bus to the people at Dharma's seminar they said 'Oh yes,' they knew that porno films were shown in buses. Had seen them themselves. They thought it bizarre. And tried to not let it be a reflection on them. Did people not object, she asked.

Then she thinks back and tries to re-construct the film she saw. It, the film they were all watching, or rather not watching, in the bus that day was maybe supposed to be some kind of a take-off porno film. Pornographic, but a skiff. But at the time, she felt as though she was being assaulted. Everyone else seemed to too. 'We are sequestrated in this bus,' she thought it almost aloud. 'We are forced to watch a porno film.' It was like a form of torture. A kind of rape. A form of jail. She started to feel she had to run away. Panic rose into her throat.

But the bus was taking her to where she had to go, so she had to stay on it. A suffocating feeling of being prisoner descended on her. Like being on a slave boat. Handcuffs and shackles. And a gag in my mouth, she thought. She tried to object. She looked around her. She felt she couldn't move. Some kind of nerve poisoning. Anger rising in her and smothering her voice. Trapped in her own rage.

Funny, she thought, I didn't used to know what people meant when they said they were scared of being closed in. Claustro.

She managed to stay on until the place she'd been told to get off at, and then managed to get off the bus and make her way from the esplanade up to Baraswa, to the Rali, where in four hours time, she would be meeting two people she didn't know.

Relieved at having escaped from the bus, and hoping that the feeling of going mad would pass, she decided to have a cup of coffee and then to walk around Sendeni until lunch time.

But instead, when she was sitting down at the Rali, she realized the feeling was getting worse, not passing. She knew the feeling was accentuating rather than passing. So it wasn't just the bus, nor just the film. It was the voyage here. Into the heart of.

This was the beginning of more torture of the obligatory porno type.

French colonial servants, professionals, businessmen and sailors, and other nondescript officials of the *metropole*, were there. They were there to meet tarted up *Reyone* girls. Very young girls. Children. And the courtship took place in a particularly vile way. Neither businesslike prostitutes, nor funseeking young girls, these poor creatures, trapped into the limbo of colonization, were actually looking for husbands by acting like pickups. The children. *They know not what.* The men treated them like toys. Like curios. Like playthings. Looked at them like you look at an animal in the zoo. Some of the men were children too. Like boy-sailors on a slave boat. Like young slave-prospectors buying new womanslaves. Sheslaves.

She realized that it was going to be hard to make the four hours pass. In no time she had read the day's papers. She had walked down to the sea-edge and back. She had walked through the park. The madness she had felt in the bus got worse. And then a physical sickness began. She started to feel bilious. Not just nauseous. She found out where the toilets at the Rali were, just in case.

And then, danger of dangers, she remembered that she could contact Rowan Tarquin and Noella. She remembered them from 1979, when she and Dharma had stayed with them for a week. Were they still in Reunion? She had had a meal with Rowan in 1982. This she remembered. Should she telephone them? She needed help. They were the only people she could think of that she knew. Yes, she would telephone them.

A wave of nausea overcame her.

She went to the toilet and vomited.

She felt she would get diarrhoea as well.

She prepared to sit on the toilet.

As she sat down, she had to stand up and turn around fast, because a violent heave of nausea took hold of her. The heave in turn, threatened to provoke her bowels.

'Funny,' she said.

The feeling of nausea, biliousness and impending diarrhoea seemed to pass.

She went back on to the verandah, and back to reading her newspapers. Should she order another coffee. Can't go too far away from the toilets now. Just when the bookshops and things will be opening. Have to stick around.

Or should she telephone Rowan, because this four hours is going to be torture in this place? He and Noella are the only people she can think of that she knows. Maybe by chance one of them's free and can come and meet her. Save her.

The minute she thought this, she felt another violent wave of nausea and diarrhoea preparing an assault on her stomach and tripe. The sicker she felt the more she needed help. The nearer she got to telephoning the Tarquins', the sicker she felt.

Back to the toilets.

Out again.

The walls began to look liquid, and people's faces began to look as though they were inside soup spoons. All distorted and inhuman. One barman's head was actually fitted on to his shoulders upside down.

Her own head seemed to swell and to contract. She felt like Alice in Wonderland, sometimes shrinking, sometimes growing immense. He must have been mad, Lewis Carroll, she thought. 'I certainly am.' The upholstery of the chairs took on the distinct texture of concrete, poured concrete.

Is it the effect, she thought, of two hundred years of colonization, dominating me in one fell swoop? 'I have taken into my body what everyone here has felt for two hundred years? The ghosts of the past are so alive that they have started to haunt me? All that Doorga ever told me about herself, and Anjalay, and Olga coming down from the mountains, and Ana de Bengal, all this allows me to feel what the people here feel and do not even know they feel.' Is this possible? That she is a medium for all dead slaves of the past? The body for the spirits?

Yes, probably. But she didn't believe this kind of rubbish. Just the metaphor sounded right.

'Or am I just getting scared to go out.' Been living in a village too long. Surinam is a small place. Must be that. Funny she didn't feel this in 1984 when she went to Belgium, Holland and England. But here in Reunion it's as if open spaces scare her.

Scared to be closed in. On the bus. Scared to be out. Out in open spaces. Jesus Christ, she thought. Bagavan. God Almighty. Sita, the fearless. You aren't afraid of anything, Sita. She heard her mother's voice.

And a wave of fear to contradict the memory. What will happen to her self-image if this goes on? 'Of course you're not scared of the dark, Sita,' her mother had said when she was three years old and she had asked her mother howcome in other people's houses they had night lamps, *veyez*, 'Fear is something you can feel or not feel. You don't feel it, Sita. I don't either,' her mother had said. 'Why? Because every night it gets dark. There's no point in being scared. In any case, you're not scared of anything, my sweet little Si'ta.' True. She wasn't. *She didn't know fear*. Never had. There had only been that fear, that exception on the way home from the demonstration on the Pwentosab road. She didn't even understand other people when they were afraid. What is it, she had thought. Why were people scared, howcome they trembled or baulked? What did they mean when they said their throats contracted and their stomachs went tight with fear. She had never understood. She had never known fear. The second time now. There was the evening of the day of the boat race and the demonstration against it. And now. And she remembered that as she had run down the road from Pwentosab into Porlwi, she had remembered something about Sendeni. 'It's the same fear,' she thought, not understanding what this meant.

She ordered another coffee.

Read the newspapers a bit more, that's what she decided to do. She was down to the ads now. It was midday. Can she wait another hour and a half? The nausea and violent cramps came back. She felt as if she was going to die. She was sure of it.

'I'll have to run away.'

Eventually, just like that, she ran away. An adult woman, in broad daylight, ran away. Like the witness Olga who saw her mother burn down the colonial headquarters and had to run away because they would kill her. Like the witness Doorga who saw her mother being assassinated by the sugar bosses and had to run away because they would kill her. Like a witness to an unknown crime, she had to run away, because death stalked her.

'Why am I going mad?' she thought.

She ran back to the bus depot.

She knew the buses were few and far between. She'd left a book about Mauritian pre-primary schools for the two people she was supposed to meet, with one of the sulky barmen at the Rali. She completely forgot that she had a telephone number with her for the men, and could easily have cancelled the appointment. In complete fright, she ran.

She got to the bus depot, and was the first person to get into an 'individual bus', waiting listlessly to fill up.

She felt relief descend. However long was necessary, she would wait. 'Escaped,' she thought.

Immediately she thought that that was ridiculous. 'From what?' Then she thought rather a porno film than real life around here. So she sat and waited for the bus to fill up over the next hour or two, which it did. The urgent sickness passed gradually. Faded. And then the bus set off and wended its way back to Senzil. Going in and out of towns off the main road. Towards the end of the journey, people began to look more normal to her. Their faces alive. Talking. Laughing. She was almost recovered. But was left with a feeling of being in flight. Fight or.

She had about a twenty-minute walk back to the hotel. She was calming down. Peace began to settle in.

But then suddenly, as if just before getting back to safety, fear started building up again, she felt afraid. This unknown feeling, again. She broke into a run. And ran all the way back. 'They're after me,' she thought. Who? Men.

She went upstairs in a state of trembling fear. And hid in her room. I stink of fear, she thought. Or is it the room?

As she had gone into the room, and then into the toilet, a strange smell had come up. The smell of humiliated womankind. 'It's coming from inside me.'

She took her panties off and washed them and put them on the window ledge to dry. She felt as though she had been raped. She even smelt as if.

She washed herself.

But she still stank of fear. Nothing could take the smell away.

The smell of fear. The smell of slavery. The smell of the fear of rape.

◆

One day when Sita had started trying to remember, in fact, no sooner had she started working on remembering what had happened in Reunion, than she had her first dream. A short precise dream. And she had it after eating a fish that makes you have nightmares, a *kordonye*, and she ate the flesh inside the head of the fish as well, which made sure she would have nightmares. She chose the biggest fish head, therefore the most likely to make her dream *kordonye*. So that she could get nightmares.

Long ago dreams told the future. Specially in myths and stories. These days dreams tell the past. Specially nightmares. They re-arrange it for you.

She had a dream. Not exactly a nightmare. She dreamt about being upset about something. She even woke up upset. When she'd gone to work at Kodan (her dream put her back near her place of work some nine years previously in 1982), Ton Tipyer had appeared out from inside the big pipe he lived in, and said: 'Someone to see you. Look he's over there. It's very important.' Ton Tipyer was straightening out his back, and also straightening out a cigarette stompie he had picked up.

She looked over to where he was pointing and there was a friend of hers called Marday who told her that his brother, Ravin, was going to bring a friend of theirs to meet her. Perhaps, he said, she could help him, this friend. He needed her help. 'Here they are now,' he said.

Then Ravin came in with the friend, and Marday, like Ton Tipyer had before him, just disappeared from the dream. A lot of introductions, Sita thought, remembering the dream afterwards. Like peeling an onion, this dream.

The friend of a friend who needed help, it turned out, was from abroad, perhaps an African, who had only just arrived in Mauritius. A

113

tall, quiet man, serious and trustworthy. Dreams tell this kind of thing. He had come in search of the truth about something, he said. A kind of pilgrimage. A quest. A personal enquiry, to look for his own peace of mind. Or rather, he said, to put his mind at rest. He had come to find out what had happened a year before in Mauritius. A kind of *denouement* to a mystery. He wanted to know what had really happened around the rape and death of his girlfriend, an air hostess, sister to Marday and Ravin. All her other friends and relatives didn't want to have anything to do with his enquiries, but Ravin had got Marday to ask Sita to talk to the man, and had brought him to see Sita. Why Sita? Because, from the dream this was evident, she was in the women's movement.

He somehow knew that she, his girlfriend, Marday and Ravin's sister, had been raped, and that her death in Trudodus a year earlier, when she was spending an off-day, as if in transit, was in fact a murder. The rape and murder had been covered up, or to use the words of the African pilgrim, they had been *buried*. He asked for Sita's help to find out what had really happened on that particular day when his girlfriend had stopped over in Mauritius.

She woke up upset.

She summarized: *The dream was about a return to a strange land and the rape of a girl, and then the rape having been buried. And the quest of a survivor.*

◆

And the very next day, worried by this dream, she went and sat under a tamarind tree. A vast tamarind tree which emitted strong alkaloid smells. And at dusk she fell asleep for a short time. Just long enough to have another dream. How many other dreams she had had before and after, that could have helped us in this story, no-one will ever know.

She dreamt that she had gone into a warehouse, which according to the assumptions of the dream, was clearly in Reunion, a large old-style warehouse, a big old shop on the model of old-style importers to colonies, a *godam*, at which many other shoppers, mainly women, absent-mindedly looked about for their wares. Basic wares like lentils and cloth and pots and bicycle tyres and salt fish. But when everyone, that is all the shoppers, mainly women-shoppers, the dream insisted on this, had finished buying what they needed and wanted to come out again, they found there was a moat between them and the road. The way that they had come to the warehouse was now no longer operative, as it were, for the purposes of leaving. Closed, they were told. Nor had they been warned that they would not be able to go back. They were all imprisoned in a kind of dungeon. The warehouse now took on the form of a dungeon. It would, of course. Any mass sequestration does. There seemed to be no way out. Then she realized that from time to time, a rope would swing past, and a woman was allowed to grab hold of it, and swing across, to the other side and out. Not any old woman. A particular woman. All the other women watched to try to find out who got the rope, who was allowed out and why. To have asked would not have been possible nor fruitful. Then it dawned on them. Of course. A woman who had paid something to someone. Sita realized that she, like the others, would have to pay in order to get out of there. But she didn't want to pay. Nobody wanted to pay. In fact they had very little to pay with in any case.

If you didn't pay, you got killed. That was the situation, the dream insisted on. Because you weren't allowed to stay there in the ware-house. There was even a sign behind them that said *trespass*, and that meant no-one was allowed there without permission. They did not have permission.

She knew what this meant, like all the other women sequestrated in the 'no trespassers' zone knew. She had to get out.

She was torn between a will to refuse to bribe anyone, and a will to get out, a will to live, a will to survive. Anguish. She thought she would rather die. And then, at the last minute, she decided to bribe the man. When she finally paid, and the rope came over, and she swung across and out, and escaped, she ran to tell Dharma. She ran and ran until she finally found him. He was in the foyer of the committee room of the Municipality of Porlwi, waiting to depone on the Industrial Relations Act, before a Select Committee. It was out of this question to tell him at this important moment. He had to concentrate on more important things. And she realized, she also had to concentrate on them. The Select Committee is more important. So, she couldn't tell him. So she just sat down next to him. She pretended nothing whatsoever had happened. 'Everything all right?' he asked. She, like Dharma, together with all the working-class organizations, had been dedicated for a long time now to fighting against the Industrial Relations Act. Priorities were priorities. Even in dreams. She went silent. 'You all right?'

'Yes, everything's fine now.' She shuddered as she spoke these words, knowing they were lies. The bribe led to lies now.

◆

Again she woke up upset.

She summarized: *The dream told her you had to pay a price to get out alive sometimes, and you sometimes could not tell about it afterwards, even if you wanted to. The dream said that.*

◆

She didn't agree. She felt ashamed of the dream.

Did she have other dreams in the intervening eight years and nine months. Dreams that she has forgotten? And if she had not slept those two nights and had not had those two dreams, where would they have gone? Where do deferred dreams go to?

◆

It was at this point that I got into trouble with them. They just flew off the handle. I don't know if they didn't like me knowing what she dreamt, or if they were upset that the bit about the rape was going to come now, and they knew they would have to listen to it. But they really started in at me.

Howcome I have the right to tell this story. Howcome I know all this? Would Sita have told me? Could she conceivably have told me? How do I know her dreams? Who am I anyway? Or was it Dharma who told me? Sita would have told him before? Why should Dharma have confidence in a man like me? That's what you ask now. Some of them even started to curse me and denounce me for what I was like ten years ago, how I had been a lazy, good-for-nothing who spent my days leaning on a bicycle at the cross-roads, and that type of thing.

The level of confidence needed in the storyteller gets deeper as the story gets deeper. They feel I am an imposter. I can't get the right to tell them something important until I prove myself. And they are furious with me.

What's my bloody trajectory in life, anyway, they ask? How did I get active in the movement?

A credibility gap yawned open like a vast *donga* between the audience and me, at this point in the story. This always happened.

I felt that they were taking questions a bit far. A storyteller's got his private life, his limitations. And, in any case, there's a story to get on with. The rape. We haven't even got to the main point of the story, and you want a story within a story. Another story within a story?

You insist? Who am I to know, you ask. How come I know absolutely everything.

117

Well, I can only tell stories. I don't know them beforehand. I only know what Ton Tipyer told me, and then I re-tell the same one anew. The words come first, then the knowledge, to storytellers like me.

Of course, my dear audience, I understand what the audience is saying now. You're saying that the important part is about to be told. And you don't trust me to tell it.

I can only, therefore, expose myself further. I will quote a story Dharma himself told about me. He wrote it, actually. Wrote it down, put it in an envelope and sent it to me. At the beginning of his story, he said. 'Maybe you should change your ways. Me too, really. Time moves on, and you just lean on your bicycle. I still do sometimes, myself. There's progress to be made, and you turn round and round in circles. We love you for it, but think about what future there is in this kind of life you lead, never getting yourself committed to anything, keeping, as you put it, your options open. And it's about time you stopped telling lies, Iqbal. I'm going to stop. Anyway it's dedicated to you, Iqbal, and to the new life ahead of us.' I swore at Dharma when I got the envelope 'Who does he think he is. Selfrighteous bastard.' But then I read the story.

And so, reader, I leave the first person and become the third. For the duration of most of this chapter. This is the first time I ever saw myself from the outside. I was very good, as Dharma shows, at seeing other people and other things from the outside. But what about myself?

So, in a way I'm glad you ask. I'm pleased about the diversion. Gives me time to think up the main story better, in any case, and to face the facts of it, while I'm telling a second-hand one. And, as you know, it's my contract with you, the reader, that I've got to keep telling the story without stopping. It's got to be continuous.

But before I go on, one or two warnings.

This story I'm going to tell is true. It's a true story. This all happened.

But this, of course, is how Dharma *saw* me, not how he sees me anymore. Because after he saw me like this, and showed me the story, I underwent a change. A kind of rebirth. To the extent that we humans can and do change. Think of it as a flashback. I wasn't even in the movement then. And I hadn't started getting the song *Iqbal was a man who thought he was a woman*, in my head yet.

◆

'Iqbal the Umpire
'Iqbal is to be the umpire for the duel at dusk: between Moonsamy Datwann, also called Moon, and Sunjay Setsu, also called Sun. Iqbal is always judging things, as if from the outside. He isn't committed to anything. He isn't even in the organization. He got these kind of watching and judging roles from his practice of always leaning on his bicycle at the Surinam weigh-in cane scales. At the cross-roads, as it were, not going in any of the four directions the roads led in. Always listening to everyone. Never wanting anything for himself, except to be amused. *Playing god*, I call it. Everyone has confidence in him. Moon and Sun both have confidence in him.
'So umpire he will be. The duel is to be *in camera*.
'But we have to go back two years to understand the duel and the cause of the duel. The cause was Bowji. It isn't clear in what way she was the cause. But she was the cause.
'Iqbal tore up to me when I, Dharma, was sitting under an *alfons* mango tree on a granite rock one Sunday morning in front of Doorga's house, waiting for Sita, who'd gone off to collect burial society dues.
' "It's Hari. He's hanged himself. Hurry up. *Li'nn met pandi*." It was only about thirty *golet* from Doorga's tin house to Hari's tin house. Iqbal added: "Bring Doorga's *laserp*, her billhook, to cut him loose. Maybe he isn't dead yet." It was only a hundred yards. And yet crossing that hundred yards seemed like crossing a whole sugar estate. Like in those dreams when something holds you back from running away from something. We were held back from running towards something. It was as if the air itself were thick, and the earth spongy.
'Even the news of the event seemed to be heavy and trapped in silence. It couldn't get through that thickness.
'Usually news of death, or drama, but specially of both death and drama in one, could at once lighten the atmosphere of Surinam up. As you turned around a distant corner, you could see from how people

119

walked or ran or just stood grouped together that there'd been a recent death, or, if they stood around in another sort of way, in bigger and more variegated groups, a recent drama. But not today. Not even a hanging could seem to get through that day. Nothing could change that determined atmosphere. Nothing could move the heavy blanket that sat on Surinam.

'Humans in aspic.

'*Is that what you want to be, Iqbal. A human in aspic?*

'Whole families of artisans wound their way back to the Sugar Estate housing in Sunday best after mass. The news couldn't get through to them partly because there was a bright white ice-cream van with loud-speakers on blaring out "*Buba*" in dismal discord. Children came running out to buy ice lollies. They even seemed to run in slow motion. It was the end of the month meaning monthly pay for all the sugar factory artisans and it was also the end of a pay-fortnight for cane labourers. The sugar estates' bosses had poured a little money into the village of Surinam: all three of the estates, Belom, Senfelix and Linyon Dikre had all paid workers. It was cane-cutting season. Respite. Imagine calling cane cutting respite. But respite it was. Respite after a year of unemployment. A little money, like a thick muddy stream, was flowing slowly around Surinam. Some reached the ice-cream van. Women in bright sarees with children all dressed up in tow, walked briskly from Kanlapay in the opposite direction, each group seeming to escort a gift-wrapped plate or China dog. Off to a wedding. Past the ice-cream lorry. A band of young men and boys were obsessed like ancient hunters and gatherers, in the canal and around the canal: they were about to catch an eel, their feet in the mud, the canal rushing past loudly, Tibay leaning expectantly into a cave, the others peering past him. No-one could hear any news. Only the sound of the ice-cream van got through.

'We had to run through this Sunday thickness. We had to try to get the news through to people. And us in aspic.

'We got to Hari first. Before we managed to tell anyone. There he was. Hanging, dangling, dead. We cut him loose. He fell heavily to the ground.'

'In his other tin room the baby was swinging in the *julwa* made of a gunny bag. Bowji must have gone down to the river with her women friends to get grass for the cow. The other kids must be playing on the *laplenn*.

' "Your mother's gone to fetch grass, I suppose," Iqbal said to the baby. "She's a widow now."

'Some said he had done it because he didn't have a job and there wasn't enough food for Bowji and three kids. Others said it was gambling debts. Others still said that he was jealous and had done it in a fit of jealousy. Bowji was a very beautiful woman. Others said you could never know what was written right deep in people's hearts. And most thought that his destiny had probably been written on his forehead, and as they said this, they moved their hands across their own foreheads, as if this were a proof, and that he would have died anyway even if he hadn't gone to the trouble of hanging himself over the eucalyptus tree that he himself had constructed into his tin house structure.

'The question as to why he did it was never settled one way or another. But one thing was settled. His wife, Bowji, was a widow. And the kids still didn't have enough food. This was a fact.

'Two years passed.

'But what exactly caused the need for a duel between Moon and Sun is also not clear. The only thing that is clear. It had something or other to do with Bowji. And the fact that she was a widow now.

'Some people said that Moon had said that Bowji entertained men, else how, he said, could she feed the mouths, and that Sun had flown into a rage. Others said that Sun had said that Bowji was the widow who had stripped naked in the circle of singing women at the *Balans* corner, late at night, so that rain would come, so that they could get grass for their cows, though no-one could explain what so enraged Moon in this. Both Moon and Sun had given her presents for the kids. This was known. There were some people who maintained that they had both, like Krishna, been peeping at her bathing down by the river, and that a first duel had already taken place. Others said they both wanted to marry Bowji, but this is doubtful. Still others said that Moon had said that Bowji had wished him impotent because he was going to get married to a young girl from Suyak, but how this linked up with Sun is not clear at all.

The question as to why there was a duel, just like the question as to why Hari hanged himself, was never settled one way or another. Quite rightly so, said Iqbal, because things don't have only one reason. They may have a main reason, but they don't usually have only one reason, he says.

'Maybe, Iqbal, but surely life ought to have more reason, more logic, more point, than this?

'But duel there was to be.

'"*Grosso modo*, Iqbal, don't breathe a word to anyone," Moon said, in confidence. "A duel by its very *res natura* has to be *in camera*. Oh, Love! How we have to suffer for thee. Oh, Venus, goddess of Love, oh, dear, dear goddess of the Moon." He looked at Iqbal, whose smile turned into a laugh. Moon was a flabby young clerk in the Ministry of Youth and Sport. He lived on the Royal Road. Well, as good as on it. He was the first person in Surinam to spurn the *datwann*, that special bit of stick for cleaning teeth, and to use a bought toothbrush and bought toothpaste, and he would lean over the public fountain every morning brushing his teeth for what seemed like hours. Toothpaste in a healthy thick paste all over the bottom half of his face. It looked as though he might have been shaving. It was because of this that he got the name Moon *Datwann* to distinguish him from the other Moon. And it was because of this standing about in his shorts, his torso naked, that the women liked him. Not just his job in government. But his naked torso and legs, all plump and hairy and slightly blue in colour, that made them turn their eyes down, shyly. As he, like his father before him, had gone bald very young, his head looked rather like a full moon, which caused Iqbal to say affectionately to him: "You really are a Moon-head, you moony old sod! Trust me. It'll be in confidence. *In camera*, as you say. You can trust me." And then Iqbal added for good measure. "It will be *in camera in toto*, for that matter, Moon."

'Iqbal said he would meet Sun separately, and arrange for the confirmation of the rules that they had already negotiated numerous times.

'"It's about the rules, Sun. Time for final confirmation." Iqbal was leaning on his bicycle at the edge of the village.

'"It's his fault, Iqbal," said Sun. "I am obliged to go into this duel. His attitude towards her just won't do. There is the question of honour. It's a matter of principle. No-one knows about the duel, I hope."

'"Let's get the rules straight. Of course nobody knows about the duel at dusk. Who would tell them? Moon has agreed to the rules, to all of them. *In toto*."

'"You shouldn't mock him like that. Bet you mock me behind my back too. On the other hand, that's why we chose you as umpire, I suppose. You mock us all equally."

'Sun was also rather rotund. The youngest sirdar at Savannah, he was. A sirdar who still ate as many *faratas* and as much rice, and drank as much dhall as a labourer on piece rates but who stood around with his smart sirdar clothes all day watching women labourers working. This made him put on weight and also get obsessed with watching women. He told Iqbal, always there for confessions, that they looked beautiful to him. Their labourers' garb. Their boots. Their straw hats. Women carrying grass on their heads, after work. Women leaning over doing *depayaz* all day, and then going home to cook and look after kids.

'"You just want to look at them all day. By the way, did he agree to the umpire's fee of five rupees?" Sun persisted with this. He said that the only way to clinch the deal, to formalize it, was by paying half an hour in advance an umpire's fee of five rupees. Iqbal said they should have confidence in him, and didn't need anything formal. And at first, Moon hadn't thought so either. But then, all of a sudden, he, Moon, had agreed with Sun on the need to formalize everything. So Iqbal had then suggested to Moon that he, Iqbal, give the money to the winner, after the duel, so as to formalize the umpire's decision without him, Iqbal, making any profit. He now proposed this to Sun. Sun thought and thought about this idea. He was the only sirdar who did his fortnightly pay to the nearest sous. Thus his name Sunjay Setsu, or Sun Setsu, "Seven Cents". Thus his popularity with the women labourers who thought this precision was just. In any case, the women knew he liked women, so they liked him back.

'"You already look at them all day. Now you're fighting over one."

'"Yes," he agreed that he looked at women all day, "but let's get the rules and the prize money straightened out. To the nearest cent. And there's one thing you don't seem to understand. We aren't fighting over her. It's to do with honour."

'"OK, OK. Honour. We meet half an hour before dusk. At Ng Yu's shop. Agreed?"

'"Agreed. And we pay the five rupees umpire's fee."

'"Yes, the umpire's guarantee money, to be paid to the winner.'

'"And it's in secret."

'"Trust me, Sun. Is the place agreed? Down by Patat River, on the bare field just next to the waterfall."

'"Agreed."

'"Trust me, Sun. Is the date agreed? Saturday, the 24th November because it'll be full moon."

'"And an eclipse of the sun on the same day."

'"Are the *kalipa* rules agreed? Indian wrestling rules. Both strip down to *lamores*, underpants. No coconut oil to be rubbed on prior to the match. No kicking or hitting below the belt, no balls-grabbing either. No hair-pulling. No scratching. No biting."

'"Agreed, for goodness' sake. This is a dignified affair. It is about honour."

'"Winner is he who pulls down his opponent, lays him on his back and holds him down, repeat, holds him down for ten seconds. I shall do the count-down. Then I shall declare the winner formally, hold his hand up in the air, and hand over the ten rupees to him."

'"Either way, honour will win." Sun concluded.

'So Iqbal immediately came to see me.

'He told me about the duel at dusk, and we at once set about the invitations. This was a duel that people would not want to miss.

'This was Iqbal's strength.

'Everyone would keep it a secret. They would do it for him. We would do it for him. People would do anything for him. Everyone had confidence in him.

'*Can you just go on using people's confidence in you as a sort of game, Iqbal? Isn't there more to life than this?*

'"Moon against Sun? Yeah, I'll come. Secret, sure. Wrestling? Wow!"

'"Sirdar against clerk. One rupee only. A bargain."

'We sold tickets for the duel at a rupee each.

'On Saturday, 24th November, day of an eclipse of the sun and eve of full moon, the spectators started to pour in. They were already laughing at the thought of Moon Datwann, the roly-poly civil servant wrestling against the stout, stingy and moany sirdar Sun Setsu, who spoke with a lisp, making his name, when people imitated him, "Thun Thet-thun."

'All spectators for the duel arrived, as per the conditions of entry, fifteen minutes before dusk, and took their places up the *alfons* mango tress, the litchi trees, *bannwar*, eucalyptus and *lakoklis* trees that surrounded the open field on which the duel would take place. All around the arena. No-one was at ground level. This too had been agreed. And no-one was to make a sound. We had sold forty-seven tickets. Mainly to Surinam and Rianbel youngsters with a sense of humour, but also to some young men from Suyak and Sime Giriye who we thought sophisticated enough for the gladiators.

'I was with the spectators, up a eucalyptus tree.

'At dusk Iqbal arrived with the two wrestlers, one on each side of him. They looked over their shoulders from time to time to check that no-one was following them. Iqbal was in seventh heaven.

'We could even hear what they were saying from our seats up the trees. Good seats, they were. The moon would be out in no time.

' "You go over there to that big granite rock, Sun, and you to that one, Moon." Iqbal told them to strip down, and to put their clothes on their big granite rocks. "No watches on either," we heard him say, in mock heroic tones.

'As they moved into the middle of the field, stripped down to their underpants, the moon came out and made their naked, fat bodies shine all chunky.

' "Come over for the coconut-oil check, both of you," Iqbal said. "You both look a bit too shiny."

'He ran his two hands over the whole of Moon's torso, and then over his legs one by one. The spectators loved this.

'Moon looked back down the path from Surinam, checking that no-one was spying.

'Then Iqbal did the same to Sun, checking him inch by inch for coconut-oil. Sun giggled and moaned at the same time, and said he was ticklish.

'The audience was jubilant. Iqbal played to the audience, from time to time, looking up at the sky, in the manner of a great umpire, but in fact just inspiring his audience not to laugh out aloud.

' "Primo," Iqbal began

'A grim reading of the rules was performed by him. He called them Thun and Moony, knowing he had an audience, when he announced the beginning of the duel formally.

'The rules attached to our one rupee tickets were that we were allowed to smoke up the trees, but not to light matches. They won't notice a cigarette end, but they would see a match light up. This rule meant that, at any one time, there was always at least one of us, within a close radius, smoking. This helped us to control our laughter.

' "My stomach aches with laughter. This before the match starts, before the duel, how will I last out?" said my mate up the tree. I could see the odd red cigarette end in the trees across the clearing from us.

' "Sh!" I said. "Rules is rules. No speaking."

'Iqbal pulled Sun and Moon away from each other, until they were about two *golet* apart. "That's it," he said. He made them stand to attention. He stood right in the middle. They had started to shiver a little, and to sweat in apprehension, and this made their bodies glisten all the more in the moonlight.

' "You're sure nobody knows about this?" Moon asked.

' "Trust me," replied Iqbal, doing a bow for the two combatants, one by one.

' "It's about honour, I am obliged to," said Sun.

' "Honour, my foot."

' "Hold it, men," said Iqbal. "Please." His hands were up in the air.

'Then he rang a bell in his right hand.

'This was the signal for the duel to begin.

'He withdrew from between Moon and Sun. The two of them looked at one another, took in deep breaths so as to blow themselves up a bit, curved their elbows outwards like weight-lifters walking down the Royal Road in Kirpip back from the gym, past the Rio, and glanced down at their pumped up biceps, and then they started to turn around in a clockwise circle.

'They didn't take their eyes off one another, as the circle diminished and diminished in size.

'Suddenly, they were both in the dark. A cloud had passed under the moon. But there they were again, highlighted like neon signs in Porlwi.

'They were dead serious, I realized. This made it all the funnier.

They continued to circle, like lions, waiting for their prey to make a false move. Getting nearer and nearer. Then I realized that they looked dignified and beautiful. They were really serious about the duel. There was really honour involved. For a few minutes I was in awe. Everyone in the trees, the entire audience, seemed to have the same sensation, because the stifled laughter had evaporated for a moment.

Moon suddenly took a wild lunge at Sun. Sun got a fright and side-stepped and Moon went hurtling down on to the ground. He saw that Sun was going to go in for the kill, but from on the ground, he threw out an arm at the back of Sun's knee, the one he had all his weight on, and sent Sun flying sideways, as his leg caved.

'Both managed to scramble up again.

'Then the circling started again. They were already breathing heavily and combat had not yet started. They were the two most unfit people in Surinam.

'We all started to laugh again. And then the match really got going, they lunged at one another, fell to the ground in a heap, pulled at one another frantically, rolled about, making a lot of noise. Iqbal was in the meantime prancing around, like one of those active and bossy umpires, with his backside pointed outwards and his hand pointing up at the sky, waiting for fouls to be committed. Then he suddenly rang his little bell. And signalled them to stand apart from one another again.

'They accepted his umpiring.

'They were so tired by now that they had to.

'We were in uncontrollable laughter by this stage. Our places up the trees were threatened.

'Iqbal gave the signal for the battle to resume. In no time, they were at one another's necks. Accusations started to fly. Moon accusing Sun of biting, Sun accusing Moon of pinching. Each accusing the other of scratching.

'The fight seemed to go on for hours, but it was only ten minutes.

'Then both were on the ground again. This time they were pulling at one another's underpants, as if the point of the game were to derobe the opponent. The stifled laughter started to get louder.

'And then suddenly, Sun being fatter than Moon, got the upper hand and sat down on Moon's tummy.

'At this point Iqbal rang his bell.

' "The match is over," he said, "The duel is done."

' "What's that sound?" Moon asked.

' "Yeah, what is it?"

'It was wild applause and laughter from the trees on all sides of the ground.

' "I have an announcement to make," Iqbal called.

'Sun and Moon were furious.

'But what could they do?

' "I would like now to announce to you both, and to everyone present, who the winner of the duel at dusk in fact is."

'There was suspense. A silence came from the trees. Sun and Moon were completely silent. Everyone waiting.

' "It's a draw."

'Wild applause.

'We all poured out of the trees, and came and shook their hands, and congratulated them both.

' "I hereby give each one five rupees umpire's guarantee to symbolize that it is a draw.

'More wild applause.

'And then he told everyone assembled, there were fifty-one of us, that he and I had bought five bottles of Goodwill rum and five bottles of Prinnle wine with the forty-seven rupees. Sun, Moon, Iqbal and I did not contribute, because we were organizers and actors in the duel at dusk.

' "We drink to honour," said Iqbal.

' "And to fun," I said.

'The party that then ensued was the best one ever held in Surinam. As Iqbal put it, it was on that day that it was decided that Sun and Moon should draw. While they each had their strong points, neither could dominate over the other. Which is why until today, Iqbal says, day and night are in perpetual harmony. They reached a stable state, he says. Which is why contradictions should be fought out. So he says.

'He was always one for a story. If I hadn't been there myself, I would never have believed it.'

◆

'When all the others had gone, you and I sat there, Iqbal, in the moonlight on one of the big granite rocks, still laughing quietly.

'"Does Bowji know about all this?" I asked.

'"Of course, she does," you said.

'"Who told her? You?"

'"Of course. I told her all about it.'

'"Well. What did she say."

'"She just laughed. She says they are fat babies and she loves them."

'"So it's true about her, um . . ."

'"Well, her little ones need food and clothing, you know."

'"But, they say, you also visit her. You haven't got a brass bean. Not a penny."

'"That's how it should be. People don't do things for just one reason." You put your head back and laughed.

'Then Iqbal, you turned around to me, and added: "I think Bowji will have the last word. We, the men, she will say, are watching Sun and Moon having a *kalipa* duel, while the women are carrying the weight of the whole of the earth on their shoulders."'

◆

His story was over. It was all true, and I recognized it. In the last part I'd moved from third person to second person. And this was when for the very first time, the song that was later to haunt me came into my head: *Jojo was a man who thought he was a woman.*

◆

At the bottom of the story, Dharma had signed his name and written: 'Dedicated to you, to life, to laughter, but also dedicated, Iqbal, to progress. Come to the branch meeting on Tuesday.' Which I did. And which I have never regretted. I don't think I would have been alive if I hadn't had the honour of committing myself like I did then, and like I do now. My life had become a dead end. The audience was right to challenge me.

◆

The Chapter in which Sita remembers, and in which she goes to Reunion, in which the rape of Sita takes place, in which murder is contemplated, and in which the burial starts to take place

◆

'Perhaps you'll need help,' Dharma said to her. He and Sita were on the beach at Rianbel. The filao trees whispered. Mosquitoes sang around them. There was phosphorous on the ripples that came into the lagoon.

Sita had been trying to remember. She had got stuck.

'Is Fiya all right? I can't remember anything.'

'Yes.'

'Are you sure?'

'Try again. I'm looking after her.'

She couldn't remember anything more. Just those few glimpses. And then blackness. Nothingness. The hole. The buriedness. No matter what she tried, she couldn't remember anything else.

She would start crying, and sometimes she wouldn't be able to stop.

And how could Dharma help her really, given the nature of what she was trying to remember. He was in it. He was part of it. His help would be bound to be limited.

'Who could help me where I am, Dharma? No, I'll work on it myself. *I alone alone must sit and pine.* Like Lucrece.'

'Why name Lucrece?'

'Just because I quote her.'

And so she stayed in Rianbel on her own. Alone alone.

And there, after lying in the midday sun on the midday sand, and after lying in the midday lagoon. Not even trying to go downwards into her mind. Like it is sometimes with birds, or with lost words. Sometimes when you're looking for birds out at sea, when they would take you to fish, what's called a *larme* working birds in formation like a battalion, and you see them in the very far distance, just a patch of grey, the only way you can really see them is to focus just *next door* to where they are. When you look right at them, they are invisible. Or like when you try to remember a word, and you can't remember it, and you try and you try, and the minute you give up and think of something else, you suddenly remember the word. She tried to look next to the grey blob in her mind's eye instead of straight at it. She tried to pretend she was giving up trying.

A shudder of loneliness came over her. The journey ahead seemed to gape into eternity. Will she come back from it? What will she find? Will it be compatible with continued life? Or will she be dramatical and cast her body over the cliffs at Grigri?

She walked out to the reef. It was almost a mile's walk. It was low tide so there were sandbanks all over the lagoon. She looked into each pool between the sandbanks, hoping to see what she was looking for. '*I wrote a letter to my love and on the way I dropt it, It wasn't you, it wasn't you, it wasn't you . . .*' She looked in each pool and said 'It wasn't you.' No, it wasn't in those pools. There were sea urchins and *banbara*, but no memories reflected back at her. And the reef, when she got to it, a wide wall with deep pools. Into the deep pools, too, she looked and saw nothing. And then she got to the edge of the reef and looked down into the big sea, which was below the reef, and which was crashing in against the reef. 'Are you there, in the deep blue sea, oh memories, oh devil or the deep blue,' she said, looking down, peering into the waves. No.

And so she went back. And she stopped looking.

◆

And there at Rianbel, after she had listened to the BBC news on a crackly radio and heard of the bombing of Iraq.

And there, after sleeping and then waking, she began the descent to hell. Instead of looking, she decided to walk in. In, in, right into

131

that part of her memory barred from her for eight years and nine months.

◆

And it was lying there. She didn't have to look for it. It had been there all along. All she had needed was the determination to walk into it, the time and space free to face up to it. To face it. To face what?

The monster.

The monstrous memory.

Unorganized.

Unlabeled.

Unanalyzed. Unfiled.

Not yet even mourned over, no tears spilt, let alone raged over. No hair pulled out. No fists into brick walls.

There it was.

This is what she found.

◆

At some point after arriving in Reunion, where Rowan did come and meet her at Zilo Airport, she found out that he and Noella were separated. There's the answer to the question from Dharma. 'Yes they were separated.' The edge of the black hole. What a simple answer. There it was.

They were separated. She got this information from Rowan. She remembered this discovery that they were separated very vividly now, and that it had alarmed her. Beyond reasonable measure. Shows how much we know and don't know that we know: otherwise why was she alarmed beyond measure. Rowan on his own. Alarming. And she had immediately controlled this feeling of alarm. She, remember, knew no fear. 'You are like a *Makonde*, Sita, you know no fear. You are like a nightwatchman, nightwatchwoman, guarding everyone against fear. Fear not, yourself, and help others to know no fear.' Words handed down by Olga Olande all the way from Ana de Bengal, words about how *Makonde* people know no fear.

Reader, here I have to come out into the open and address you again. Whether Goldswains agree or not, I must do it. This may be the place, the very point where Sita made an error. Should she, on finding out that Rowan Tarquin was separated from his wife, have immediately said: 'I would rather stay in a hotel, thank you.'

This may have been better. Surely, she should have said it. Or would this, on the other hand, have been rather silly on her behalf? Even paranoid. Would people think she needed her head read if she refused to stay in his house just because his wife was not there? What was his wife or ex-wife in that case? Some kind of a bodyguard for other women against her husband's aggressiveness? Or was his wife just the buffer who took his violence? Maybe Sita should have said that then: Oh, I would rather stay in a hotel.

But then, can we be sure that in any case all the events that followed would have been significantly different if she had just said: 'I would frankly rather stay at a hotel, thank you.' Maybe they would have been. But should she have said this? This may well be the break-off point. Here may be the culpability. Inasmuch as there could possibly be guilt. But, then again, not necessarily. It would not have been the fool-proof preventer of history. He could, for example, have said to her, well, in that case, if you won't stay, please be kind enough at least to come around to my place for a nice cup of tea. And then it would be hard for us to say that she should have said 'no' to that as well. And maybe the scenario would have continued the same. Because she would have been in his house with him alone.

Should a woman never accept to go into the same house as a man is in on his own, even a man she knows? Should a woman never accept an invitation for a cup of tea? And what about the lift? When she steps inside and then, before the doors have time to close, a man comes along, either a friend or a stranger, should she, because she is a woman, leap out of the lift? And take the stairs. And what about the stairway? May she not meet a man alone there? Should a woman take a taxi? What should a woman do if she misses the last bus? Should a woman take the last bus? Or the second last? What time is trespass for woman? What place? Should a woman accept to get into a car with a man, any man, alone? If a second person gets out of the car, should a woman just dive out after her? Should a woman visit a friend at his house? Just pay a visit, you know, to see him. And can no woman ever

133

share a house with a man, a man who is a friend, an acquaintance, or just a person?

Remember, Sita knew Rowan. He was if not a friend, at least an acquaintance. Longstanding.

He had separated from his wife.

He had, he said, got himself a flat of his own in the very same complex in Sodron that he had always lived in. Noella and the children had kept their previous flat (where Sita and Dharma had stayed a week) but they were not in Reunion at the time, Rowan had said. When she thought of it now she wondered. Was he really separated, or had he just got himself an additional flat for his private use? Even for private misuse? Or private abuse? Howcome he answered his old telephone number? Were Noella and the children all along near at hand? So, it wasn't such an easy question to answer. That's why the answer had fallen into the black hole.

Rowan said that his parents were also not in the country. They also lived nearby in a big house. Sita knew them. From 1979. She, his mother, a woman afraid of her son, and ashamed of him. She remembered now, the way his mother looked at him. Sita had thought of the pain mothers go through when their sons provoke that expression in their faces. They had, Noella and the kids and Rowan's parents, both lots, allegedly gone to France for a while.

Was Sita right to have assumed that this was true? It certainly may not have been. But then, these colonizers went to and fro a lot between what they still call the metropole *and what is still the colony.*

So, Sita would stay at Rowan's flat. A wave of anxiety blew over her. Like a passing smell. Completely under control, it passed.

'Nonsense,' she thought.

And then, 'Trapped,' she thought. *Was she socially trapped. Should she have given in to her feeling of passing momentary silly anxiety? Should she have tried to escape from that moment on? She thought of his name Rowan, like Rawan, and Targuin. Should she have run? Or would this have been over-suspicious on her part? And based on superstition. What's in a name? It is not his fault he is called Rowan or Rawan, the ravisher, is it? And Targuin is the name of many people, not just Lucrece's rapist. What should she have done? I do not know, dear reader. Only you can judge. Moral dilemmas have no answers.*

The dilemma is sweet. Bitter sweet. Of itself. And maybe the dilemma is not individual for just our Sita, or you or me. Maybe the guilt is not Sita's, but all of ours. Where do we accuse her of trespassing? And at what time of day forbid her to venture out?

◆

Rowan Tarquin was distant and rather cold on the surface. But a slight agitation in him, underneath. She was perplexed. He had always, if she remembered rightly, sort of admired her. Looked up to her. Gushed over her. Even sometimes, seemed to seek her out, and under the surface, to hunt her down. Until 1979 that was. Until the last time she had set eyes on him.

But now, he was frigid. She remembered the words '*lightless fire*' coming to mind, and then other words like '*pale embers hid*', as though the pallid surface hid dread. 'Where are those words coming from?' she thought, 'What are they out of?' She shuddered: *lightless fire with pale embers hid.* The words themselves, like a song that scratched itself into your mind when you don't want it. (*Iqbal is a man who thought he was a woman* automatically comes to my mind as I tell you this.)

Maybe he's got a headache, she thought. Splitting migraine or something. Sita thought he'd probably had a lot to worry about, having separated from Noella recently. Probably got a splitting head. Perhaps he was thinking about his kids. He certainly wasn't interested in her, his visitor. Perhaps she bored him now, she thought. And underneath this veneer of distraction, ran a torrent of turbulent aggression. Better the bored veneer. But, well, he could show interest in some sort of subject matter, if not in her, she thought. Just for the sake of politeness. But he was interested in nothing. Nothing whatsoever. Neither in his own life, nor in hers. Neither in politics nor in his work. She tried to talk about probation work in Reunion. No interest from him. Pre-school playgroups. Nothing. She mentioned the children, how were they, and Noella. Coldness remained. Buried in his own thoughts, she concluded. '*Jayde*', let him be. Certainly no political contact here. No contact whatsoever. Bloody waste of bloody time. Be better off at the airport hotel, she thought. But it's too late now.

Anyway it's only a matter of hours. A couple of hours and a meal at a restaurant and it will all be over, she thought. That's where the lie came from, that's where the line came from, she realized. She thought that before. That was the hope. That was the fact that might have been, if only.

She has this memory of his having been introverted and hard to talk to. A person lost behind his glasses. Still blinking suddenly and a little too noticeably. She distinctly remembers thinking that perhaps her presence was a nuisance of some kind to him. Put him out. Conjured up anguish for him. He wanted to move backwards but couldn't. Agitated. Cold and distant. Maybe he had had to cancel something that interested him on account of her phone call and on account of her inviting herself to stay overnight.

She hoped she wasn't putting him out in any way. She was vaguely sorry to have imposed herself. He should have said. But as it was too late to do anything about it, she decided to put up with his mood. She decided it must be a bad mood of some kind. Or, the words came back, a splitting head.

She can't remember what they did in the afternoon. After lunch at a restaurant, the bit she had always remembered. Perhaps, yes, she remembers, or rather there is a vague feeling. Perhaps he took her to see a film. She has a memory of a movie theatre on a downhill road, going down towards the sea. A piece of memory which she can't place anywhere else in her mind. The cinema on the left hand side of the road, on a kind of bluff. And of being in the foyer of the cinema, and then being surprised that when she went through the door that the screen was facing the way it was. The trouble is even the bits that are not necessary to have buried are now lost in the ordinary mists of time. Eight years and nine months is a long time. *Try and remember, dear reader, what you were doing on 30th April, 1982 at two in the afternoon.*

Sita has a vague memory of a borderline pornographic film. A bad film, she thought, without much point, and with a lot of sex scenes. Couldn't place that thought anywhere else in her memory. And of thinking at the time that, having lived in Mauritius for eight years, she must have been sheltered from such sex scenes in movies. Stricter routine censorship, maybe, she thought. A vague shadow of a memory.

But perhaps this memory is from another point in time. But if so when? Funny that expression: point in time. If not then, when? If not here, where? At what point in space? At what point on the globe?

Everything round this memory is disjointed and unrelated.

Perhaps, she thought, she just rested at his flat, put her feet up, because he had something to do at the probation headquarters. There is a distinct feeling of regret that she had not done something when she had been on her own in the flat. Not contacted a neighbour, say. Therefore she must have, for a while at least, been on her own. Must have been. And of Rowan's being cross: '*So you used my phone to phone his brother, to phone Lutchman?*' 'Of course, I did, I just told you. I've left the money next to the phonebook.' Where does that memory come in?

In the evening, after eating out at a restaurant again perhaps, she remembers getting back to Rowan's flat with him. Going inside. It was night. '*Night, the mother of Dread and Fear.*' Since when was night the mother of dread and fear. Hadn't her mother said that it's dark every night, so there is no dread nor fear in it. '*Lightless fire*' and '*pale embers hid*'.

The realization was sudden. She remembered, with horror, where the words were from. 'Oh no!' It was right. Both dread and fear descended on her and wrapped her up. The words, they're all from 'The Rape of Lucrece'. It's like the spine-chilling write-up of a horror film. The words from the Shakespeare poem, when she realized what poem they were from, were what caused her to have her first experience of fear, the very first in her whole life.

A second wave of anxiety had crawled over her. 'You know no fear, Sita,' and she had known none. And yet, she thought, he had behaved so oddly. Was this coldness of his a good sign or a bad one?

It was planned, she remembers, that she was to sleep in the room they were standing in, the lounge, when they got back to his flat. Too much junk in the spareroom, he had said. She would, she thought, have to evict him from it at some point. Her hand-bag, a fawn-coloured one with decorative writing of some kind on it and that had been her mother's, a sturdy cloth bag that Doorga had liked, was in the corner of the room, where she had put it down; she started keeping it in view, in mind, in case. The feeling of being a hunted animal caught her in waves, and she controlled it.

He put on a record. Too loud. Why so loud, she thought. Drown out the screams. She remembered with horror how in 1979 he had taken off the record Noella had put on. What a terrible thing to do to someone. Take off the record she had put on. Sadist, she thought. He's a sadist. Don't be silly. It's nothing.

He looked at her in a strange way. Blank hatred or something in his face. She stayed standing. Then he had fear in his eyes. She saw his fear. And it went through her head that fear and aggression are the same thing. An odd thought.

And then, as if all this had only been in Sita's mind, he clapped his two hands together and said: 'What about a cup of coffee.' She jumped. Like a dog at a firecracker. Then covered up her fright, even at the very time that the fear rose inside her. Then, quietly, he offered to go and make the coffee. 'You have to get off to an early start tomorrow, so you must go to sleep now.'

Yes, it was all in my imagination, she thought. After all.

She felt sudden and overwhelming relief. Relief at this clear-cut statement. He would make coffee and let her go to sleep in peace. She felt herself shaking as the adrenaline kept on going round in her veins. Sweat on her palms, still glistening.

The music was loud. Bad French pop music. But still she felt the relief through the noise. Relief overwhelmed the sound.

Reader, I must interrupt to make a statement again. At no point had he shown any interest in her. None of the signs and signals. No courtship rituals, as they are called. Not just he didn't say anything pleasant, but he hardly said anything at all. He neither touched her hand, as if by mistake, nor looked into her eyes, nor made any kind of spoken or unspoken advances. He didn't offer to take her bag or her jacket. He didn't do anything. No intimation of anything. Not even warmth. Women know these things. All the different forms of proposition, various kinds of proposals, hints, invitations, suggestions, offers. By word. By look. By touch. By action. There were none. None of the usual informal signs that he would, if she were not married, be interested; or, if she were interested, he would be. Nor that he was interested, but not free. But then, she thought, on the other hand, there had been no clear signs that they were just friends either. None of the usual signals to break the courting code that the two of them could have been molded into by the nature of the evening.

But still, when he spoke, she was relieved. She clutched on to this relief with all her might. He would make coffee, and she would get to sleep early.

This absence of warmth had triggered alarm bells in her head without her even realizing it. Until she felt the coast was clear and he would make coffee.

She sighed, a silent, pallid sigh, as he went out of the room. She was overwhelmed with relief at this neutral, ordinary statement. *This, in itself, is alarming, when you think of it, reader. He was announcing that he would leave her to sleep. Leave her alone. Leave her in peace. No eviction necessary.*

She didn't offer to help. She left him to make the coffee on his own in the kitchen, the adjoining room. Give him space to himself, she thought. He looks low. He looks grim. He looks odd.

She went over to his bookshelf, caught sight of a book, a copy of T.S. Eliot's *The Waste Land and Other Poems*, and she tilted it backwards with the middle finger of her right hand, pulled it out, went over to the Madagascan chair and collapsed into it and began to read. '*Corpse buried in the bottom of your garden.*'

He went into the kitchen. There he shook. Like the original Tarquin, a violence rose up like nausea inside him and he was '*madly tossed between desire and dread*'. His head was splitting more than before. His visual field went wavy over half of his right eye. Sweat formed on his brow.

He took up the flint gun, to light the gas stove with. He forced a spark from it, and said, '*As from this cold flint I enforced this fire, so Sita must I force to my desire.*'

'*Here pale with fear he does premeditate the dangers of his loathsome enterprise, and in his inward mind he does debate what following sorrow may on this arise; then, looking scornfully, he does despise his naked armour of still-slaughtered lust, and justly thus controls his thoughts unjust.*'

Rape, he thought, is the vilest deed. Destroy her. 'My head will split in two. I feel it now. Why harm her, hurt her, dirty her with my filth?'

He went to the door and looked around it, at her, reading peacefully. 'A child, like my child. A mother, like my mother. A woman. I will not do it. In any case, there's my own future. I will be ruined if I am found out. Lose my job. Prison. But I won't be found out. She won't have any proof. Came here herself. The music's loud. She's a whore. No neighbours are home. And what if Dharma finds out? Will he kill me? If only she were married to someone else. Anyone else. He is too strong. He makes me envious of his demeanour.' Jealousy rises like bile. 'I loathe him. He's got everything in life. People love him. He is part of history. Sita loves him. And what if he accuses me? *O, what excuse can my invention make when thou shalt charge me with so black a deed? Will not my tongue be mute, my frail joints shake, mine eyes forgo their light, my false heart bleed?*

'I have no excuse, no quarrel with her, nor even with her family, specially not her husband nor her child nor anyone else,' he thought in his childish way. As if there could be an excuse somewhere, someplace, if he could only find it. 'Hateful it is,' he thought, and then '*There is no hate in loving; I'll beg her love*,' but then 'what if she says no, she will say no. How could she, so perfect, ever love someone like me? She will say no.'

He looked at her again around the doorway.

This time, like the grim lion, he saw her as his prey. 'I'll hunt her down and kill her.' But his vacillation went on and on. And so it was that, as he watched her reading, the peace on her face, the composure, the restfulness, his feeling abated: '*His rage of lust by gazing slacked, yet not suppressed.*' It didn't go away. It possessed him. And then the beginning of justifying his act to himself started. He shrugged his shoulders. He put on a macho expression on his face, he picked up the kitchen towel and put it pointedly over his shoulder, useful item, he knew, and stared at her again. 'I'll take her.' He hated her and all women, with a deep hatred that began in his loins and moved up into his chest and threatened to smother him if he didn't act. 'Annihilate her.' He blinked into his glasses, moving his head back suddenly, as if he was about to be clouted across the face. And he took the glasses off. Rather not see what I'm about to do. Although, in any case, he thought, '*The blackest sin is cleared with absolution.*' Yes, that's what I'll do tomorrow. He decided there and then to go to confession the day after. Yes, that's what I'll do. My head aches, but whatever I do, my deed will be absolved. He, He, He will forgive me. God is a man. Adam was right. Eve tempted him. What if she screams? Then what? Is the record player loud enough? He looked at the three kitchen knives, an expensive heavy set, just opposite the door.

She, meanwhile, had got engrossed in the long poem. She forgot where she was.

For the first time since the beginning of this Rowan ordeal, as she had come to see it, she lost her concentration. Her defenses went down. She was not vigilant. His offer to make coffee so that she could get an early night, had worked. She had even felt passing guilt that she had suspected him, the poor pathetic, spectacled, sad male creature. The hurt, blinking little boy, backing up slightly all the time and trying to escape harm, to escape criticism. She had relaxed.

Should a woman ever, dear reader, relax her attention like this? Be off her guard?

Or should a woman always be vigilant. Always be, as it were, peeping over the top of T.S. Eliot's poems in order to make sure no harm is coming around the corner?

Because harm was coming around the corner.

From the kitchen.

She didn't look up. She didn't see him coming towards her. She was reading calmly.

◆

He came in and struck her across the face with a flat hand. Before she even knew he was there. Hard.

141

◆

In the beginning there was the pressure of the blow. She hears the clout. Sees lights. Dull nothing. Head heavy. Now pain. Now confusion. *Wasteland* flying across room, like lost soul, *Wasteland* knocking over ashtray on carpet. Is it a stranger got in, attacked her? Her hand to nose, like newborn baby. Blood. Red blood. Her blood. Her own birth? Her periods? Giving birth. No. Hurt. Death.

◆

Then she knows, she realizes, she sees it all. 'I was right,' she thinks. 'Must get away now. Is it too late? Too late already? Keep calm.'

Try to get up. No, it is too late. Weight on her. Nightmare of being stuck down.

He's already there on top of her, holding her down, by her neck with both hands. He presses her down into Madagascan chair with all his weight. Trapped. A snare. Animal caught in trap. Fly in web.

'He going to kill me.'

It's a murder. So, this is what murder is, she thinks. Everything happening slowly now, she realizes. All slowed down. All fall down. Down came a spider sat down beside her.

Thought that someone else got into house attacking her, thought left co-existing with knowledge Rowan Tarquin himself. In his own house. What? In his house? He on his face look of deep terror. Mask of fright. This chills Sita. He feels fear. Out of fear, he is violent. His eyes ice. A blind stare. She thinks of Y chromosomes. His violence looks pathological. Is he sick? He is transmogrified into demented lunatic. His glasses off, she realizes. Maybe that why she thought it someone else. No, it was that his head splitting in two. And horrible side growing.

It is host attacking. Host attacks guest. Striking out at her as if she threatens his very life. As if she threatens to kill him. And always, cold and calculating, always keeping her pinned down by neck with other hand.

This negative man, cold, distant, and pathetic, now, at same time, enraged bull. 'Mindless,' she thinks. His eyes are glazed with hatred and fear. He fears his head burst into two. He violent like possessed by devil. His mouth set hard and cruel. Fear stuck on his trembling face, a mask. A mixture, humiliation and hatred, fear and cruelty.

◆

'What are you trying to do, you fool!' she cries out, 'You'll kill me. Why do you want to kill me?'

In one second, a split second, she sees it all. Her whole position. She has seen it all along, so it isn't surprising that she sees it in that split second. She knows no-one in nextdoor flats. She doesn't even know if there is anyone in nextdoor flats. If she screams, and no-one hears, he gets more enraged and kills her. At what point will he stuff a gag into her mouth, will he smother her to death. She gets scared of her own scarf. On his shoulder, with horror, she sees kitchen towel. Is this what murder is? Will neighbours break door down, save her, if she screams? Are there any neighbours at home? Is there anybody there? Will they hear?

◆

Should she have screamed for her life at this point, reader? Yes, definitely. This could have brought someone.

But then again it is the screaming that could have brought her death?

◆

Instead, she chose rational confrontation. Speak to him, she thought. Try to break this icy outside: 'What are you trying to do, kill me?' But the words didn't get through the armour of his mad rage. The Rowan

143

she had known, at least known a bit, was not present in this animal. Her father, Mohun Jab may have been able to dissuade bruisers from beating him up, but she, a generation later, had no such luck with reason. Her mother, Doorga, would have beaten him up much earlier for his sullenness, but she, a generation later, was trapped. 'Doorga, why did you die? Why are you dead, oh mother?' Can we be getting worse at living our lives, she thought.

She looked towards the door they had come in by, slyly by turning her eyes around behind her. Locked. No key. He saw her looking. Saw what she found. She looked in front of her at the glass door leading out into the small bit of unkempt veld that was his garden, and it too was locked. No keys. He saw her see this too. He saw her see the towel on his shoulder. And he even saw when she caught sight of the three kitchen knives opposite the kitchen door, hanging on the wall. He saw the two thoughts the knives provoked. Both doors locked. In any case, even if she knew where the keys were, how would she get to them, how would she get enough time to unlock the door, open it, run away. He would kill her.

And if she did get out. Say, she managed. All this went on inside her head. If she did escape. It didn't seem possible. But supposing she did. She thought of the bleak, always half-deserted flats she was in. The colonizers' bleak unpopulated houses. A colony in the middle of a slum in the middle of a colony. An endless series of tarmac roads, and little car parks, all the same. It was like a maze. Worse. In 1979 she and Dharma never knew which way to walk when they got out of the car to get to the flat. And when they came out of the flat again, they never knew which way to walk to the car. And now, it was worse, because it was a different flat. Would she find a way out of the maze? Again she contemplated screaming. Would anyone hear her if she screamed really loudly just once? Once, before he tied her up. After screaming once, he would gag her, death by strangulation or death by suffocation, are they the same thing? She went over this again. It was obvious. Evident. Maybe strangle her. 'That's how he'll kill me.' That's how they all do it. A sort of accident. They get scared of the screaming and can't stop the noise. So they try and stop the noise. Death by strangulation. Or by smothering. And if they heard, if any neighbour heard over the loud music, would they come and help her? Or pretend they hadn't really heard anything? Just loud bad pop music. Or that it was not their business really? She came back to the same question: How would they get in? At most, they would knock, and she would be gagged by then, and he would either not open the door at all, and say there's no problem through a closed door. Or shove her into the kitchen, and open the door to answer their question. Say he hadn't personally heard anything. Must be coming from somewhere else. He didn't hear anything, he would say.

Her bag was on the other side of the room. It seemed a world away. *Should a woman ever let her handbag get that far away from her, if she's in a foreign country? Or more to the point, why do women carry handbags? We men keep our passports and wallets close to our bodies. Why?*

In her handbag, her airticket for the next morning, her only way to escape, her passport, her money. She would have to get to it, to run away. Not just to the keys. Get to the keys, to her handbag, and get enough time to open the door, and get an advance. Could she run fast enough. Yes, she thought. She looked down at her shoes in dismay. A sandal with a heel. Not a very high heel, but a heel. No back strap. Handicapped. Could she run fast enough with this handicap? Rather barefooted. She didn't know anyone in the whole of the place. Where would she run to? To where? To who? In which direction? East or west? North or South? Up or down? Right or left? He would be after her. And then, would other men who she didn't know find her, a woman running around in disarray in the night without reason, and attack her? If those you know want to kill you, maybe those you don't know also want to. It was an hour of night when most people out would be men. Nearly all. What percentage of men, what proportion of men could be relied on to help her? What proportion to harm her?

She would have to do much more than just throw him back for a second. She needed a plan. Fast.

She tried to prepare a counter-offensive. She would need to get a major physical advantage. 'I'll have to half kill him myself,' she thought. 'I may have to kill him. Will I kill him? I will kill him.'

Then she would have to get hold of her bag, or should she forget that, and, say, break the huge window pane in the back door, with, a chair. She couldn't even get out of the chair. But he would have to move later. Unless he just intended to kill her right now. She still couldn't see any keys anywhere. Then she could get an advance on him. And then, when she was out there. In which direction would she need to run to get out of the hideous colony within a hideous colony? If she could get out of the compound onto the main road, she could remember the Gendarmerie on the left on the way down to Sendeni. How far away was it? Could she get there? Would she be safe there, if she did get there? Or would the police be more dangerous for her than this present threat by Rowan? Yes, she thought, they would be. Much more. Would they rape her or just arrest her? Even if they didn't, would they let her get on her plane? Would they let her get to the Labour Day meeting? What a fool to think she could sacrifice her life for a Labour Day meeting. Would they, the thought came back, rape her in the Gendarmerie? Like the police at Pwentosab did Véronique? When she, in disarray, ran there for help?

And on the way to the Gendarmerie, if say, a car came past, would she hide from the lights, in fear that a carload of men were in it? Men who would see her running away, helpless, hunted. Barefooted. Would they turn into hunting men, would they, like a pack of wild dogs, attack her, trap her, and kill her? Rape her. Or would the lights be a sign of help at hand? Would she jump out in front of the lights, waving and shouting for help. How do you cry for help here, in this land? Or would she hide behind a bush or in a canal all on her own and wait for morning.

This also, dear reader, is a question worth asking? Should a woman stop an unknown pair of lights at night, when she is in distress, or hide from it? Makes you think, doesn't it. I mean the question makes you think.

'Would he strangle me if I started to scream?' Again her thoughts came back to the hand on her throat. 'His hands are right at my throat right now. He wants to kill me.'

Surely she could get through to him somehow. Break through this barrier of hysterical violence.

He's someone she knows.

This can't be happening, she thought. 'Dharma,' she thought, 'why are you not here to save me.' Thrown into the position of the downtrodden woman, she became one. Sita the brave. She thought she had to be saved. For a moment. Because how could she save herself? No knight on horseback to pick her up and carry her away safely. Like a Kay Nielsen poster. No Hanuman and his army to the rescue. No Mother Mary. No miracles. No-one to act out the plot of saving a damsel in distress. It always was lies. Her mother Doorga knew it, howcome Sita didn't. Howcome I'm not a bruiser like her? What oppression have I accepted long before this night of the attack.

Then the three knives. They appeared in her mind's eye. She didn't let her eyes give her away this time. Would they save her. Not by themselves, that's for sure. She would use one of them. The middle one. Last resort, her mother had said.

Were they curios, or were they kitchen knives? Three in three sheaths. Sita couldn't remember. 'I will kill him?' She remembered Dessie Woods. Life in prison for killing the man who raped her, killing him with the very knife he threatened her with. She remembered signing the letter of support for Dessie Woods. 'I too am going to be raped.' That was the first time the realization of, the notion of rape entered her head. She had thought he was just beating her up, torturing her, and was going to kill her, and bury her body in the bottom of his unkempt garden.

Only then, after all these thoughts, while he held her chest down with one hand, did he start to pull roughly at her clothes with the other, pulling her skirt up. He's going to rape me, she thought. 'He's not going to kill me, he's going to rape me. Or maybe both. But he's going to rape me first. This is my chance. Have to try and kick him in the balls. Impossible where I am now.'

'No. No. No. I don't want to,' she cried out, pushing his hands away. 'For Christ's sake, Rowan, stop it. I don't want to.'

'Well, I do,' he roared. 'I happen to want to.'

'Stop it. Don't, Rowan.' She spoke with authority. 'Take your hands off me. I don't want to. Do you hear?'

'I want to. That's it. I want to. You don't want to, but I want to. One of us has to win, one to lose. I'm not going to be the one to lose. I want to.'

'That doesn't make sense,' she cried.

'If you agree, it won't be rape. Agree, fool.'

'But I don't want to. Can't you see it's not right?'

There she was, *a voice that pleads in a wilderness where there are no laws, to the rough beast that knows no gentle right*.

But no. What on earth. What's he doing? He's gone mad. He put his head down on her tummy. Still he was in an uncontrollable state. Old words like *lust* and *ravish* and *vice* came to her mind. And *foul appetite carnal*. What is he going to do? She couldn't understand what was going on. He's gone mad. What's he doing? She couldn't get up out of the chair. Pinioned. She was pulling at his shirt. A button popped off. With the other hand she pulled on his hair, but if she pulled harder, she knew it, he'd go even more berserk and kill her. She still didn't know what he was doing. Pulling at her skirt. Pulling at her underclothes. She pulled his hair harder, and he tightened his grip on her throat. He started, like some kind of a pig, to slobber into her groin. Spitting and slobbering. Spitting and slobbering. Well, she thought, he's mad. He's a lunatic.

She tried to talk reason again. 'What on earth are you doing?' Tried to stop him, to make him snap out of this hysterical rage of hatred.

It was like being trapped in a cage with a wild animal, like a lion, or a tiger. Any false move and you're dead. Maybe you're dead whatever you do. Or with a maniac. A raving mad man. He was a wild animal or a maniac. He was a predator. The wolf and the lamb. The hawk and the chick.

The ineffectual struggling on her part, the hair pulling, the trying to reason: *Think but how vile a spectacle it were to view your present trespass in another*. The refusing, refusing refusing, the trying to get out of the chair, the being shoved back roughly, the trying reason again: 'Someone in your job, bring ill repute of lust, dishonour, shame, on yourself,' it went on and on as if without end. The grip he had on her throat ever tightening. Nightmare without an end. He was animal-like, proceeding with homicidal, trembling rage in his absurd act of spitting and slobbering. She shouted at him to stop at once. But he went on and on. *Spitting* into her groin.

She realized that she would get tired, too tired, She had to try something else.

She played dead. Stopped struggling. She lay still. Seem to give up. Pretend it's all over. Maybe you're dead. She thought, 'Just stop. Stop it.'

Which he did.

Maybe that would be all, she thought.

What false hope. Stupid innocence.

Why waste time with false hopes, Sita. Why give benefits of doubts?

Of course that would not be all. No. How stupid to think so. He pulled her out of the chair hard by one hand, into a standing position, and, like a madman, asked her if it had been good. Was that good? Violently asked. A charade. A ploy. The whole thing was a ploy. She looked at him, seeing him as he was. He has done it before. The loud music. The isolation of the victim. Young girls in probation under his charge. She realized it. Noella, her haunted, raped eyes. Noella had tried to warn her, she realized, long ago. She remembered having seen him with two of the girls under his charge, in 1979. Now she realized she had been right. He had hunted them down as well. At the time she had suspected it. Vaguely, somewhere in the back of her mind. But then had put it down to his colonial relationship with the girls. Perhaps the revolt she had felt on the part of the girls was not against a rapist, but against colonization, she had thought. It was both. They are the same thing.

She was thinking fast.

'How do I escape? Where is my bag? Where are the knives? Can I kill him? Can I kill this sick person? He's not right in the head.' Pity. She felt pity, even as she was about to be raped and killed. Even as she prepared to murder him.

'Can I get into a position to kick him one really hard donkey-kick right in the balls? Really hard. Enough to knock him out. To send him writhing on the ground. That'll give me the time I need.'

She knew that if she tried and didn't get him a direct killer-hit, a full blown knock-out kick, he would then go wilder and avenge her in this uncontrollable rage he was already in? Would he have killed her?

He was still in this woman-hating state. A state. The state. The colonial state. The capitalist state. The state of power. The state of repression. The patriarchal state. The state. *Something rotten in the state.*

She actually didn't know what would happen next.

Then it was obvious.

It was age-old.

It was the show-down.

He was going to undo her clothes. To undress her. He started to pull at her blouse.

She felt the rape of centuries against women descend on to her shoulders. Like the weight of chains. Like the head-locks fastened on women slaves. The patriarchy was what made her the victim. Only in patriarchy is rape a weapon. She knew it. She'd often learnt it before. Now she was being made to go through it.

She knew the relativity of it all. Did she not know the women who have no fear of rape, and who believe they cannot be raped? Who therefore cannot be raped. She thought of the women from the matriarchal world of Chagos. Women from Diego Garcia. From Peros Banos. From Salomon Islands. Part of my country. Theirs the matriarchal islands of Mauritius. What would they do in these circumstances? 'Oh Sibyl, oh Alexsina, oh Annzli, tell me what to do.' Of course, Sita knew. She had learnt all she knew about a lot of things from them. One year before they had told her what they had done.

She had learnt.

'Leave me alone. Take your hands off me. I can take my own clothes off. Don't you dare touch me,' she shouted. Matriarchal confidence in her voice. 'Take your hands off me. For god's sake. See what you can do, boy. I'll take my own bloody clothes off.'

Which she would. She stood there like a wild hunted animal that has suddenly seen the way to survive the hunt. She grew tall. She stood dignified. She then started in an angry, defiant, winning drama to rip her own clothes off. She tore them off. Like Alexsina. Like Sibyl. Violently.

'I am a woman. Watch out. I am a woman. Beware of women.'

With utter disdain and a wilful confidence, she coldly and threateningly took her own clothes off and threw them on the floor. She stood there primeval. Woman. Naked and defiant.

Rowan shrank. He quaked. He was terrified. He trembled. He whimpered. He lowered his eyes from her body. He blinked backwards again and again. He was struck impotent. Shame descended on him. He looked around to see how to escape. There was no escape for him. Patriarchy gave him only one road ahead. He couldn't escape because he was in his own flat. He put a hand to his aching head. 'For what I am about to do, I shall be the most harmed,' he thought. *Lust, the thief, the poorer.* His self-will had deflated. He had lost his nerve. His energy drained. And then with *lank and lean discoloured cheek, he hung his head in shame.*

For a while, her confidence had worked. It is possible, she thought. But now to get away, to get away, I'll need even more of a physical advantage. I'll need time to get my clothes back on. *Thou shalt not, a woman, seek help naked.* It is against all social laws. That she would see to later. But right now?

She had won an advantage.

Women are stronger, in some way, and she had learnt it from the women from Chagos. From Annzli and Alexsina. They were right, after all. From Sibyl.

He was scared of her. He was dwarfed. He was scared of his mother. She, woman, was his mother. How could that ever end for him, really end? Born from inside her womb. Suckled at her breast. Give the milk, withhold the milk. Woman, the giver of life and the taker. The creator and the destroyer. Kali. Tongue sticking out. Head of newborn babe appearing from her yoni. Ten skulls threaded in a necklace around her neck. Six-armed goddess Doorga. And so he cowered.

He is scared of Sita too now. Suddenly.

The fear he felt made his lust evaporate. He at once became calm and hangdog. Like a little boy. Shaking a little. Ashamed of himself. Already ashamed, before the act of rape, for now *against himself he sounds his doom, that through the length of times he stands disgraced.*

He won't kill Sita now. She knows it. He has lost. On that she has won. It was out of the question. To this extent she had won. She knew it at once. All fear passed.

She had gained the upper hand psychologically.

But how long would it last? And what about the rape. She was naked now. Would she have to pay the price?

When would he go homicidal again? Like a chromosome man gone berserk? And how would she get back into her clothes and out of this place and to somewhere safe and to the airport and to the Labour Day meeting. All this for the Labour Day meeting, she thought?

Here, reader, is a moral dilemma. The Chagos women had shown her how to take the initiative against rape and murder. She had done

151

as they would have done. And it had worked up till now. But in what circumstances had she done this? Did the circumstances permit? Nothing else was in her favour. She was out of her geography. He was in his. She didn't know the language here. He did. She didn't know anyone. He knew lots of people. She didn't even know where to run to. He would know where she would run. Her shoes were a handicap. He knew this. She had no money. He knew it. He knew all this. The balance of forces were against her in all ways. (In our society, aren't they always, when it comes to women?)

Should she, under these circumstances, have torn off her own clothes? Was it, reader, a wise decision. Was it the safest thing to do? What will happen now?

If she humiliates him any more now, as he stands there desemparé, will his hatred of women erupt all murderous again?

'I am surviving this,' she thought. Play it cool.

He hesitated. What should he do now? Then like a contrite idiot. Like a harmless robot, he started to take his clothes off.

She didn't look.

He disgusted her.

Should she try to kill him now. The knives. She was standing up, she began to move, but he looked at her. The violence started to erupt in his frightened hce again. In the look a threat. Do not move, he said.

'I'll forget the whole thing as soon as it's over. *I alone alone must sit and pine.*' The minute this thought went through her head she knew she was a raped woman. Already raped, and still to be raped. Which part of this is the rape?

But she must survive.

She wasn't scared anymore.

She was dogged.

Determined to survive. Stubborn. Hard as nails. Murderous. But only commit your murder, girl, only take the step of murdering him when you're going to succeed. Take no risk of missing, or you'll die.

So now it's the rape, she thought. It had all slowed down. She no longer knew horror. The horror was gone. She would survive now. 'I am strong,' she thought.

'Dharma will heal me. Dharma will give me strength to overcome this. Dharma will say: "It's over now." It's as if he's here with me.' If she did not associate her love for him with her own body, perhaps this would not be so vile? To go through this rape is to go through the rape of her body, her own body, and she would get over that. But also the storming of the temple of her love for Dharma. A double rape. What is in a body, she thought. It is but a shell. 'No, it is me. I am my body. But then shall I not heal? And will not Dharma heal me?'

'Like a lamb to the slaughter,' she said almost aloud, of herself. Is this consent?

In a parody, he took her by the hand to lead her up the stairs to his bed. To the gallows. To the gaschamber. The slave taken in shackles. Making sure she would not get away or make any counter-attack. *Like a thievish dog he crawls sadly with his meat*, upstairs. My body become meat.

So this is what rape is, she thought.

Of course.

It's what it has always been like. Since the first rape.

'Will I survive? Dharma, I'll be back soon. Will I get back to Mauritius? My little girl. My Fiya. Will I get to the airport? He probably won't let me out. He'll keep me sequestrated.' She thought all this. 'Cut me up and bury me in a shallow grave at the bottom of the garden.'

His patheticness struck her again.

Like a nine-year-old.

Now it's a matter of getting it over with.

'I'm not on the pill,' she lied. Childish delaying tactic, hoping something would happen inbetween to prevent the rape. So this is how we give consent? Or was the rape itself already over? Without consent. And now it was only allowing him a way out without killing her?

He turned the light off. *His shame folded up in blind concealing night.*

She turned her head away. He put a condom on. He's done it before, she thought. Raped others before me. He even knows to keep the proof. She heard him preparing. More spitting. At himself now. He pinned her arms down at each wrist with his two harsh hands, he kept her legs down and apart with his dead knees. She was crucified. Nails in each hand. In both feet. She lay completely still. Thought of all the women of the world that suffer this disgusting spectacle from husbands, night after night. The children forced into incest. And the ordinary rapes like this one. 'Jesus Christ.' Spear in the side. Forced in. She thought of Noella. Domestic violence, like a contradiction in terms. Pain. 'I hate him.' Speared. Over and done. He reproached her not struggling. 'Why are you so inert?' Pig, she thought.

He went to sleep, lying with one heavy arm across her, one heavy leg. The kind of weight you tie a body down with to drown it, and keep it under after it's dead. He weighed a ton. He is checking that she doesn't move.

Was she an accomplice in this rape, reader? Or worse still, did she give consent? This is the question. She invited herself to stay. She took off her own clothes. So what is rape? Could she have avoided the rape? What should she have done? But the rape was done now. Done. Never to be undone. Only the murder was in doubt.

She lay awake.

She lay there the whole night. With the weight of a dead man on her. His head by now had split. He's dead. A dead man. If she kills him, she'll have a dead man on her hands. She's going to kill him, so that he will really be dead. The will to vengeance, like an ancient ritual, for the first time in her life, rose in her. 'The rape is over, and yet I want to kill him. Kill him dead.' Dessie Woods sentenced to death for killing her rapist with the knife he threatened her with. 'He didn't even threaten me with the knives. Not in so many words.'

Pinioned by him. She knew the exact spot between two ribs on his back slightly to the left, where, if she slipped out from under his arm and leg without waking him up, went downstairs and fetched one of the three kitchen daggers, the longest one, she would place it. Place it, position it with her left hand, and then raise her right fist into the air, and like a block of iron, punch down hard, really hard, all out with the right, throwing the weight of her entire body behind that one fist. Power. In one point. The dagger would go through his heart. Arterial blood would pump out of him. She was pleased at the thought. Revenge for rape.

Her body desecrated. Not of itself. Just a shell. But, her being. Sacrilege.

Ravaged against her will.

She lay there a knot of anger and hatred. Burning. The whole night. Seven hours. Four hundred and twenty minutes. Twenty five thousand two hundred seconds. One by one ticked by. She wanted to kill him. O this dreadful night. Please turn time back. Take this night away. Sequestrated. Fury knows no bounds.

◆

That is the ball of anger she had found when she dived. The first memory that came back after eight years and nine months. It was the rage, as she lay pinned down. She heard the *Desert Storm*. And she saw this very anger, her own anger, this murderous desire, this murderous will to kill Rowan. Her own anger.

That whole night long, long night, anger and trappedness. Sequestrated with nothing but her own anger. An anger too great. A desire to kill. Her contemplating killing him. Killing a man in his sleep. Would Eve have killed Adam under the circumstances?

At first light, she crept out, he didn't wake up, fetched her clothes and her handbag, looked at the knives, went past them, and went and closed herself into his bathroom. She walked to and fro, a caged lioness. Should I kill him? She asked. Paced the small bathroom. Looked up at the tiny airvent instead of a window. No, it's dawn. I'll wash it away.

Then she had a bath.

Wash his shame off her. Wash the filth off. Out.

The water burned her lacerations.

But never the desecration, she thought, it doesn't wash away.

Wash the proof away. Slight bleeding. Still painful. To bath, an error. The police doctor would say so.

She was still in a rage.

Would he let her go to the airport?

Would he let her out? Or did he intend to sequestrate her here for a long time. How long would he get away with it for? Would he have to kill her then? Lutchman knows I'm here and he'll tell Dharma, she thought.

Would he decide it was too dangerous to let her go in case she filed rape charges?

She would never win a case, she thought. Never. She knew how hard it is to win any rape case, but this one harder. She had invited herself here. He would plead consent. How could she prove the contrary? On what evidence could a judge send a man to jail for nine years? But would even the fear of the possibility, the dread of the chance of rape charges not be enough to make him terrified? Did this mean she was still in danger of being murdered? She would still have to be wary. Murder was still possible.

She'll pretend everything's normal.

While she was in the bathroom, she heard him moving about. He came up to near the bathroom door, and said, as if nothing in the world were wrong: 'Did you sleep well?'

'Yes,' she said. She decided not to talk much to him.

The same voice as the offer to make coffee. So, it was probably all over. Back to the cold and distant Rowan from before the rape. Take up where he left off.

'Would you like a cup of coffee?'

She had no other line, she had once again to say it: 'Yes, please.'

She was still in the bathroom. She took her mascara out of her handbag. She hardly ever used it. But she put a heavy line above and below each eye. I need it, she thought. Two lines to demarcate everything she would see.

She felt the heaviness of being human. Her vertebrae balancing precariously one on top of the other, and all her weight suspended, ridiculous, on the front side. Her arms floppy appendages balancing this way and that, as she stood still. Her arsehole feeling the weight of gravity of all her innards pushing down on it, and on her lacerated parts. Her tits, worst of all, balancing downwards, nipples, tender, pointing forward towards the enemy world. She dressed quickly. 'No wonder we are the only animal to wear clothes,' she muttered.

A regret took hold of her. The pathetic weakness of patriarchy became clear again to her: 'I could have caught his balls in a vice-grip, or mule-kicked him, or bitten him. Of course, I could have.' Yes, it was only in the idea of patriarchy that she was weak, not in the physical struggle, one to one. One to one? That's the question. One to how many? Whose side does society take in the confrontation between man and woman?

She went out, dressed, and stared at him. Could you call it hate? Or disgust? Or pity? Or was it just a sort of nothingness she felt?

156

He did make the coffee. The same water he had put in the kettle the night before.

They drank their coffee, she picked up her bag, and he did drive her to the airport. 'I've got a terrible headache,' he said.

She was silent.

'It's a migraine. Makes me feel as if my head will split in two.'

She was still worried as to whether he would in fact take her to the departure lounge. But he did.

◆

She saw the French police. A telegram came into her head. *Tell them. Accuse him.*

'No, they're worse than him, the French police force.'

She wanted to go home.

To Dharma.

The May Day meeting seemed far away now. And to her daughter. She feared for Fiya. If she was weaker than Doorga, would Fiya be weaker than her? What was happening to history, she thought?

He made sure she went out, he watched her go towards the departures door, and through it. He was wary. He glanced guiltily at the policeman at the door. There were policemen everywhere. You could see Reunion was still part of France. The air stank of a police state. Uniformed men everywhere. No culture between humans. No rights. He made sure she got right on to the plane. He blinked, moving his head backwards. Behind his glasses. Now he was safe. He had felt in as much danger as she had.

She still felt as if she were running away. Still running away. Running as fast as she could. As she had thought she would do down the road that curved in towards Sendeni, with the Gendarmerie on the left. Only she had to be stealthy. A beast of prey was after her still. And she deep inside the animal fight or flight state. Her adrenaline told her.

On the flight, she still had the feeling of being in flight. She was running so fast now, that she had taken off and was flying away from the danger. Flying over the Indian Ocean. Over the turquoise sea.

She kept running. Heart pounding with fear on the aeroplane.

She ran off the plane.

She ran to the car waiting for her. Lutchman, Dharma's brother was there as planned. 'Am I looking after you well for my brother then?'

'Of course, Lutchman.'

And then when she sat down in the car, she felt estranged from everything in the universe. For the first time in her life. And why was Dharma not here to meet her. Resentment. She felt resentment for the first time in her life. Of course, she thought, of course, he's at the mass meeting.

She kept on running. Until she ran through the thick crowds gathered at the meeting. She ran through the thick sounds of loud speakers. She ran to the Rond Point at Rozil. She looked over her shoulder from time to time, checking that Rowan was not behind her. She ran up to Dharma. She felt she was still running away. She hadn't thought about what had happened, she didn't think about what had happened. She just knew that as soon as she met Dharma she would say: 'Something terrible happened in Reunion,' and then she would stop running and then, in telling what happened she would think about it for the first time herself. Then she would be able to absorb the knowledge. In the meantime, she was still in flight.

She saw Dharma. All calm and radiant. She went up to him. She had no voice. She couldn't say anything. She seemed so far away. He hugged her, and looked at her to try and understand why she looked so strange.

'Everything all right?'

A silence. Then 'Yes.'

'Are you sure?'

Then, 'All is well, my love,' she added. In a way, now it is, she thought.

He took her hand in his, and looked at her. She looked troubled. He looked deeper into her eyes. Yes, troubled. He knew there was something wrong. Perhaps it's because of all the crowds of people, he thought. 'Let's go and meet friends in the movement.'

◆

Ton Tipyer had decided, after all, to come to the meeting, and had been in the tavern on the corner, and saw Dharma waiting for her. He knew Dharma was waiting for Sita. So he also watched and waited. When she came running past him, looking over her shoulder, he knew there was something wrong. What on earth has happened. I must find out, he thought. He started to run towards her to ask her what had, what was the, what on earth, why was she, but as he started to run, the crowds surged between him and her, and, struggle as much as he could, he couldn't get nearer to her; like in a nightmare, he was washed by the tide of the crowd in the opposite direction.

◆

'The article,' thought Sita, 'should really be called "Who was raped before me", but I'll just call it "Who was raped before".' This first title, which she thought was rhetorical, she suddenly rejected. It was 22nd December, 1990 that she was doing her preparations. Yes, the title would be 'Who was raped before.'

But it would also be about who wasn't raped.

Say, thought Sita, preparing an article in her head and scratching down notes as she thought, say. Say, that we human beings have been on this planet, have existed as a species, for a million years, or maybe two million. It depends on what you define as human. Well, say one or two million years. With its noughts, that makes 1,000,000 or 2,000,000 years. A long time. And yet the first rape was probably only about ten thousand years ago. 10,000 years. That means just the other day, in historical time. That means for one or two million years there were no rapes. That means that for 1,990,000 years there was no rape. The concept didn't exist.

Or am I going to be writing nonsense if I say this, she hesitated. Can it be true? And then she went on. The act was not a category. It was absent from ideas. It was absent in reality. Rape was not possible in human society until males came to dominate females by force. Until males gained control over weapons, ownership of land, private control of the food supply, ownership and control of property as a whole; will readers believe such a thing? Until males found out about their role in reproduction and then somehow got control over the process of reproduction, this symbolized by concepts like virginity and rape and a male god of a punitive nature, and then thought they could start to own children individually, control women one by one themselves, and impose inheritance laws to get their things to pass on to their sons. Maybe it was like that. That kind of ownership and control only

160

happened for the first time in a number of places on the globe from about ten thousand years ago onwards. And then, in any case, pockets of civilization live on until today, until right now, where rape is still not possible. She knew one such pocket, Alexsina. Not a category. The Chagos women, the women from Diego Garcia and Peros Banos and Salomon Islands. Rape is impossible because women are stronger than men in one-to-one fights. Women have no balls, as it were, to weaken them. Because women control reproduction collectively, so men cannot afford to attack them by band. Most ill-considered, it would have been. May have seen themselves – ourselves, think I, *Jojo was a man who thought he was a woman* – expelled only to become lone males, wandering in anguish upon the earth, like the lone elephant in the Savannah, like the lone whale swimming from ocean to ocean.

Iqbal was a man who thought he was.

That is why all gods long ago were women.

And then she began to think about her namesake.

And even in Sita's day, she thought, our Sita thought, the goddesses weren't ravished. The other Sita was threatened with it. In any case, she was a modern day human not a real goddess, the long ago Sita, *the* Sita. Sita, wife of Rama in the Ramayana, stolen because of her beauty and dignity and goodness. Stolen. She shuddered as she wrote the word, like a slave, she thought. Stolen by Rawan because he was like that. Stolen despite the care taken by Rama's brother, Lutchman, to protect her. He had difficult dilemmas, Lutchman.

Promises his brother he will look after Sita while he, Rama, is away hunting. Gets news Rama is in dire trouble. What to do?

Anyway it turned out, she was carried away and sequestrated. But she was saved because Rawan had feared his head would split in two if. And it would have. Because it had been prophesied before. She was only stolen, only ravished but not raped. She, in her case, would have had to say the word 'Yes,' because it had been prophesied that Rawan would not take her by force. And she refused to say 'Yes.' She, like a damsel in distress, was rescued. Whole armies came to the rescue. Armies of monkeys freed her. Hanuman included.

What is the moral in here, Sita thought. Could, of course, write something without an easy moral.

There was Lucrece. She was the wife of Collatine. Raped in the dead of night by her husband's friend, Tarquin, of royal blood, the king's family, jealous of Lucrece's beauty and virtue. His threat: that he would kill her, and throw the dead body of a servant on her, only to claim that he had killed him as he was raping Lucrece.

> 'Lucrece,' quoth he, ' . . .
> If thou deny, then force must work my way,
> For in thy bed I purpose to destroy thee;
> That done, some worthless slave of thine I'll slay,
> To kill thine honour with thy life's decay;
> And in thy dead arms do I mean to place him,
> Swearing I slew him, seeing thee embrace him.

And then, quoth he,

> 'And thou, the author of their obloquy,
> Shalt have thy trespass cited up in rhymes,
> And sung by children in succeeding times.'

And she, meanwhile, trying to stop him, trying every argument, and every ploy,

> Pleads, in a wilderness where are no laws,
> To the rough beast that knows no gentle right.

How much he understood, she thought: 'I purpose to destroy thee.' Odd, that. Most people four hundred years later still haven't realized that rape's to do with 'destroy'. Lucrece's only way out afterwards was through suicide. Then her husband and father took their revenge. They paraded her dead body through the streets of Rome to show what Tarquin had done. Brutus had proposed this. This was the political ending: the people agreed to Tarquin's everlasting banishment, after which they were ruled not by kings, but by Consuls. But what kind of a personal ending is this?

There was the lock. The Rape of. Pope's poem. Where lady's honour had got so reified as to rest in an object. This is what rape means in a way. We become the lock, wrote Sita. Then she decided to leave out the paragraph from Pope's poem. Must know what not to put in.

There were the rapes by de la Montagne, the *kolom*, at the Bel Bel Sugar Estate. The rape of Kawlawtee Bindoo, of Jinnta ke Ma, of Rita

Sekismal, of Manntee Beedassy and of Sakoon Beekoo. These were the known names. How many others is not known. 'Tell that short girl, Kawlawtee, to work on the far side, Ramkelawan,' he said to the sirdar. '*Wi misye*; yes, boss.' Then Jinnta ke Ma. 'Yes boss,' again. Then, he didn't mean to, but all of a sudden, Ramkelawan refused to obey Misye de la Montagne's orders. Sirdars are sometimes like that. Rarely. But sometimes. '*Non, misye*, I can't do it. I won't tell her. Tell her yourself.' The next day Ramkelawan was fired. *Gandya* found in his work *tant*. That was how it had to be. In those days. He walked home, with his head sunk low into his stomach, half the way home, and then, when he reached the mid-point on the road home, he changed his deportment, and he held his head high like a stag for the second half of the way home. The truth is like a myth sometimes. He, Ramkelawan, the Sirdar, would, in fact come to help in starting the strike. But not before the new sirdar, Pillay, had called over Rita, then Mantee and later Sakoon. And Sakoon was only thirteen. A girl child labourer. A *chokri*. She was the last one raped. And then the strike broke out. It literally broke out. It was like a *tit-albert*, a poltergeigt. A strike that you couldn't get a hold of, if you were the boss. Today in Basin section, tomorrow Tamarin, the next day Medinn, and the day after Basin again, then Bel Il, and then again Lamek. Strikes that stopped in one section and took up in the next, day after day after day. One day, two days, three days, Sunday came, four days, five days, six days, seven days, eight days. And then the cane would be burnt down the night before in the *karo*, the square field, that would be most affected by the strike the next day. The sugar turned into syrup would ferment in the fields. This made the sugar estate owners quake. The entire cane cutting process was completely disorganized. The strike seemed capable of going on endlessly, section by section. The bosses panicked and started what iffing. What if they couldn't put a stop to this? What if mutiny broke out everywhere? What if they lost control? What if there was a revolution? They pretended not to have known what was wrong. And to find out. And then, finally, to get rid of their protege de la Montagne. He was fired.

Then, of course, work started to get back to normal. Ramkelawan says that even god took his revenge and struck de la Montagne lame in one hand and leg. This history was as recent as 1969, so myths go on being made. No, said Ramesh, the cane labourer who'd organized the strike: the gods probably couldn't give a damn one way or the other. Dirty old fool had high blood pressure and had probably had a stroke. Even good people have high blood pressure and strokes. Why does god strike *them* down? Said Ramesh. And he added, that is why at the Bel Bel Sugar Estate we would ten years later be the back-bone and driving force of the 1979 strike committees. After running the de la Montagne strike, he said, we workers could run a nation-wide strike, and any workers who can run a nation-wide strike, can easily run the country's economy. Some sort of moral begins to emerge in history, she thought. But what moral?

Then there was Dessie Woods. She was an American woman who was being attacked and raped by a strange man, who was forcing her submission by threatening her with a sharp knife. She succeeded in wresting the knife from him and then she stabbed him with it. He died. She was charged with murder, and found guilty of murder. And sentenced to life imprisonment. The knife she used, curiously, was actually proven, during the course of the case, to in fact be the man's. A racist jury found her guilty of murder. What could the moral be in that one?

Then there was the rape of Mantee. Mantee's family was poor, and having difficulty getting her off their hands, or, as they put it, getting rid of her. The family of a man from Triolet in the North came all the way to Surinam to look at her, bringing their young man in tow. No-one in the North wanted to marry him. Which was strange because the family had an arpent of land under sugar cane and only this one son to inherit it. They brought him for Mantee to see. She could not stand him; it was hate at first sight, she told Sita later. 'Do you find him to your liking, Mantee?' Her family was poor, so she said, 'Yes.' What she said 'yes' to had a double meaning: the word 'to your liking' was '*kontan*,' the very same word for 'love'. Her family was not only poor but also progressive. The young man said, 'Can I take her to a matinée next week?' Yes, they said, being progressive. So he came on a motorbike, and took her off to the matinée. Only he stopped on the way, 'at the house of a friend,' he said. It was a deserted house, and in it, he raped her. She cried, and when she got home, she told her family. The menfolk of whom made up a posse, and caught a bus up to Triolet in the north. An ultimatum was put out: if he did not marry Mantee within one month (what, they said, of a possible pregnancy?), they would come around again by taxi this time, and, they said it frankly, *kup so grenn*, cut his balls off. His family believed it, and so did he. And they were quite right to because they would have. So Mantee was married off to her rapist. Sita sighed about how to write this up. She felt guilty about not having prevented this marriage herself. Me too. I went and ordered the marriage invitations from a letterpress printer in Porlwi for her marriage myself, because I was working in Porlwi and her family were poor and kind people. I, Iqbal, am guilty of this.

Iqbal was a man who thought. The invitations had a drawing of two happy young newly weds looking at one another inside a heart.

Ton Tipyer arrived at the wedding. He knew the boy's father from being a batman with him in Egypt in the war. After half an hour, he came over to me and said, 'I'm getting out of here. There is something wrong and I don't know what it is.' I also left.

What, my dear audience, is the moral in that one? How could Sita's story on rape be formulated around such examples?

But she went on.

There was the rape of Véronique Soulier, a young woman, and her rape took place in the Pwentosab Police Station. She was raped by four policemen inside the police station, behind closed doors. On the off-duty policemen's resting bed. She had gone to the police station in times of trouble: a violent row of some kind had broken out between her husband and his father. Mother Mary didn't come to her. Nor did Hanuman. She was raped when she had gone to get help from the Pwentosab police station because of this fight in which her husband, a violent man when he was drunk and he was drunk at the time, was about to kill his father, her father-in-law, with a dagger. The policemen, when they heard about this left the men to kill one another. They raped Véronique instead. How did they reach this decision? Was it consensus, or did they put it to the vote? Or are some of the men so weak-willed and spineless and immoral as to just do what is easiest, to follow suit, once one evil colleague has acted out his devastation? Destroy. Destroy by band. Destroy by default. Véronique was raped by all four policemen in the Station. Howcome their sexuality was operative under these violent circumstances? But this quadruple rape was just the first rape she, Véronique Soulier, would suffer. Sita cringed and felt her insides shake, when she thought of her.

So did I and so do I: *Iqbal was a man who thought he was a.*

What was the moral now? How could she deduce any moral from this story?

The court case in the Banbu Court was her second rape. Sita had been a witness to this rape. Not in the case, but in the court. After rape by the policemen, rape by the judiciary.

The Banbu Court room is the most beautiful court-room in the world, and Sita's not the only one to say so. I also think so. Should she describe it, or would this be a diversion? It is a gem. The geography gives a false sense of hope that the trial may be a just one. The Court House is simple and useful. Mango trees outside, with benches molded around their stems. Shade and cool. While you wait for your case. Bright turquoise lizards play up and down the trees. A thoughtful hut outside for families and friends to wait in in case of rain. There is a lot of waiting at courts. And inside the wooden benches carved and spacious for friends, family and public. A ceiling fan just above the public gallery. Most considerate. Usually just for the magistrate. Shutters open letting wind waft gently past the magistrate, past his clerk and note-taker, past the prosecutor and defense lawyers, even past the public, and out again.

But the setting was not enough. The prosecutor and defense lawyers, the magistrate and his clerk and note-taker, hooted and laughed about the rape as if it were so many jokes cracked one after the other. Rude jokes were enunciated, sides were held, and laughs spilt out like slobber. Véronique, eyes blinking back tears, looked up at the ceiling then at Sita, then back at the Magistrate, as she had been told to do. Sita was the only woman in the court. Everyone else was male. And smelt it. Sita shuddered at the smell. Men humiliated by men. A most clear smell. Mixed in with it, she and Véronique emitted another smell. Women's *fear of men* smell. I as a man recognize it. *Iqbal was a man who thought he was a woman.*

It was through Sita's presence at this case that she got to know Véronique. Should she write this up in the first person. No. She had heard about the case, turned up and told Véronique just before that she was there 'for the Women's Movement,' as she put it.

166

The sniggering, and joking went on endlessly. The defense lawyer's main line was 'Why did you go to the police station? Why? What did you want to give? What did you have to offer? At night and all? Why should a young woman go to the police station at all? What do you usually give men? Have you ever offered men anything? To give what?' In Kreol '*lanket*' means 'a deposition', so Véronique had no other way of saying it, but saying '*lanket*'. But in Kreol 'cunt' is '*langet*' with a 'g', and the defense lawyer's entire case was this joke. The magistrate roared with laughter every time, took off his glasses, and wiped them. As did the prosecutor from the *Parquet*. They nearly fell off their chairs when the defense lawyer, seeing Véronique's pregnancy, asked if it were the result of the alleged rape: the rape had been eighteen months before the case. The fact that they, the judicial system, were all responsible for this delay didn't occur to them. The joke about the pregnancy caused all the men to look at Véronique's husband, who, by dint of circumstance, and for having been obliged to sell out men's solidarity, was forced into being the ally of womankind, hung his head in shame. Sita lost track of her article now.

I lose track of telling about her article too. I hung my head. *Iqbal was a man*. The true shame was mine. Ours. I was in the court by chance, because I had been going up a one-way street the wrong way in Albion when I went to a political meeting on my motorbike one evening. And there wasn't a street sign to say it was one-way so I was going to plead not guilty.

Véronque chose silence. She seemed to go on a kind of strike and stopped answering questions. Even those put by the prosecutor, who was after all prosecuting her case against the rapists. She had given up. This was her second rape. In fighting in the courts, on her own, she had suffered the second rape. Bad as the first, she told Sita.

The next day, when the court case continued, and the defense lawyers brought their case, Sita turned up with fourteen women friends. All from the women's movement. Fourteen is not many, but then, on the other hand, it is. Fourteen mobilized women, fourteen women in court, fourteen women acting in concert, is many. They all went into the court room early. Took up the central seats. Changed the very smell of the place. I was there too again that day. To take sides with Véronique, this time. Her article and this book are getting muddled now. I take sides with Véronique and become a woman. Because it was the women who did it. They all had notebooks and pens and hand-bags and sarees and dresses and scarves and fury written on their foreheads. Two had brought their babes in arms. One woman was seventy-three, *Bonnfam Linet*. She had thick *fon-butey* glasses, after her cataract operation. Although she couldn't read, she also had a notebook and pencil. She looked as though she could hit someone with them. Her head was tilted slightly backwards so as to get a better view through her round glasses.

Today, the defense lawyers, the prosecutor, the magistrate, his clerk and note-keeper, the whole lot of them, were on best behavior. Not a snigger out of them. They were shamed by the presence of a group of women. They felt individuals now, up against womankind. The previous time they had been a group up against an individual woman.

But, for Véronique's case, it was a bit too late. Véronique's words were the ones that should have secured a conviction against the policemen. She had withheld the necessary words because she and Sita were on their own against the rest. But Véronique won her own private case. Her grace was saved. Even her husband raised his head, a proud man, a pipe-fitter, with shoulders to prove it. Véronique said to Sita that day: 'In our way, we have won now. See the way they cower, the whole lot of them. I could not have fought them alone,' she said. 'Nor just you and I. We all needed to be here.'

There starts to be a moral here. The nearer the rape, the more she knows. But the more difficult to write it up.

Then there was Véronique's third rape.

Her husband left her soon after the policemen were found not guilty. And so she went back to live with her father, a docker who had just got his mechanization redundancy pension, when sugar-loading started to be done by pumps instead of on dockers' backs, and with her step-mother. Her father had taken his bulk-loading pension money and spent it. He had bought a fridge, a colour TV, a motorbike, rented a house in Ward Kat in Porlwi and he paid twenty thousand rupees to get his daughter to go to France. This last expense was his only investment against poverty. No work in Mauritius, no jobs. No money to live on now. Poverty drove you to look for work abroad. So he had paid twenty thousand to a '*Franse*'. To the Frenchman, for the ticket and the getting of a visa for France. So Véronique had set off for. Her father's hope. 'Fi' he called her, for daughter. Via Zaire and then via Belgium it was to be. In their group there was Véronique, also known as ⁿi, another girl called Marie Claire, and there were eighteen Plenn Vert boys, all very goodlooking young boys, she had said to her father, seeing nothing strange in it.

Three weeks had passed since their departure from Plezans Airport. A big send-off party had been to the Airport.

'And just look how she's come back now, Sita. All thin. Did you know she was back, that's why you came? And my twenty thousand rupees gone down the drain. All my money gone. And all our hopes. Just look at her. Fi, come on, come and say hello. She'g been in Zulu wars.'

'What?' Sita said.

'Yeah, Zulu wars. And no rice anywhere there. Not even bread. Look how thin she is. Would you like some Coke. Go get her some, go on. And my twenty thousand down the drain.'

Lies, thought Sita. Politeness says she must listen. One of those family conspiracies to tell lies.

'Would you like some coke?'

'Yes,' she replied to Véronique's step-mother's offer, a large untidy mother with no milk powder, she said, for her baby and could Sita buy her a packet of Everyday just for today's milk. The coke was already being poured. And I must remember to buy a packet of Everyday from the shop at the corner before I go, Sita thought.

'Zaire, Zambia, Zimbabwe, Zulu wars everywhere. Zulu armies.' It was like a refrain. Sita had enough experience not to believe a word of it. All made up.

They went on endlessly, appearing to fabricate as they went along, looking to Véronique who bent her head forwards, and nodded. Confabulations. An unconscious conspiracy to invent something to cover up a failure, she thought. And a whole lot of racism mixed in, she thought. Véronique had been a strong, upright, proud woman. She looked in bad shape now. Every time Sita asked Véronique something, her father and mother chimed out the reply, adding the main themes again: 'No rice, Zulu wars, and the twenty thousand down the bloody drain.'

When it was time for Sita to go, she had already said to Véronique, walk to the bus stop with me, will you, her father said: 'Twenty thousand rupees for that passport to go abroad, and it's ruined. Ruined. Might as well throw it away. Fetch your passport, Fi!' Sita stopped dead in her tracks. Then she went back to her chair and sat down in it again. Proof?

The passport was brought. Illegal immigrant stamped into her passport in Zaire, Zambia and Zimbabwe. The British High Commission in Zimbabwe had repatriated her and would claim from the Mauritian government. All stamped and written boldly.

On the way to the bus stop, after Sita had bought a pound of Everyday, she said quietly and calmly, 'Raped again, Véronique?' The thin Véronique bent her head forward, and then lifted it slowly and, woman to woman, mouth closed and crooked smiled back at Sita. That smile has never left Sita's mind. It was news too heavy for Sita. She felt a mounting wave of anger, and then a passing despair. Then, she said, 'Ahn', in the Indian intonations of communion. They held one another's gaze. Then Sita turned around to go.

They never met again.

Thought getting carried away. Can't put all that in a story, Sita thought. That smile. 'Where can I start to write about this?'

It's almost as though there's men making up for lost time, one or two million years lost.

What is the moral?

Then there was the boy gang-raped and killed at Be di Tombo.

He had always been a bit cooks. Used to sing funny songs and beg in the United Bus Service buses at the Kirpip Bus Station while they filled up before leaving for Kan Leziz, Site Malerb and Labrasri. Had funny hair. Prematurely thinned, as though he had some illness. A funny voice, too high, like a eunuch's. Everyone knew him. Everyone knew he was a harmless loony. His family in Kannmas had tried to interest him in staying home, tried to get him to learn a simple trade, like fixing bicycle tyres, but he liked nothing better than singing and begging in buses. That's what he liked best. That's what he was best at. And that's what he did. He annoyed the bus conductors from time to time, delaying them as he collected money; up and down the aisle when they wanted to set off. But a passing annoyance. Part of everyday life, he was.

He was raped by a group of picnickers. Ordinary men on a picnic. Nine of them. A mixed bag, as they say. Middle-aged and young. Of various skills and trades. An *ad hoc* group, for the purposes of the picnic. Raped and abused to death, he was. Died of gangrene in the Civil Hospital some days after his admission.

Sita stopped writing, stopped thinking, put her head down on her desk.

And I once again, intervene. How did they come to this decision, this group of ordinary men and boys? And how did they perform? Did they stand in a queue beforehand? And what did they do afterwards? These are the questions we all have to answer, dear reader, for what if we were one of those men? Would we be among them? Would we be like them? Would we be them? Are we, by any chance, them?

And this is when the song words come back: *Iqbal was a man who thought he was a woman.* Is this not the song that all men should sing. Until men can be men.

◆

Long before dawn on the day of the meeting, on 1st May, Dharma's father, Dasratha, the man who worked in his own fields, got into his lorry and went to his hunting grounds near Black River Gorges. A forestry guard stopped him in the pitch dark, as he got to the edge of his land.

'Someone been burning chillies in the Crown Land, driving deer into your land, Mr. Dasratha.'

'You know I don't do that kind of thing.'

'We know, Sir.'

'So, why tell me.'

'Your new partners, Sir.'

'No defamation, please. My new partners? Of course they wouldn't.' But he knew it. Instinctively he knew it. It was them. Mohun Jab and Extra Large had been driving government deer into his hunting ground. He started regretting that he had invited them to be partners. Two weeks of partnership, and regretting it already, he mused. 'If you have your own land,' he had told them, 'in a partnership with me, you pay your annual rent like I do, and you have your own hunting ground and your own deer, like I do, you don't have to be poachers anymore.' They had said it was a good idea.

When at crack of dawn on Saturday, 1st May, he met them at the hunting hut on stilts, a strategic look-out post it was, he said: 'What you go burning chillies on Crown Land for then?'

Their answer was inevitable. He realized it. It was inevitable. 'Why kill our own deer? What's the point? Especially if we can kill government deer?' They would stay poachers. They didn't like *hunting*, it dawned on him. They liked *poaching*. They were addicts. They didn't like owning land, nor even renting it.

'Well, let's get going,' Dasratha said. Extra Large would go with the

172

dogs and raise the deer on the windward side of them, and when there was a fork in the grasslands between the bushes and trees, Dasratha would control one fork and Mohun Jab the other.

Extra Large and the floppy-eared dogs, exulted at the knowledge of the hunt and with noses to the ground, set off. Dasratha and Mohun Jab parted further and further as they looked for better vantage points for their part of the hunt.

When they met after a whole morning's hunting, Dasratha said to Mohun Jab: 'And what was that shot I heard? You got a try.'

'Yeah,' Mohun Jab said coyly, 'not a very good one.' And then he added two words which aroused Dasratha's suspicion: 'A miss.'

Mohun Jab did not miss deer.

And so they went home, without any kill.

Dasratha was a wily partner for them to have. and he had as much energy as they did. He came back after dusk by foot, gun in hand. He took up a hiding position on the track that Mohun Jab had been hunting in.

He waited.

Sure enough, the brothers arrived at about midnight, and loaded up the dead deer and went off. They were happy. They were still poaching.

'Obsessed, they are. They are interested in nothing else except poaching. They only know how to poach. They even poach in their own land,' sighed Dasratha. 'Imagine poaching from yourself. I'm the fool to have taken them on as partners. Well at least I know now. And there isn't much I can do about it, until the ground lease expires.' He laughed and went home to tell his son Lutchman, who hadn't come hunting with them because he was going to fetch Sita from the airport.

Mohun Jab and Extra Large went back to their house behind the police station and cleaned up the venison. In the morning their mother cooked them a good curry, and they gave away goodly morsels of meat to everyone they knew. They never sold a single pound of venison in all their lives. Just like they thought hunting land shouldn't be owned, not even by themselves, so they thought food too, was outside the market. They laughed at the very thought of making money out of the forest.

Dasratha didn't know his daughter-in-law was running away like a hunted animal that same day. Mohun Jab's fine daughter, reduced to flight. And Mohun Jab didn't even know. Would never know.

◆

Running away, to the airport, running away, on to the plane, running away, flying away, flying upwards, still running away, running away flying downwards back over to Mauritius, the one-hour flight being only up and down never on the flat, still running away, out to Lutchman's car, being driven to the public meeting, still running away, and weaving her way through the crowd to Dharma, she was still breathing like a hunted animal. Not a deer. A meerkat, she was. A scared, hunted down meerkat. After the sound of gunshot. Frozen in flight. Eyes wide open. Nostrils flaring. Turning over her shoulder. And then again running.

Then stop.

She had escaped. She had survived. She hadn't been murdered. She wasn't in prison. Like Dessie Woods. She wasn't buried in the little bit of veld. She was alive.

She was back in time for the public meeting. After all that. She, insisting on being present herself, being there, experiencing history herself, going to the meeting. Being there for the birth of the organization. Here she was. Arrived. In time. In flesh and in blood.

◆

And yet she missed that meeting really. It wasn't worth anything to her anymore. She felt it like ashes in her hand.

The meeting and the crowd and the historical importance of the birth of the organization, none of it was alive for her anymore. Not then, not at that moment anyway. In getting back, she'd lost it. She'd met things that made being back in time for the meeting into something unreal, reduced all this to the level of scenery.

175

◆

Naked human alone. Reduced to animal flight.

◆

How are we humans going to make progress, when there are such handicaps placed on us? Individual handicaps, like a horse in a horse-race. She, who wants to participate in making history, goes out of her way to, quite literally, only to get pulled down, brought down, to the level of an individual attacked by another individual. And the attack is one thing. It only took a few hours. But afterwards, wasn't she brought down by her own mind, reduced to a state of incompetence. Reduced to a state of shock. Reduced to a state of lonely hiding.

◆

In Dharma's arms, at last. At the round-point.

She tried to tell him. She tried to tell Dharma. The words were all composed, ready to be spoken: 'Something terrible happened in Reunion.'

But she couldn't get them out. They were stuck. And she was frozen in her tracks, she was, like a meerkat.

He looked her in the eyes, and was shocked.

He saw something there, something terrible. He looked deeper. Couldn't fathom it. He took her by the hand, took her hand in both his hands, and then, troubled, led her to their other friends. As if she were someone a bit frail or even sickly. And she couldn't say anything or say she had something to say. *And that deep torture may be called a hell, when more is felt than one hath power to tell.*

They went past in front of me. They looked estranged from the meeting. She estranged, and he, by the effect, estranged. And they stopped and looked at one another, right there in front of me, in the middle of that tightly packed crowd.

Both stood like old acquaintance in a trance, met far from home, wondering each other's chance. Dharma noticed she was very disturbed. *At last he takes her by the bloodless hand*, 'Everything all right?' He thought maybe, maybe to arrive from abroad right into a big outdoor public meeting was difficult for her. Too many people. He thought maybe she didn't enjoy the flight. He thought maybe the conference in the Seychelles may have been difficult for her. She didn't always like that kind of thing. She was sometimes a bit of a savage, he thought, and didn't like the atmosphere of that kind of conference. He thought maybe she had had bouts of jealousy about him when she was away. He thought maybe she was tired. 'Sweet love?' he asked. She was silent. She looked ahead. Like a meerkat. He felt a wave of fear ripple over him.

So it happened that at the round-point she didn't tell him. She wasn't in flight anymore. She felt a calm descend on her and all around her. But not inside her. She was exhausted. And felt a deep, deep need to sleep. But her adrenaline was still making her shake.

She couldn't say what she had to say. Like a child who couldn't find the way to open a conversation. As if when her mother said 'And why, may I ask, are you late?' to a little girl who had been raped on the way home from school, all the little girl could do was be quiet, not finding any words to speak. Not capable of making the space for the words she needed to say. And it was thus that Sita, already a mother herself, was at that moment just like a little girl, and that was how she started being seized up in a limbo.

◆

What should she have said, reader, morally speaking. Should she have said: 'We have to leave this meeting, Dharma, for I have something very important to tell you.' Obviously. She is an adult. She must find time and space for her paragraph. No-one had ever taught her how to find a time and a space for herself if she was in distress. She didn't know how. And then again, reader, it, the something to tell, only happened because it was so important for her to be there for the May Day meeting. She hadn't had time to realize that the importance of her being there had been destroyed.

And so she started to miss her cue. A split second. Not knowing how to make an opening, nor what she should say, nor how to say it.

Did the consequences of some words frighten her. What would be the consequences of telling this? For her? For Dharma? For their friends? For the political priorities of the day? Could she judge this properly?

◆

And another split second passed. Another hesitation. She went on getting nearer to missing her cue.

And did she know that in not telling Dharma, she would end up not telling herself? How could this ever have been a possibility? Should she have known that you don't know anything yourself really, unless you think it over, digest it? Did she have a duty to tell of the rape, because in not telling, she would hide it from herself? How was she to know this?

She missed her cue.

Like a conundrum, the fact of her very thinking about the dilemma was, at least in part, the cause of her missing the moment of a good decision in the dilemma. And she missed her cue.

And life went on as if she did not have those words to say, as if there wasn't anything waiting inside her head to be said. Life went on.

◆

She can't even remember anymore what happened in the hours immediately after the meeting. Were there other people around all the time? There often were in those days. Did friends come around to their house that afternoon, that evening? They often did. Or had she already started to clam up? Started the burial. Fiya wasn't there at first, her little girl. She remembers when a friend brought her around, taking her in her arms, as if some harm had, in her absence, threatened her, not herself. 'You look well, Fiya,' she had said, 'You look so well.' Fiya had looked surprised by what she had said, as if her mother had expected otherwise. The mother, being hurt, feared immediately for her daughter.

◆

Dharma. He remembers they took a shower. Sita and him. Close together, as always. And yet, she seemed far away. The word 'disturbed' came to his mind. And then they came to their bed. Did they make love? He thinks not. Odd.

◆

She remembers folding herself into their bedsheets, after that shower, or was it that night? And knowing that she was safe. She could stop running. She could relax. And she would bundle the whole unthought-out thing up. She could reclaim her body to herself. Shrouds for the death of her memory. Shrouds for death of part of herself. Swaddling clothes for the comfort of the newly born. And the regressed.

◆

Had her mother still been alive, she would have thought it over, imagining telling her, planning every word she would use, knowing her mother's every response, and then have actually told her. Or if Fiya had already been bigger. If only. Like a sister. Or maybe she could even have had Dharma's mother, who she had been very close to, to go over it with. But both mothers had died recently. Was she still in mourning for these deaths? And her daughter was still too young. And her sister scatterbrained.

She couldn't tell Devina either.

Devina was herself too upset about things. At that very time. Like a mirror to reality she'd gone all highly strung. This made Devina's memory of the time clear as a bell. She had become hyper-observant. It was Devina, herself, who would later tell Sita why she, Sita, had not told anyone. Devina knew why she hadn't. Like her name suggested she might. The diviner.

Later Devina helped. 'Impossible to tell us,' she said. 'Not at that time. At any other time, you would have. Not then. No. It was impossible. You could not possibly have done it. There was no other thing for you to do but to bury it. It was like living hell at the time.'

She got out her diary for proof and to get exact dates. Toni, one of their closest friends, had tried to kill himself a few weeks before. 'Look at the date. That Friday night. Drinking from a bottle of Round-up. Not only that. You remember why? He wasn't normally a candidate for a suicide, Sita,' she said. 'Last person that anyone'd have expected to. Why? Remember the why. For goodness sake, how could you have come home and told him that? The reason why was that Suzie had told him she had had a "rencontre", to use her word, with someone, a man, when she was abroad. Suzie had come home, told the truth, and this had led to unpredictable disorder. Almost a death.' She was cross at the truth now. That Sita had no-one to tell. 'And you couldn't tell Suzie either. She had been arrested overnight, because how did the police know it was a suicide attempt and not attempted murder. Women get arrested real quick around men's suicide attempts and suicides. Could you,' Devina went on, 'have contemplated, after Suzie's bringing home disorder, bringing further disorder home with you as well? Because rape is worse disorder. It is the ravenous personification of disorder, drawing, like gravity, further disorder around it,' said Devina.

'Can't you see,' Devina said to Sita, 'that your rape was like the living parody of an affair, of an encounter? Is rape not the parody of the man-woman relationship as we know it,' Devina asked. 'The woman passive, victim of the man's will to act. The woman supposed to say "no". At least never say "yes", and most certainly never approach the man. The woman prisoner of her passivity. Is not rape excusable and possible in our society only because the woman is not free to move towards the man, to propose, to say "yes". Until we can say "yes" in complete freedom, how can we convincingly say "no"? Our noes only mean a form of yes. Until the shackles on the word yes are broken.'

Thus spake Devina.

'There was an atmosphere at that time, when you got back from Reunion,' Devina said to Sita, 'at the time of the alliance of the socialists with the social democrats. An atmosphere of total disorder. Even of personal disorder knitted firmly into political. You were the only one everyone leaned on. So how could you arrive home, and announce you'd been raped? How? I tell you you couldn't do it.' She almost shouted now. 'We all needed you not to. I, still, for one don't want you to tell me, with a part of myself. I'd rather not know. I don't know what to do about it.' Devina was in a rage.

'Some friends were,' she went on, 'in the meantime, euphoric. I mean it,' she said, 'euphoric, in reaction to the disorder, euphoric, in the midst of crisis. It was their response. How could you tell them anything when they were in that state? Others just switched off. So telling other friends was difficult,' Devina said. 'You, Sita, were the only one who seemed whole. You had to help everyone else. Who would have helped you? Even Iqbal wouldn't have,' she said. She was right. I wouldn't have been able to handle it. I still can't *Iqbal was a man who thought he was a woman.*

'Maybe,' Devina said, 'your All Women's Front friends, including me, would have gone on and on at you to go to the police in Reunion and press rape charges, and go for a court case. Quite likely,' she had said, 'because we were like that. But,' Devina added, 'you would have known. You knew the moment in history that we were all in, the political moment. You understood it. I, for one, didn't know it then. I only know it now. You knew it then. At that time, you would have judged the situation correctly, Sita. You would have known it was not the right time? The very week when the organization was being born? To talk of a rape? You, of all people, to tell us, you'd been raped. No. You couldn't have. And you knew you couldn't. You knew that objectively it was a difficult police case. No getting around that. Not a one to win.' Devina went on, angry. She said: 'You would have known it wasn't appropriate to make this case a priority at that time? And that you would have been right. We would all have got upset about it, and been impotent with rage,' Devina said, 'We would have thought of nothing else, we may have wanted to catch a plane across and attack the man. But court case for court case, you have to be reasonable now, Sita, after all these years even I am,' she said, 'it *was* a bad case, and you knew it. We may not then have realized what a bad case it was. I know I wouldn't have. I know what I would have said. I would have said, Go and make a statement. At once. I'm coming with you. We would all have said: "Go ahead with a case." But what would we have done, all of us? Taken flights across to Reunion, ten of us at a time, each time there was a hearing? We wouldn't send you over on your own, would we? We aren't millionaires, we're just the women's movement.'

Dear audience, here is a moot point. Should Sita have gone to the police? That is the question here. Should she? Are the police on your side? What does it mean for the state to prosecute for and on behalf of a woman victim? And if your case is a bad one, should you go to the police in any case, to put it on the record? And does this take precedence over other things you're doing in your life at the time? Personal things, like say, you're going to be getting married, or to have a final examination for some course you've being doing for three years? Or more generally, at the time you are helping to set up a street committee to get running water in a village somewhere? Or when you're helping to found a new political organization?

And then Devina got really cross. 'When is a rape case ever a political priority, let alone a personal one?' Devina asked. 'This is one of the problems for the whole women's movement. When is any aspect of our movement a priority? Of course, it is a priority, Sita, but when? That's why you didn't tell anyone, Sita. Because it all went through your mind in a flash. It was useless, at best, to tell, and harmful, at worst. The extent of the harm it would bring was immeasurable. Would we not all have felt raped? Does a rapist not rape all the friends of the victim, at the same time as the victim?'

Maybe Devina was right.

But why, Sita asked herself didn't she at least tell Dharma. She had meant to tell him.

She didn't even tell herself, how could she have told him?

But, say, she did know somewhere in her mind. Why didn't she say? Maybe she protected him from the rape. Are not all rapes against the man who loves the woman, a rape of him, as well as of her? Why hurt Dharma? He knew the man, this Rowan. What would he be supposed to do? Go and beat him up? Like some kind of an old-fashioned male impersonator? Like John Wayne. Or was he supposed to ignore the whole thing? What was he supposed to do about it? Why give people knowledge that is so heavy a burden to carry? Why tell someone something when there's nothing they can do about it? It was all over.

Maybe, she thought to herself, she didn't tell Dharma, supposing she knew enough herself to be able at some point in time to 'tell' Dharma, because she thought there were probably some things in his life that he didn't tell her, she didn't know what, so why should she tell him things that only affected only her, in the final analysis? Maybe he would then tell her things that she didn't want to know, in return. A void of unknown things rose up like nausea, as she thought of it now.

More simply, maybe she was just scared in case he blamed her for it. Even part-blamed her. She blamed herself, after all. She had invited herself to Rowan's house, in point of fact. The fact speaks for itself. She had gone ahead and stayed on even when she found out that Noella wasn't there. And she hadn't even screamed or put up a fight. She was a very strong woman. Her mother would have fought him off. She, by contrast, had stripped her own clothes off. After all. So maybe Dharma, if he was in his right mind, wouldn't believe her that she was forced. Was she really forced? What is rape exactly?

And then, as if by juxtaposition, her rape came immediately after Suzie's silly confession of a silly 'rencontre'. What did such a juxtaposition in time, mean? How can one event come and muddle another completely separate one?

Maybe she didn't tell, in part, for practical reasons. She was a practical person. If she told even just herself, let alone anyone else, she would need a few days, she would have known – she wasn't in the women's movement all that time for nothing – you need a few days to cry and rage. All rape victims do. Even if she told just herself.

She didn't have a few days.

She never had a few days really free. Until now. Until the United States armed forces raped Iraq. There was always Fiya, the young one, and there was always the movement. Other people always needed looking after.

And Dharma, himself, she would have thought, would need a few days to work out what he felt about it, if she told him. He didn't have a few days either. Not to himself. Not for himself.

There were public meetings in Maybur, Senpyer and Kirpip on three days the very next week, after the rape. Both Dharma and Sita had to speak in them. They did so. Yes, Sita, straight after the rape, got back to work. She addressed small crowds in Maybur, Senpyer and Kirpip. And after the Senpyer meeting, there was a small private meeting of Socialists in Kan Sami in Moka, that ended in a violent row, with the agents of the Socialists trying to make everyone do a walk out, but leaving half their members behind to join the new organization.

And Fiya got measles, and she played guessing games with her in the bedroom in the dim light that the doctor prescribed for a few days.

The organization had its first big newspaper interview, its foundation interview with the big Sunday newspaper. Dharma, his brother Lutchman, Lex and Sita were to be present. I remember that I was the one who arranged the interview, even the time and the place for it. They were present. Sita was there, but strangely, she had asked not to have to say anything.

Dharma had to depone in front of the National Remuneration Board for the free zone workers, against their obligatory overtime. The Monday after the May Day meeting. He did. On the Sunday, Sita had helped him prepare his dossier.

Sita had to give a hand preparing things for the colloquium of the following Sunday.

◆

Did she have time to announce a rape?
Worse still.
Did she have space?
Worse still.
Did she have time and space to absorb it herself? Of course, she must have had time to tell at least herself? Why didn't she, reader?

◆

She didn't tell me.

She didn't tell Ton Tipyer either.

But then again, why didn't we ask her what was wrong at the time? It was obvious that something was wrong. I knew it. Ton Tipyer knew it. Devina says she knew it. Dharma obviously knew it. But we just shut up. Didn't want to know. Were we scared that it was something grave, maybe something disastrous? Something that would upset us?

184

If she didn't want to know about it herself, why would we want to know about it?

Did the rape from the time it was happening already start to bury itself from Sita herself? Do terrible experiences always run this risk? That there is a mistake in the recording process itself? Not just the memory afterwards? Does a rape get stored into limbo files, secret limbo files that are stored detached from the conscious mind from the time of childhood, get stored there from the very moment the rape is taking place?

Because in fact Sita never, ever thought about the rape itself. Never. She remembers, during the assault, during the sequestration and during the rape, thinking she would work it all out with Dharma afterwards. She would absorb it later. She would submit to it later. Go through it later. 'I'll cut myself off from the experience,' she thought. This was how she, on purpose, didn't think about it even at the time it was happening. She did not think about it at all. Neither in the plane when she was still in flight running away, nor when she got back, nor at any moment until she dived and dived for it. At the very time it had happened she had taken it, the whole horrible deed, all unthought-out and raw, on her own shoulders, carried it to a hole and buried it. She never, ever thought about it herself again. Never ever.

Is this how amnesia sets in?

Experience misfiled at the time of the occurrence itself. Or filed in a special limbo file. Buried in an inaccessible drawer, under everything else.

She didn't just forget about it

She lost it.

For eight years and nine months.

Until the corpse she had buried started to sprout in the garden.

◆

Time. Time the healer. The timing of it all.

There is something about the timing of her remembering. *There is providence in the fall of a sparrow.* Something very timed. Somewhere in her mind there had been a decision right at the time. She had made an original time bomb. It was as though it had been prophesied that she would remember and that she would tell Dharmi on the very day when remembering and telling him would leave equal periods of time of their life together before the rape and after. Eight years and nine months. The day she remembered was that day. The day she told him was that day.

◆

Open letter to God Almighty from Sita

> Dear God, or god, as the case may be,
> Dear God, or Gods, as the number may be,
> Dear Sir or Madam, as the sex may be,

Thank you for being so kind as to. For want of a better being to address myself to. Hope it is a timely epistle. From one unknown quantity to another.

I, Sita. Age, address, profession, hobbies. Wife of Dharma. Mother of Fiya. By way of introduction. Never know what they already know about. *Must remember to keep the tone formal. Not be emotional.*

What exactly, you may well ask, what exactly is my petition, my demand, my reclamation, my reason for writing? Multifold? Manifold? Or singleminded? Monomaniac? Or olygofold?

Make me a good girl for christ's sake amen.

Are there guidelines? Do you, any of you, have anything further to say? Shouldn't think so. May have stopped having anything to say by now. Prophets over and done with. Stopped communicating, or stopped existing?

Reason for writing in this case obscure.

Is there a case for writing, to you or You? Open letter is open. Rules is rules. Thus open to all. Many of whom believe in you. To some extent or. They think perhaps you do not know, are not informed, have not been petitioned, otherwise you would not turn a blind. They think you are perhaps emitting signals which we are not, so far, receiving, not loud and clear, anyway, perhaps for want of finer tuning, a higher frequency or shorter waveband. No doubt a mere hitch. Communications problem. Two-way, I should think. You neither receive nor emit.

187

For women, I ask. I petition. I write. For all the daughters of the earth.

What are your guidelines? Do we have recall to any courts concerning freedom of the person, of the body?

And bluntly speaking, are we allowed out?

Should we stay at home, for a start, or go out and work? From whom should we seek permission? This is not clear.

Are we meant to be sequestrated? Are houses really jails run for the government by individual men? Keep us in the nick. Private enterprise in prisons. Some with day parole? Go out to work, with permission. *This formulation may be faulted as too rhetorical.*

What exactly are the property laws as regards trespass from your/ Your point/points of view. Whose land is it anyway? Is there a curfew on it? Is night time illegal? This makes much work illegal? And hospital emergencies illegal to look after. And yet we must. I am getting emotional. The question is, do we need permits to break a curfew when we go out at night? Or must we be chaperoned by a prison guard? 'What,' said the defense lawyer in the rape case, addressing two adult women, 'What were you two doing on your own out at night?' 'Our own.' Would fifty women also be 'on their own' at night?

Place. Freedom of movement. What places are illegal? Are deserted roads illegal? Short cuts out of the question, if isolated? Are beaches, cinemas, provisionally legal only, for us? 'What,' asked the judge, 'were you doing there, all on your own?'

◆

Should we wear long dresses, high heels, and pretty things to ornament the place, or should we prepare to fight, strengthen up our muscles against the dangers, prepare for flight, in tracksuits and tackies? Is it dangerous out there? If not, why can't we go out when, where, how we want to. If so, why are we encouraged to wear apparel designed to trap us? If it is dangerous out, why do we put loops pierced through our earlobes? To tame the bull, they pierce a loop into his nose. My nose is pierced. When I blow my nose, snot comes through the hole. I did it to myself. Could you intimate on this. Why do we carry weights on our arms like the faster horses at Sennmars have strapped to their stomachs? Or, please tell us, for gods' sakes, is it more dangerous indoors, in the privacy of our own families' homes? Who is more likely to kill us? Statistics, please. Or rape us, or beat us? Husbands, brothers, fathers, friends, acquaintances? Or complete strangers. Where do we need to be armed most.

Where should the safe house be?

Peace from whom?

◆

And why the rule not to hit below the belt? Who made it up and why do we keep it? Perhaps new rules could be promulgated. Thou, woman, in self defense, shall hit below the belt. Would you/You agree?

◆

Why have you forsaken me?

◆

What are the guarantees for us? Freedom from cruel and inhuman treatment. Who may mete it out, and under what conditions? Father, husband? Who are the prison guards? Brothers, men-neighbours? Where is the Court? And who sits in the seat of judgment? Where the judgment? Why are there assumptions against us? Would I put a false charge of theft on someone? Maybe. No more nor less chance than a false charge of rape. Maybe more chance. Because to be stolen from is no shame.

◆

And why, in this petition, I ask in the name of all women is the shame ours?

◆

Wait for the silence, girls.

◆

For the gods if they ever spaketh in the past, hath stopped in the present.

◆

Amen.

◆

Sita.

◆

Sita sat at home in the *godon* and thought. Dharma had taken Fiya away for a few days. 'Give you a break,' he said to Sita.

Three nights and three days, she thought. And then there was a breakthrough.

Sita decided to kill Rowan. Murder him. In cold blood. Hang his head on a string around my neck, she thought. Maybe kill first him, and then others, other rapists. String their heads all up on a necklace. And wear them in public. Woman the creator, woman the destroyer.

The day before, Sita had thought of killing herself, putting an end to her own life. I knew it at the time. At one point I was convinced I would be the one to find her body. Knowing I would be attending her funeral, even organizing it. Like I was at the wedding of Mantee, after she'd been raped, I would have been at the funeral of Sita, after her suicide. She had thought of the cliffs at Grigri again. Then thought she might end up swimming instead. Her life instinct may be too strong, she had thought. Had also thought of the bridge at Montayn Ori. Popular place for suicide. Then thought maybe someone she knew would go past and stop her. Maybe Rada Kisnasamy. Then of poison. Perhaps insecticide concentrated. Say, Rogor. Drown in her own secretions. The revolting smell for the people who cleaned up the mess. And so had concluded that stabbing would be better. Between her own ribs. Like Lucrece did. Aim well for the heart. Sharp knife. Fall onto it.

Yes, Lucrece killed herself after Tarquin raped her long ago. But that was long ago. Even at the time Brutus thought it was a mistake.

And so it was that after three nights and three days: 'I'll kill him instead,' she resolved. 'Kill him dead.'

No point in killing myself.

And then, only then, did the full weight of eight years and nine months hit her. Because for killing him now, only now, it was late.

191

What did that mean 'late'? She felt it was late. Eight years and nine months. Better late than. The other Sita got rescued, she didn't need to kill. Dessie Woods killed him on the spot, and that wasn't the answer. Not stealthy enough. Véronique took them to Court, and then they got away. Back into their jobs in the police force and maybe lying in wait for other victims, who knows. She kept them at bay though, for the second part of the second rape, when we all went to the court case together: together we won a victory of sorts, she thought. And then Véronique again let them get away, because she, like Sita, was in places she didn't know. Trespassed.

All over the world, there are so many rapes to venge. How, like Hamlet said how, to venge a deed and by the vengeance put an end to the something rotten in the state of. How, like Hamlet said, to not just make it worse. How to make it better.

Catch a plane over. Only a half an hour. Kill him. Commit a murder. Knife or gun. Catch a plane back.

The mafia do it for lesser reasons.

But would it end rape? Would her act, like Hamlet feared his might, just add more disorder and more rot? Not venge things clean. Not change the direction of anything, the state of anything.

Would the murder help anything or anyone at all? 'Will it even help me?' Would it help womankind? That pathetic Rowan Tarquin and his glasses. Blinking backwards, still trying to get away from the blows of a brutal father, blows struck at him in the cradle. 'Could I kill someone who has glasses on? Such a little boy. A sick little boy. And how would this stop rape? He is himself not rape.'

Would this act of murder stop men thinking they could rape women? Stop them sequestrating and raping women the world over? Thinking they own the place, and its women? Stop them strutting around hands in pockets waiting for prey?

'Or should I, should I?'

'Should I rather,' she thought, 'join hands with the children of the Sodron? Their hands are accurate but inexperienced. Their targets are approximative. Their reasons hardly formulated. Should I venge against their rape, against the rape of the colonized? Should I catch a plane and help in venging a kind of rape that perhaps can be eradicated. Independence of a country. A collective independence.'

But would they, the children of Sodron, even having been raped, maybe even specially having been raped, would they in turn, the boys thereof, become rapists? Who are our allies? 'Other than Dharma, than Ton Tipyer, and you, Iqbal?' she said addressing me.

Of course, dear reader, the question is where does rape come from? From Rowan Tarquin himself? The one bad man, you can tell by his name, preordained, individually bad? Or is it in the nature of the body politic? Is Reunion rapist and raped? The colonizer and the colonized? Is the cure to cure the place?

Or is it not also in the general balance of forces in the sex war that rape lies?

Trespass laws for women only. Don't go out at that time, nor to that place. You're a woman. You'll be hunted down. This makes you afraid of running for help. Nowhere for any woman to run to. No money at hand. Shoes not built for running. Don't wear this, nor that. Don't be young nor old. Don't be late, for god's sake. And don't take short cuts. Why are your things in a handbag? And why is your handbag at a distance? Passport in handbag. Not sure which direction to run in. Not sure whether shouting will bring help. Not sure that it won't bring harm. Not sure of help from passers by. Not sure who else may turn out to be rapists. Maybe the police are. Maybe the state is. No-one to understand your language, in a manner of speaking. No case to win. Law makes rape seem to be to do with sex not to do with assault. You the accused, you the victim, one and the same. You are at fault. And the rapists? Who, in this case, are they?

All of us men? Or just most of us? How do we know it is not us?

And what is the normal if not a parody of rape as Devina said? Man invites woman. Woman cannot easily say 'Yes', if she means yes. For saying 'Yes' may mean you are a bad woman. So when you say 'no', 'no' has two meanings 'Yes' and 'no'. Let alone woman proposing to a man. Would you, a woman, like to kiss your friend, a man? If yes, do not. He will think you a bad woman. So how is he supposed to know you want to kiss him? Until your 'yes' is free, woman, your 'no' has no conviction, and rape is implied in every manwoman relationship.

Women are two. Mothers, wives, virgins, nuns, and sisters. Whores, prostitutes, bad women, mistresses. Why are women two? Until women are one, there will be rape, because some rape is supposed to be less culpable than other.

Is it a lesser crime to rape one's wife? It is not illegal here. To rape a prostitute? Difficult to get a conviction. Some judges even think prostitutes deserve it. So, in this case, rape is relative? Depends who you rape? Therefore it is everywhere. In the mind of man, in the body politic.

She thought of sand dunes. How to find where the trade winds of change will blow from? And when will the watershed come for women? How to add a drop of water to the dam, filling up for change?

◆

'Sita. Look at my head, Sita. Look at me Sita. Help.' The voice, the everpresent voice of someone wanting help. The voice, not audible to Sita before, gradually got clearer. The voice was at her front door in Surinam. I could see from the lamppost I was leaning on.

'I have been calling you for three nights and three days, Sita, and you would not hear me. Tonight would have been the fourth night, but you have started to hear me now. You were as if in a dream. But you did not turn away from me.'

'Who are you, it's dark outside.'

'Help, Sita. The others turn away from me. You were only deaf. You have begun to hear me now. You know me not. I need help. I come because you are of the movement, in the movement, I come to you. Let me in.'

'Oh, Mowsi, Mowsi, you are Everywoman. Look at you. What have they done to you. Oh, Mowsi, come in, come in.

'Oh, Mowsi, they have shorn your head with shears. Oh, Mowsi you are bleeding. They have beaten you. Oh Mowsi, your throat has bruises and rope marks. They, did they, did they try to kill you Mowsi?'

'I have eaten nothing, no rice, for three nights and three days, Sita. They all turned their backs on me. I am afraid. I hide by day in the woods and by night I call for help. They all turn away.'

'Here is soup, Mowsi, leaf soup made with rice water. I hear your every word. Your quiet strong words. Drink this soup.'

'I have to speak, Sita. I have words that must be spoken. They want to come out of me. My hair is shorn, so I cannot hide what they have done to me. Put the soup aside for me. Later.'

Sita, I peeped through the window and saw her, did a strange thing. She went out of the room, and came back with a hairbrush, and started to brush Mowsi's crudely shorn hair gently. Brushing it, brushing it, slowly. Only then, after this ceremony of care, did she take up a cloth, wet it, and wipe the dried blood off Mowsi's shoulders and arm. Only then did she put aside the blooded *horni* and fetch her a clean one. Only then did she caress the strangle-marks on Mowsi's throat.

'And now, Mowsi, time has come for your words.'

Mowsi stood up and sort-of looked upwards as if up at Bhagwann, in passing. 'They say I am a witch, Sita. They say. I make their children ill they say. I caused the cyclone they say. They formed a band, fourteen men and five women, there were even two young children, and they jumped at me, caught me and held me down and tied me up and beat me and forced me to drink something which I closed my throat to and they tied a *horni*, all twisted into a rope, around my throat, and tightened it cruelly, and they cut my hair with big scissors, my hair that has never been cut before, and they threw me in a ditch for dead.'

'You are the smallest woman, Mowsi, and you are beginning to get old.' Sita stroked her head again with her bare hands now, standing behind her.

'Who were they, Mowsi?'

'That is the cruellest part, Sita. They are my neighbours. They are my actual neighbours. All of them. And there were others who came and stared, and didn't stop them. Will I have to leave Surinam, Sita? My landlady is saying I am not to come back. She needs her house, she says. My own nephew has refused to speak to me. He says I am bad luck. No one talks to me or cares for me. When I call for help, they turn their backs, and talk behind my back. They say: 'Who knows, maybe she is a witch.'

'Will you be a witness, Mowsi? Will you stand up and say this, if I stand by you? If our movement stands by you?'

'I, Sita, I give you my word. I shall stand firm.'

'There are many things to do, then, Mowsi. So drink the leaf soup first.'

She drank it.

'Sleep here, on the *nat*. I shall put a blanket over you, because the shock has made you cold even on this hot night. I shall sit by you the whole night on this *pirha*. For I too have a decision to make. My deafness to you must be turned into attentiveness. For time is passing by, Mowsi, and we owe life a lot. Tomorrow we start the defense of Mowsi. You will leave neither Surinam nor your house. Your hair, as it grows out, will be more beautiful than before. You will stand up tall and hold your head up high. People will lower their heads in shame, and pretend they did not turn their backs. Hundreds of women will stand by you in public.

'You, Mowsi,' said Sita, 'have come at a time that helps me. I was in the dark, Mowsi, and you have brought light. For I have decided what to do now. Your courage makes my courage. Let life be praised that I had ears for you, Mowsi. And that I am in the All Women's Front, and in the movement. For without you and your courage, and without past women and their courage which formed the Front and the movement, what would become of the future?'

And then they heard a faint sound. The sound of the beautiful music of a flute.

'What is that, *Beti*,' Mowsi said to Sita.

At the door, appeared Ton Tipyer, playing a simple flute. He was blue in the night light. He was transformed. He had given up drink, so they tell me, and become sweet and kind. He had become a flute-player. He played a bamboo flute, which had cost him twenty rupees. A young man called Choko, who sold flutes at the Kirpip bus station, had sold it to him. And Ton Tipyer now played soothing tunes to Mowsi and Sita. He settled in for the night with the flute. Mowsi, sleeping in bouts between tunes, and Sita, sitting on the *pirha*. From that day onwards he was called Ton Tipyer, the Flute, or *Bolom Laflit*.

That night, as I approached Sita's doorway, she got up from the *pirha* she was sitting on, came over to me and said: 'Iqbal, there are lots of true stories for you to tell. Didn't I teach you to read and write when you were only three? Was it for nothing? Or will you write down the truth for other people. You heard most of Ton Tipyer's stories night after night with me and my sister. Why don't you write down what has to be remembered? In your own way.'

◆

And it came to pass that it was that phrase that brought me to tell the story of Sita, and to write down the story of Sita so that you today, dear reader, can know all these things. Otherwise I would never have thought of it myself. But, then again, in any case, I owed Dharma a story. Didn't he write me a short one, so that I would mend my ways. From gratitude to Dharma, I write this long story for him. Consider it a bunch of grapes, Dharma, that I hold above your mouth, and one by one, chapter by chapter, you break them open on the roof of your mouth.

◆

And since writing this story, dear, dear reader, the endless song has stopped running around in my head. I no longer sing to myself *Iqbal was a man who thought he was a woman*. Progress has therefore been made. I am a man now. And I am a woman. Like we all will be. With the good trade winds, and with the fine water that falls from the heavens. And with one or two cyclones from time to time. And with our minds that work together. And in unison. We will all be man and we will all be woman. And we will love ourselves as we are.

And we will have wanted to be free. Freedom. And then we will be free. And we will have wanted to be equal. Equality. And then we will become equal.

Such are the hopes of Iqbal for another story. Another history. In the future.

Maybe Sita will write that one down. Who knows? And leave it as inheritance to Fiya. To balance all she inherited from Doorga.

the end

THE AFRICAN WRITERS SERIES

The book you have been reading is part of Heinemann's long-established series of African fiction. Details of some of the other titles available in this series are given below, but for a catalogue giving information on all the titles available in this series and in the Caribbean Writers Series write to:
Heinemann Educational Publishers,
Halley Court, Jordan Hill, Oxford, OX2 8EJ.
United States customers should write to:
Heinemann, 361 Hanover Street,
Portsmouth, NH 03801–3912, USA

BIYI BANDELE-THOMAS
The Man Who Came in from the Back of Beyond

Maude, a strange schoolteacher, tells the tale of a man from his girlfriend's past. As the naive student Lakemf listens, a tale of incest and revenge slowly begins to unfold.

CHENJERAI HOVE
Shadows

As the war for liberation rages around them, two young Zimbabweans must decide whether they will continue to live and love in such a barren land. A telling portrait of rural life and the strictures of colonial law.

NIYI OSUNDARE
Selected Poems

This collection contains the very best of Osundare's poetry. The verse testifies to his commitment to a popular 'total poetry' – words to be listened to in conjunction with song, dance and drumming.

TIYAMBE ZELEZA
Smouldering Charcoal

Two couples live under the rule of a repressive regime, and yet their lives seem poles apart. In this compelling study of growing political awareness, we witness the beginnings of dialogue between a country's urban classes.

NGŨGĨ WA THIONG'O
Secret Lives

A new edition of Ngũgĩ's collection of early stories revealing his increased political disillusionment and foreshadowing the novels which have made him one of Africa's foremost commentators.

ALEX LA GUMA
In the Fog of the Seasons' End

This is the story of Beukes – lonely, hunted, determined – working for an illegal organisation, and of Elias Tekwane, captured by the South African police and tortured to death in the cells.

CHARLOTTE BRUNER (ED)
The Heinemann Book of African Women's Writing

A companion piece to the earlier *Unwinding Threads*, also edited by Charlotte Bruner, this anthology of writing of the post colonial era provides new insights into a complex world.

CHINUA ACHEBE & C. L. INNES (EDS)
The Heinemann Book of Contemporary African Short Stories

This anthology displays the variety, talent and scope to be found in contemporary African writing. The collection includes work written in English and translations of francophone stories. The magical realism of Kojo Laing and Mia Couto contrasts with the styles of Nadine Gordimer, Ben Okri and Moyez Vassanji.

AMECHI AKWANYA
Orimili

Orimili takes his name from the great river that flows through his home town of Okocha. But while the river flows on to the wider world beyond, Orimili is anchored to his home town, and yearns to push his roots yet further in. His ambition is to be accepted in the company of elders, to wear the thick white thread of office round his ankle.